UNDULATING FLESH

JESSE PULLINS

Published by arrangement with the author.

Copyright © 2025 by Jesse Pullins.

All rights reserved.

YOU'RE READING ANOTHER TERRIFYING COLLECTION FROM

**FOLLOW VELOX TO KEEP
THE NIGHTMARES COMING:**

CONTENTS

UNDULATING FLESH

I seem to have misplaced my pills. Not good. Their regular spot in the medicine cabinet was empty, a tiny little space much like the one I felt in my stomach. It's been so long since I missed the scheduled doses, and I fear what will happen if I go without for too long.

I've been doing *so good*.

How did I fuck this up?

I ring the office as I gather my laundry, listening to the dial tone as I pack t-shirts and jeans into a garbage bag. It rings and rings, feeding my anxiety as I contemplate whether I should even go outside. Is it even safe? Is it safe for me to be around other people? It keeps ringing, and I feel the racing in my mind held back by a tiny leash. Voicemail.

Please leave a message after the beep.

God, how did I fuck this up? Pure stupidity.

I mumble my embarrassing apology to the answering machine, disguising my begging smoothly so I don't seem like an absolute wreck. I pocket my phone and grab my keys. I throw the bag over my shoulder and put my hand on the knob, and hesitate.

I should just stay in.

I don't have any clean clothes.

I have to do laundry.

The laundromat is only a block away, anyway. I'll go do my laundry and come back home. We'll sort it out then.

I leave the apartment, trying to keep my head high. Maybe I don't even need the pills anymore. Maybe I'm better now.

Down the steps, and on the street. People pass and I give friendly nods. They all look so cheery. The fresh air is nice. It feels good not to take the pills. I hate taking them anyway. The air is crisp today; the snow is melting. Everything looks pleasant. I'm glad I left the house.

The laundromat is empty.

The laundromat is empty.

The laundromat is empty.

The laundromat is empty.

I pushed through the door and pick my machine. They're all 8 load monsters, an entire family's worth in one go. I pick one on the back wall, so I can watch the street through the window. I check the time: 3:15pm. After the jeans dry, I could probably be home by five. Gotta hang the shirts up at home. Drying makes them shrink.

I toss the bag at my machine and start loading everything in. I think of my pills and how I don't have them. The feeling of failing crawls up my back like rats. I need to call the office, let them know I misplaced them. I'll get the load started first.

A waterfall of clothes. Shake the bag out, get everything. The knob on the machine is satisfying. The metallic drag of the coin drawer is satisfying.

I'm satisfied.

The washing machine groans and fills with water. It's always so pleasant to wash, especially when the soap mixes in. The walls are meat. I look at the soapy water. So soothing.

I ring the Doc's office, can't forget that.

"Hey, yeah, I don't really know where they went. I think it would be a good idea to get a refill, as long as the Doc thinks it's alright. I haven't gone without for a while. Gimme a call back at—"

I grab a seat and watch the street. People pass by, some busy, some not. Parents with their kids. Couples holding hands. A woman jogging with pods in. An old man in aviators, looking a bit like a grumpy frog.

I stretch and look at the tumbling laundry, the soothing soap drizzling over the glass. The soft sunlight from the outside is relaxing.

I can't... I can't think.

I watch the tumbling clothes and my stomach starts sinking slowly. There's a man agitating in the washer, tumbling over and over again. The washing machine bucks wildly, thrashing against the other units next to it. The noise peels the paint inside my skull.

WAM WAM WAM WAM WAM WAM WAM WAM

The man looks at me from within the washer. He's trying to reach for me, and even in the blur I can see his piercing eyes, his white teeth. He's talking to me.

Let me out.

I rub my eyes. I'm sweating bad. The cool light from the street soothes me, the blood in the washing machine is soap again.

Get it together. You don't need the medicine. You're fine without it.

I'm fine without it.

I rub my eyes, tapping my feet on the floor.

God, how could I make such a mistake? Stupid. It's just stupid.

I get my phone out and check the recents, clicking the number for the office. Weird, it's saying this is the ninth time. That can't be right. *It's lying.*

I dial and hold the phone to my ear, standing up. I'm pacing a little bit. It's ringing.

I watch the people on the street as it keeps ringing. They look so happy. Why can't I just be fucking happy?

I watch them pass by, and the dial tone is getting quieter.

I man with a suitcase is walking past like he's in a hurry. I watch him walk, and the dial tone is gone. It's silent. The phone is silent.

The man with the suitcase stops and looks at me through the window.

Please leave your message after the beep. Please leave a message after the beep.

The man with the suitcase is mouthing the words, but I can't hear him. I feel the trickle of sweat on my back and I shiver. When did it get so fucking cold in here?

The man with the suitcase puts his hand on the glass. His hands must be hot, they're fogging the glass. His eyes. They look a little too far apart.

I lower the phone, making sense of the words he's mouthing. The same word on repeat.

Sunday.

It's Sunday. The doctor's office is closed.

I look at the washer; the clothes have stopped. I sit in my chair, hands over my ears. I can hear them. I can *hear* the walls. I can hear them writhe around me.

Gestating, undulating flesh.

The street is dark outside. The light is gone. Nobody is walking the streets now. Not people anyway. I'm trying not to look at them.

The walls are meat, and I feel them getting closer. Shifting slowly. They move when I'm not looking. I can see them in the corner of my eye. The flesh... it's coming.

I get the courage to check my phone and ignore the smiling reflection in the black screen. I check the time. It's 9:30pm.

I seem to have misplaced my pills.

Somebody help me.

Help me.

Please.

THE WANDERING SAW

The wind whispered across the infinite plain like a great black hand, casting waves of shadows over the dancing grass. Each individual blade curved under the whirling gust, almost as if it cowered under the silent chorus of tortured screams it seemed to bring with it. Each breeze was filled with an acute sense of pain, a wail of eternal anguish inaudible to normal human hearing. The grass swayed back and forth before abruptly standing straight, pulsating in response to the arrival of a wanderer in this sea of gloom. The endless grass could sense the danger, the *violence*, oozing from the very pores of the man who trudged through the valley. Under his step, the blades bent beneath his oppressiveness, flattening under his boot without really knowing why.

The wind whipped at his long-matted hair, ratty from a lifetime of blood and grime caking the strands without as much as a single wash. His face was obscured by a crude metal mask; an emotionless expression shown on the rusted iron. He was heavyset, but carried it in a way that made it powerful. What was once a white cotton shirt was heavily stained with dirt and a faded crimson color; with a black leather apron tied around his waist and neck. Both hands wore long butcher's gloves, one squeezed in a fist, the other gripping a sticky chainsaw. He moved his head across the dark grassland lazily, as if he hadn't seen anything interesting in days. He didn't eat. He didn't sleep. His only regime was the endless wander, to find someone worthy of tasting the jagged teeth of his saw.

Without direction or any inclination of where to go, he simply walked forward, the chainsaw swaying in his low grip. When the teeth grazed a taller blade among the rest, the foliage seemed to silently scream, withering away like ash in a windstorm.

On he trudged, one heavy booted step after another. It was a determined walk, each step filled with unspoken purpose, silently drawing closer and closer to a blind goal that made sense only to him. The chainsaw was heavy in his left hand, but he held on, patiently waiting for the exalting pull of the ripcord. Despite the nagging desire, it remained calm, like an itching gunslinger's hand eagerly waiting to draw the machined blade.

Creatures lurked in the shadows of the tall grass, watching the wanderer in frightened silence. Not a single organism looked identical to the next, aside from the recurring theme of twisted gore and limb amalgamation. Occasionally, the masked man would stop and slowly browse the horizon and the things lurking would duck out of sight, trembling under the metal gaze. He would look for only a few seconds, but the concept of time was lost on this plane. The single blink of an eye could take an eternity to observe, and to the hidden pests in the grass all they could do was wait for the roar of the living chainsaw.

But there was no cord pulled, no hostility brewing. The masked wanderer simply turned back to his course and continued his slow march, leaving the critters be. Concern was not a capable feeling for the wanderer, nor were any of the normal human feelings one would once experience. Deep within the expressionless face of the rusted mask was the ability to sense the power of those around him, as if he could see an aura of strength radiating from the creatures he passed. If something were to lurch from the grass and attack him, he would *know*, and he would reach for the cord in the same instant his opponent took a single step in his direction.

Over many hills and slopes walked the chainsaw man, with nothing but more grass and the weak hiding around him. He could sense them trembling, but he paid them no mind. They were not worthy of tasting the teeth. The more he walked, the more he felt the itch, the urge to rip the chainsaw to life and let it scream. The want of the vibration in his fist was what he existed for, but it was pointless if there was no one worthy of feeling its shredding embrace. As the masked wanderer reached the top of a hill, it gave him eyes on the plane ahead, one of twisted metal and stacked husks. A junkyard.

The Chainsaw man looked over the newfound area with calm excitement, wondering if a worthy opponent was hiding amongst the nooks of scrap. He cracked his stiff neck, feeling the wear of constant travel in his demented bones. He wasn't tired and there would be no rest. The win of the next fight was enough to keep him going, and it was more nourishing than any morsel of food or relished depravity he could indulge in. Without further delay, he descended the hill and trudged into the walls of scrap automobiles, seeking the reward that lay within.

The destroyed vehicle frames were stacked well over his head, looming over like skyscrapers of burnt metal. The vibrating grass thinned and eventually gave way to a slop of mud, each step sucking at his boots as the journey grew more difficult. The weaker pests watched from their posts in the distorted steel, watching him work his way through the walls of scrap. Off in the distance, a scuffed up Jester with bleeding eyes watched from atop the wreckage, a bloody skinning knife squeezed in his linen glove. The Wanderer could sense his gaze, but didn't give him as much as a glance. With his sense of power, he felt the Jester slip into the surrounding abyss, withering away until the aura was lost.

Deeper and deeper, the masked man descended amidst the walls of skeletal automobiles, each passing row growing narrower until he found himself in some sort of hallway of broken steel. Every step planted brought him closer to his reward. The chainsaw was ready, *begging* to come to life. He idly ignored the plea, his boots slapping through the mud that came up to his ankles. An aroma of stale petrol wafted down the tunnel of stacked cars, the fuming scent welcomed to the congested nostrils behind the mask. Ahead there was a standing pool of gasoline, its oily shine reflecting on the mud's surface. With a silent nod of acceptance, the masked man trudged his way towards the collection of fuel. Without a sound, the man knelt before it, the swampy ground soaking his pant leg. He tilted his mask upward, long locks of dirty hair obscuring his face as his chapped lips kissed the surface of the potent liquid. He slurped loudly, taking in mouthful after mouthful of the burning water. He drank greedily, for it was perhaps the only other indulgence he allowed aside from the wandering hunt. The fluid stung his cheeks, and with every gulp he felt the fire shriveling his insides.

Behind him there was a thud, followed by the clang of metal. He paused his quenching thirst and slowly slid the mask down, swallowing the last bit of gasoline that continued to stab at his rotting gullet. With the sound of wrung leather, he squeezed the hilt of the chainsaw as he returned to his feet. He could hear the hissing of his visitor lurking behind him. He turned to see half a man, hunched low like a wolf ready to strike.

The man was perched on his hands, holding himself upright with bent arms. The walking torso took a hand-step forward, dragging his body that was obliterated from the waist down. He had a mess of tentacle-like intestines where his legs would be, and he slid himself over the mud's slick surface like some sort of grotesque octopus merman. His face was upside down, and a toothy mouth served as one hollow eyeball. His actual eyes looked as if they had been gouged out ages ago. The butchered merman looked over the wanderer with his sniffing nostril, trying to size him up without actually seeing him. After a series of reverse smells, the merman shrieked, his coarse growl bouncing off the walls of cars that sounded like a chorus of tortured men. After his lungs emptied, he puffed his muddy chest out, letting his growl of intimidation sink in.

The wind whistled as the chainsaw man looked down on the merman, his locks whipping wildly. He stared intently from behind the rusted mask, the closed eyes on the iron burrowing into the walking torso. He took a powerful step forward, his boot striking the mud so hard it seemed to shake the ground. The air around them seemed to crackle, and suddenly the merman wailed in fear, like lightning had struck inches from his face. In a series of screeches the torso fled, burrowing into the wreckage with his flailing guts trailing behind him. The masked man watched until the pest was out of sight, and when he was satisfied with the dismissal, he continued his journey down the iron corridor.

The air grew thicker the closer he got. He could feel the growing intensity with every step, and as the metallic taste of victory was in reach, he felt the ever-evolving itch of the ripcord demanding attention. He silenced the need and focused only on the whistling wind as he waded through the energized atmosphere. His breath wheezed against the mask. His boots sloshed in the mud. The apron slapped in the gust. And as he drew toward the end of the corridor, he heard the first sounds of his opponent's presence.

The tearing came first. It was a loud, shrewd hiss, like someone was ripping carpet from an old floor. It was slow, painfully drug out. Whoever was causing such a commotion was taking their time, enjoying every step of their cruel endeavor. Each tear was followed by a muffled groan, like magma suffocating under a hard shell. The Masked man drifted in, eager to see the scene of his next battleground. So close to the reward, he couldn't pass up savoring the discovery.

There was a loud *pop*, accompanied by a grunt of relief. The chainsaw man could hear the sudden gush of fluid peppering the mud, a shower of blood without question. It was a familiar sound, one common in a land such as this. Then there was the sound of a thrown object slapping on the wet ground. The next grunt was slower, almost aroused. Whatever task had been completed had just as easily been forgotten.

Unable to wait any longer, the masked man reached the end of the metal hallway, arriving in a round dead-end clearing. It was a miniature coliseum, and the junk cars were stacked much higher. The walls of scrap reached almost thirty feet, towering high to keep out any unwanted attention. Only a few brave crows watched from the pinnacle, blood red eyes waiting for the inevitable feast. The masked man watched silently, the source of the noise being everything he wanted it to be. Alas, the long journey had paid off. He had come to the right place.

Directly in the center of the clearing was a chiseled mountain of a man, his muscles flexing as he worked on his prey beneath him. Beads of sweat trickled down his brow as he twisted the giant spiral gear of a two-handed crescent wrench. He adjusted the mechanical jaw on the oversized tool, his beady eyes never leaving his victim. A faded yellow hardhat was strapped to his head, a color that matched his reflecting fireman trousers. He was shirtless, showing his natural armor of bulging muscle and suspenders that stretched over a broad chest. With the sound of gnashing molars he worked his jaw, a complete lack of skin and tendons from his cheeks down, showing the complete lower half of his skull. The hulking worker was so entranced on his prey he hadn't yet noticed the masked man observing in silence.

Beneath the weight of the muscular fiend was a body so horribly mangled the only features telling its gender were the pair of pale breasts pressed into the mud. Both legs had been wrenched off mid-thigh, as well as the right arm. Each stump was a torn mess of broken bone and warped gristle. The only limb intact was the left arm, frozen in a final reach of despair, contorted fingers grasping at the unknown possibility of rescue. The masked man watched as the helmeted fiend lowered the cold-forged steel jaw on the last limb, spinning the gear to get the perfect clamped bite on the tender flesh. The Laborer's bony jaw *clacked* with excitement when he stood and gripped the wrench in both hands, giving view to the outline of a large erection in the tight fireman pants.

Just as the fiend was about to throw his man-made lever he stopped, suddenly transfixed on the face of the mutilated female. With one hand holding the wrench he crouched, his clicking jaw inches from the girl's face. His free hand caressed her matted hair, moving the strands from her brow so he could see the side of her face that wasn't buried in mud. Her cheek wore the streams of a hundred dried tears, beneath a single bloodshot eye that was locked into the distance. Through twitching eyelids she stared at the Masked man, who watched in silent savoring.

As the beady eyes found the rusted mask, a ghastly scream erupted from the skeletal jaw, so loud it shattered every window in the makeshift coliseum. In a rain of glass, The Laborer rose, tearing the wrench from the ground and letting the heavier end fall into his palm. With a single stride he stepped in front of his prey, as if to block the path of the chainsaw wielding trespasser. There were no words spoken, only the invisible rules of the fight that would now have to unfold. The Laborer flexed his entire upper body, veins popping like straw across the board. The masked man reached for the cord, his wrist and fingers cracked from prolonged disuse. When his digits curled around the cord's T-handle he felt his whole body come to life, suddenly reawakened from a long-lost slumber. He waited for the opponent to make the first move, and as the helmeted fiend took his first sprinting stride, he yanked hard on the rope. The chainsaw roared to life and the battle began, the jagged teeth moving in a blur as they cut through the air.

The Laborer jumped and brought the wrench down hard, aiming for the metal mask in his aggressive rage. Another ghastly scream exploded from his bony jaw as the tool crashed into the ground, throwing chunks of broken earth and splashes of mud in all directions. The Wanderer had moved out of the way at the last second and was thrashing with the chainsaw, swinging wide at his opponent's face. The Laborer tucked his chin and caught the screaming blade with his helmet, feeling the teeth dig into the tough plastic before it glanced off. The masked man worked with the momentum of the saw, holding it outstretched in both hands, pivoting his feet in the mud so he spun with the weight of the power tool. Turning on his heel, the masked man turned and brought the saw down harder this time.

With a frustrated grunt the Laborer yanked the wrench free from the earth, bringing it up just in time to stop and absorb the saw's impact. The chainsaw burrowed into the wrench with a flurry of dancing sparks, the unnatural teeth shaving a divot into the steel. The masked man leaned into his attack, gripping the shaking blade like a heavy sword. The Helmeted fiend buckled under the vibrating weight, his boots sliding in the mud as he fought for traction. He looked into the expressionless mask of his mysterious challenger; the wrench shaking so hard it tore the skin on his palms. Toxic black smoke billowed from the engine as he teetered into the cut, rocking back and forth like he was finishing a fallen tree. The mask shielded any signs of fatigue, only adding to the power of the maniacal blade. This angered the Laborer deeply, and he flexed again to unleash his own power, fueled by the interrupted climax of his prey.

The Laborer dead lifted the weight with his massive legs and repelled the saw with a wild swing, rearing back to bring the wrench down on his opponent's skull once again. The masked man stepped in quickly, tossing his weight into a haymaker with his defense wide open. His gloved fist buried into the Laborer's face, bony knuckles crushing his nose and digging into his left eye socket. The wound bled immediately, crimson tendrils seeping from half of his face the instant he withdrew the punch. The Laborer echoed another ethereal scream, much louder than before. The mangled female on the ground burrowed her face away from the noise and the crows perched above flew away in fright. The Laborer clacked his jaw rapidly and his eyes glowed red, his veins pulsing like living worms across taut muscles.

The next punch came before the Wanderer had time to react, a straight-armed slug smashing into the mask like it was shot from a 75mm cannon. The impact jarred his neck, and the shockwave sent his body reeling, hurtling across the mud like a skipping rock. The Wanderer crashed into the coliseum wall, embedding into the warped metal in a flurry of dust and debris. As the dust cleared, he shouldered a broken sedan door that tried to envelop him in an attempt to break free of the junk's embrace. The saw still throbbed with life, a feral cough of digested fuel surging through the machinery. The Wanderer raised his head just in time to see the helmeted fiend rocketing toward him, already at half-swing with the muddy wrench. With glowing evil eyes blinding his vision, he felt the excessive force of the wrench crushing his plump stomach, several ribs cracking under the colossal weight of the blow.

The wall of trashed cars shifted under the immense power of the attack, and the Wanderer felt his body being pressed further into the broken steel. A shower of metal and fiberglass rained down from the walls of their arena, dozens of sharp pieces sticking into the mud around them. Winded, the Laborer reached a thick arm into the wreckage and grabbed the Wanderer by the shoulder, ripping him from his twisted encasement. The masked man latched onto his opponent's arm and squeezed, digging his meaty thumb into the soft flesh opposing the elbow. With shattering strength, he broke the Laborers arm and twisted, feeling the sinewy *snap* of the joint under his butcher's glove. The Helmeted fiend sucked in for a cry of pain but was stopped short as the Wanderer burst from the wreckage, driving mask-first into a full body headbutt. The blank mask drilled into the Laborer's face like a battering ram, the rusted iron splintering the hardhat to several scattering pieces.

Distraught from the surprise attack the Laborer stumbled, retaliating with an awkward one-handed swing of the wrench. In the staggered blink of his beady eye, the Wanderer squeezed the injured arm and broke it backwards, followed by a chainsaw swing that swatted the wrench away like an annoying fly. As the Laborer flinched from the Wanderer's inhuman recovery, the masked man let go of the ruined limb and smashed him in the face with the pommel of his mechanical sword. The hardware broke multiple teeth from the skeletal jaw and the Laborer fell like a rag doll, inches from the bloodshot gaze of the tortured female. He locked one eye with the girl, his other one swollen shut from his opponent's haymaker. As he stared at her, he struggled to lift the wrench once more, pouring all of his strength into a final attempt to reclaim his domain. As he looked into the girl's mocking eye, he heard the scream of the chainsaw, accompanied by the heavy footsteps of the masked Wanderer.

Despite his odds, he tried to lift the wrench again, only to feel the immeasurable pain of the teeth chewing through his flesh as the Wanderer side-swiped him. The wicked blade ate through the muscular arm with ease and dug into his ribcage, shredding meat and bone alike as if it didn't exist at all. The wrench fell to its murky grave, taking the severed arm with it. With nothing else to hold himself up, the Laborer collapsed into the mud with a wet smack, just as immobile as the abandoned girl that lay beside him. The Wanderer stood over him, wet locks dripping on the Laborer's chest as the blank mask looked down on him. The power of his gaze was suffocating, and as the rusted mask stared from above, he felt just as much like the prey he hunted. The fight was over. The Laborer had lost.

Without a single word, the Wanderer planted a rubber boot on his heaving chest. He held him firm, just enough to keep him in place for the final blow. The Wanderer did not receive pleasure from cruelty, nor did he enjoy toying with those he defeated. He only did what was *necessary* to move on. He took a closing look at The Laborer, and as he squeezed the chainsaw's trigger the blade's edge screamed into motion. The Laborer released a clacking hiss as the Wanderer thrust the saw downward, plunging the weapon underneath the bony jaw. A gurgling rush gave way to the grinding of marrow, the hot chain kicking up a spray that spattered the black leather apron. The Laborers husk bucked under his planted boot, and he ran the blade upward, separating the skull in an explosion of broken bone and brain matter. The saw screamed until the rush of blood and gore gave way to tilled mud, and only as the corpse ceased all movement did the chain stop its grind.

The Wanderer yanked the blade from the mess in silent satisfaction, pausing only momentarily to savor his victory. He looked up to the eternal overcast sky, blood running down the rusted iron that lacked all visible feeling. There was a deep breath, and as he exhaled, lightning cracked across the sky in a bright flash. Sheets of rain followed, showering the wreckage of the junkyard arena as if it tried to wash away the madness. Raindrops seeped past the mask and trickled down his shielded face in cool streams. There was an instant of solace, but it was only temporary. When he finally lowered his head, he knew it was time to move on. Rainwater trickled down the caked blade, leaving a red trail in the mud as he made his exit. A booming thunderclap sang across the sky as the Wanderer left the destruction behind him, continuing his unending search for a stronger opponent.

THE HAWAIIAN SHIRT

Clyde watched the falling snow through the large windows in the thrift store, heavy flakes dancing in the parking lot's light. He watched them gracefully flutter, tired 90s music playing faintly over the store's speakers.

"Babe?" Hunter said, startling him with a touch on the shoulder. His wife looked at him with raised eyebrows.

"What? Sorry. I was miles away," Clyde said, watching her put the worn paperback with the rest of the old books, each with cracked spines and yellowed pages.

"*I said,* I'm going to go look at dresses. Do you want to go look at button-ups? You might find something good. You don't dress up anymore," she said, grabbing the cart.

"Uh, yeah. I'll take a look around. See what they got," he said, scratching his head. He looked over the aisle for the men's section, at the wall of shirts hanging on the outside perimeter of the store.

"You used to look so cute in those," she teased, wheeling the cart around to head in the opposite direction.

Clyde walked past the rows of jeans and khakis, the wall of shirts looking more disorganized the closer he got. He started picking through them, metal hangers screeching against the rack as he waved the clutter of faded beer t-shirts and long forgotten sports jerseys, surviving a hundred washes just to rot in hand-me-down hell. With a sigh he nearly gave up, but halted when his hand grazed an oddly smooth, pleasant fabric. The hangers squealed as he pushed the surrounding shirts away, to get a better look at his discovery.

It was a Hawaiian shirt.

Clyde lifted the hanger off the rod and brought it close, his fingers indulging in the soft cotton-silk fabric. It was navy blue and covered in white orchids, which was unusual to the norm of parrots and palm trees. It was perfect, aside from a faded red stain on the front of it, near the middle button. He ran his thumb over it, the ridges of his fingerprint dragging across the tainted fabric.

Clyde's surroundings blinked to black, the store's music replaced by a whirlwind of terrible screams. Visions flashed through his mind, a torturous channel-changing revelation. Taut rope constricting a man's throat, his face strained and blue, his eyes bulging red. Rushing water and a capsizing sailboat, helpless cries drowned under the weight of water.

Sniffling cries muffled by duct tape, tears streaming from puffy eyes. Ankles bound to chairs, fighting wildly against restraints. The splashing spew of a jerry-can, pungent fuel trickling down wooden stairs. The 'clink' of a Zippo lighter, followed by the strike of its flint. The slithering *whoosh* of ignited flame and billowing smoke in a burning house. The crack of a hammer beating nails through wood, as sirens blared in the distance.

A steady hand inspecting a kitchen knife in a dimly lit shed, the light glinting off the blade. Only to be set down gingerly and replaced by a beat-up chainsaw. The pull of a rip cord, an engine sputtering to a scream. Two hands tightly wringing a rag in the sink, red seeping through white-knuckled fingers. *His* fingers.

"Babe? You alright?" Hunter asked, and Clyde blinked.

"Yeah, just tired I guess," he said, and with a shaking hand, hung it back up.

"Wanna bring the car around while I check out?"

"Y-yeah," Clyde said, trying to shrug off the fever dream.

They loaded the bags into the car and left the parking lot, headlights pushing into the night. On the way home, Clyde rubbed his eyes, feeling the beginning throbs of a migraine forming. After massaging his eyelids, something caught his attention in the back-seat, and he checked the rear-view mirror. One of the bags tipped over, and he could faintly see the floral pattern of the Hawaiian shirt.

YELLOW BALL

Woodrow ran as fast as his little legs would take him. He huffed down the grassy hill and away from the other kids, trying not to fall as he picked up more momentum than he expected. On this cool summer day the wind was just right; when one of his classmates kicked the ball as hard as he could, he wasn't surprised to see it fly out of the field like it had. Woodrow was positioned out in the field for this game of kickball, and even though he knew the classmate got a home run, he had gotten caught up in the excitement and the thrill of retrieving it gave him the energy he required. It wasn't until he reached the bottom of the hill that he spotted it. The vibrant yellow ball had rolled to the stop at the edge of the weeds, right before the dark line of trees that started not far behind it. Woodrow hunched over and caught his breath, feeling very winded now the hill had leveled out.

Wiping his brow on the sleeve of his windbreaker, the boy started towards the yellow ball. It looked so appealing in the grass, sticking out amongst the blowing weeds. The sun hit it just right, making it seem like a shiny gumball like in the machine at the store. With squeaking sneakers, Woodrow jogged toward it, feeling the cool breeze of the wind pick up as he grew closer. The boy slowed down, arms reaching out for his prize. He was eager to have the ball for himself, and to show the other kids he was cooler than them for catching it himself. Before his fingers touched the cool rubber, there was a shout behind him, and he jumped in surprise.

It was the gym teacher, gasping for breath with a red kick ball held in the crook of his arm. He straightened his ball cap and held it out for him, a worried smile on his face.

"Hey Woodrow! Here, I found it. Go ahead and take it back up. Recess is about over anyway," said the teacher, and there was an *Aww man,* from the boy. His spirits seemed to lift when he got the red ball, and without a second thought he scurried back up the hill, the teacher breathing a sigh of relief as he watched him go. When he was far enough away, the teacher turned back toward the woods, a single bead of sweat trailing down his temple. He wasn't sure what disturbed him more; what the boy had been reaching for in the grass, or the dark shape of teeth and eyes that was slowly disappearing into the woods.

DRUNK DRIVE

Dan understood he had made a grave mistake. With the nearly empty whiskey bottle in his lap, and the pistol pressed against his head, he stood frozen at the edge of his bed. His friends had warned him time and time again not to drive after so many drinks. They called him reckless; they called him lucky; they called him stupid. He knew they were right, but he only lived a few minutes from the bar. It took no time at all to get home, no matter how foggy his head was or how blurred his vision became. Night after night he pounded drinks until his words slurred and his legs grew weak. Each time he got behind the wheel, each time he made it home. He understood tonight was different. Tonight, he had made a big mistake.

He sat on his bed, seeing the remnants of the whiskey in the bottle, wanting to drink more but finding himself unable to.

Dan understood tonight he had ruined his life, and the life of another. When he limped his truck into the driveway with one working headlight and a crumpled hood, he decided what he would do before he even made it to the front door. He would take the easy way out instead of seeing the heartache on so many faces. He didn't want to see, he just wanted it to go away. He just wanted it to be over. But as he sat on his bed, gun to his head, he found himself unable to close his eyes, unable to hide from what he had done.

Dan understood he didn't see the woman in time. She was unlocking her car on the oncoming side of the street, and when he swerved in her direction, she had nowhere to go. He knew when he looked down at her wheezing body that it was too late; there would be no way to save her. He understood when he got back in the truck and left her there to die that his life was over as well. So he went home and got the pistol out of the closet, along with a drink to go. He understood it was the end. There was no going back.

He didn't understand, however, how she appeared before him now, horribly mangled, head cocked as she stared at him a few feet away. He didn't understand why she was moving closer, and why he couldn't look away. Each wheezing breath getting closer and closer as her disfigured legs limped her forward. Worst of all, he didn't understand why, when he pulled the trigger, the gun didn't fire.

PLEASE PAY INSIDE

Payton turned into the small gas station, cursing at herself for not getting gas in town when she left the campus. She was halfway through her six-hour drive home in the middle of nowhere, and she would be totally lost if it wasn't for the little blue line on her phone GPS. It was after midnight, and she was tired and weary from the road. She unplugged her phone from the dash and grabbed her purse, looking around outside before stepping out. It was a shitty little two pump station, with a faded sign that left out any recognizable franchise. There were no other cars, and no traffic as far as the eye could see. She didn't really want to stop, but the fuel light was on, and the GPS said there wasn't another opportunity for thirty miles. She didn't want to chance it, and she made a mental note to think ahead next time.

With a sigh, she swung her door open and stepped out into the brisk night. The overhead fluorescents flickered softly, and the cool breeze waved at her long hair as she walked around the back of the car, already fishing out her debit card. When she came to the pump, she let out a heavier sigh at the paper sign taped over the card reader. Scrawled in pen was a simple message: *Please Pay Inside.*

After a quick glance around, she headed in. The door jingled as she pushed through. The gas station smelled of bleach and stale air. An elderly man with glasses and beady eyes offered a wave as she passed. She nodded awkwardly and headed to the refrigerated section, deciding to get a caffeinated tea for the rest of the drive.

She walked down the closest aisle, twirling her hair on her finger as she walked. She passed the candy bars, overpriced medicine, and a corkboard littered with flyers. She scanned the drinks, seeing rows and rows of brands she didn't recognize. She grabbed the most expensive one and hoped for the best. On her way back to the counter, she couldn't help but stop and glance at the corkboard. Aside from the local ads, it was filled with missing persons. She looked from picture to picture, still twirling quietly. Some photos were clearer than others, some were of grainy quality, others faded with age. They were all women, each in different poses and different angles, like they were shot while on a vacation or something. Just as she went to pull away her twirling stopped, and she noticed a strange similarity between them all. They all seemed to be taken in or around this gas station.

Payton turned to leave, just in time to catch the flash from a polaroid camera.

SOMETHING TO WEAR

Wet leaves and pine needles squished under Joshua's boots. Slowly and carefully, he hiked the backwoods of his property, his trusty German shepherd "Cage" trailing close behind. They moved together through the forest in silence, Joshua panning a lantern and Cage following his nose. Joshua ducked under some branches, maneuvering his old Mosin on his shoulder so it didn't catch on the twigs. A shiny stainless hatchet hung on his hip under his heavy coat, which he used occasionally to hack away big sticks and brambles that created an impasse. He was looking for a deer out in the woods, or at least that's the story he gave his wife.

He didn't know why he lied to her; it was just something that happened. He never lied to her.

But on this night he was looking for something in particular, something he was trying to keep a secret. When the bright glow streaked down from the sky, he just *knew* it would land on his property. *He* had to be the one to find it.

A brief crunching and rustling of brush made him jump and the dog barked. Joshua shined the lantern at the source, only to see a deer staring at them through the trees. It just lingered there silently. That was until Cage barked again and it promptly scampered away in leaping bounds. Joshua shrugged it off and pressed on. Through trees and crowded brush they hiked, and such a time had passed he was starting to lose hope. Just as he was starting to get worried, a smell came wafting in the trees. Smoke. He followed the smell, and it wasn't long before he found what he was looking for.

The turquoise glow shimmered in the night, shining and fading every few seconds as they drew closer. Cage started to whine and Joshua unslung the rifle, pressing it against his shoulder as he crept forward. He could see it now, the molten rock sizzling in the mud with smoke dancing from the tiny crater. When he arrived at it he stood there for a moment, before deciding he would nudge it with the gun. Cage started to bark erratically, and Joshua heard something in his mind; not a sound nor voice, just something he seemed to understand.

BRING ME SOMETHING TO WEAR

"Honey? I'm home."

"Oh great, dinner's almost done. Did you find the deer?"

"Yes, I did."

"Where's your coat? And where's Cage?"

"He's on the leash. But hey, I need your help. With the deer. You got a second?"

"Sure. Let me turn the burner off."

Joshua stood in the doorway, holding the door open for his wife while she grabbed her coat and zipped it up. As she stepped outside he followed behind her, the hatchet tucked behind his back. He gripped it tightly, blood stained and matted with fur.

DEAD MALL

"I'm no chicken, I'll do it," Larissa said, looking up at the cracked little window in the alley. She found herself regretting these words. She looked back at her two brothers, both older than her, and currently very amused. They smirked and crossed their arms expectantly, gesturing to the window and giggling to themselves. She sighed and looked back at the tiny window, flashlight in hand.

"Well, at least help me up."

They were standing in the tiny loading alley of a dead mall, in an otherwise bustling town in Indiana. The large building had been emptied for years, no store or restaurant able to thrive in its shell. The dare was simple: sneak in after hours and grab something from one of the abandoned stores. In and out, they had said. It seemed easy enough, but now that they were lifting her up and she could see into the dark mall, she was getting nauseous. Standing on their shoulders, she shoved at the window. The window was broken, merely sitting on its track. She slid it open and crawled through, not giving her brothers the satisfaction of tormenting her further.

Larissa landed on the tile and turned on the flashlight. There wasn't much sound in the building, with everything being so dusty. She found a stack of boxes and scooted it by the window so she could get out easier, then shined the flashlight behind her. She was in one of the main stretches of the mall, and it was picked completely clean save for a few trash bags and CLOSEOUT SALE signs. The cage shutters were pulled down on every empty shop, leaving nothing but the long hallway ahead. At the far end of the corridor lay an old mannequin, directly under the gutted entrance sign of the old Penny's. It turned out she wouldn't have to go far after all.

Quickly and quietly she scurried down the hall, her breath in quick gasps as the adrenaline kicked in. It was almost thrilling, the rebellious feeling of doing something you shouldn't be. In the Penny's entrance she stood the mannequin up and pulled out her phone. Pressing her face next to the life-size doll and she took a selfie, the flash bright and blinding as it went off. Feeling satisfied, Larissa promptly sprinted back down the hall, leaving the mannequin behind. She booked it to the boxes, keeping the flashlight on the exit without looking back. She climbed the boxes and wiggled out the window where her brothers were waiting to help her down.

"Well?" they asked. She unlocked her phone and held it out so they could see.

"So cool. How'd you do all that?" They asked.

"Do what?"

She turned the phone back and studied the picture, feeling immediately sick. Behind her and the doll she posed with stood dozens of other mannequins, all posed and looking directly at her.

SAND BAR

Cool water washed over Ryan and Bianca's feet as they stood at the shore. It was a bright summer day, and with the gentle breeze and the sun gleaming down it seemed like the perfect day to put toes in the sand. After laying their towels down and cracking a few cold beers, all they had left to do was enjoy the view and listen to the calming sound of waves caressing the beach. It was wonderful; exactly what they needed after a long and hectic work week.

What started as playful splashing led to the inevitable chase into deeper water, and soon they were up to their knees. Ryan splashed Bianca and she shrieked at the chilly water, starting a back and forth of mischief until Bianca tackled him into the water. Together they came up gasping and called a truce, and it was only seconds until they found an embrace and watched the horizon together. Seagulls cried in the distance. Yards away a jet-ski soared past, sending an echo of waves in the water. Ryan was so caught up in it he almost didn't hear Bianca speak.

"Do you see that?" she said, pointing at a boat slowly wobbling in the lake.

"The boat?" Ryan asked.

"No, *that*." He followed her finger to the lone fisherman casting a line into the water. He held the rod loosely, ball cap and shades fighting the sun, Hawaiian shirt blowing in the wind. Not a care in the world. It took Ryan a moment before he saw it, but when he did, he felt his stomach twist into knots. Half obscured by the lapping waves was something pale and veiny, holding onto the ladder with white knuckles. And it was trying to climb up.

Ryan and Bianca looked at each other and saw the color drain from each other's faces. They didn't know what it was, but it looked *wrong*. In an unspoken agreement, they took off into the water, flailing their arms and shouting at the fisherman. The water got deeper and colder as they trounced further, over their knees, then waist high. They shouted for his attention, and as they reached the end of the sandbar, their voices finally reached him. With the water at chest height and their toes approaching the drop off, the fisherman turned, offering a smile and a wave.

Now that they were closer, they could see the pale humanoid shape climb another rung. Its chest heaved as it climbed, dual sets of gills widening like jagged slashes. In terror they looked from the being to the fisherman, who was now taking off his sunglasses, his face wrinkled with concerned confusion. He dropped the pole and pointed at them, yelling something they couldn't quite hear.

Ryan looked worriedly at Bianca, but found nothing but bubbling water. She was nowhere to be found. Before he could yell for her, he felt the icy grip on his ankle, and he was yanked under.

BRICK HOUSES

When the lumberjack moved to the small, wooded town of Murer, he purchased an empty plot in the middle of a long stretch of beautiful mason houses. The outskirts of our town were heavily overgrown with lush trees and vegetation, effectively enclosing the entire community in a beautiful, natural embrace. Every backyard was filled with trees of all sizes, and the growth would reach as far as you could see. When he got out of his vehicle the first time, he looked perplexed, and it didn't take long for him to flag one of us down.

"Why do you all have brick houses?" he asked.

We told him our ancestors had worshipped the trees long ago, and it was considered a sin to harm the forest for such selfish reasons. We told him they had taken from the earth instead, harvesting clay deposits and fertilizing in their place so the trees could thrive around them.

"Huh. How about that?" was all he said, and proceeded to set up a tent on the land he bought.

It wasn't until the next day when he went to the diner for breakfast, he had shared his plans. He told us he was a retired logger, and he purchased the land to build a cabin from the trees on his lot. Once finished, the cabin would serve as his summer home. We promptly looked at each other in disbelief, then told him he was making a grave mistake.

"The trees are not to be harmed," we told him. "The trees wouldn't like that."

He promptly stated that it was his land, and he would do with it as he pleased. We warned him as he left but he did not listen, and it was that night when he fell the first tree. In silence we watch him drag the log from the woods, wipe his brow, and turn in for the night.

In the morning, the lumberjack showed up at the sheriff's station. His clothes were torn and dirty, his face disheveled and wild-eyed. He spouted off about being attacked in the middle of the night, that "tree people" had drug him from his tent and into the woods at night. He said he was terrorized by them and tied to the stump of the fallen tree, fastened to it with vine and his face glued to the stump with sap. He was stuck there until almost dawn when he managed to free himself.

The sheriff dismissed him and we laughed off his "crazy talk", but in the end he relinquished his property. He was packed up and gone just as fast as he arrived.

We were glad the costumes made of loose bark and sticks had worked. We hung them back in the closets, where they would sit until the next new arrival. After all, we are getting too old and tired for the old way. It's much easier than grinding their bones into mortar.

DON'T GO PAST THE TREE LINE

When the chickens died, I thought at first it was raccoons that did it. Maybe one had got into the coop and made quick work of them. But if it was a raccoon, it would've been a total mess. They would've been torn up, feathers everywhere. They just seemed to kind of keel over, some blood leaking from their poor little beaks. It made no sense. I was deeply saddened by the loss of my chickens; it was really the only thing that made my house in the country a "farmhouse".

When I started finding the dead raccoons in the yard not long after, I thought maybe there was something a little bigger on the property. They would be covered in little bites from head to toe. It was strange, like nothing I'd seen before. I have ten acres, but half of it is divided by a thick tree line that leads to five or so acres I really don't mess with. Nothing but trees and bushes, so thick you can't see but a couple of yards in. I contacted DNR and they told me there was a coyote problem this season, and to shoot them on sight if I saw them in my yard. I'm not much of a hunter, but I keep a 12 gauge around just in case things get crazy. From then on, I kept it loaded by the door.

It was when the coyotes started showing up that I started to get worried. I found them in the same fashion as the raccoons but worse. Their legs would be twisted, chunks missing, jaws broken. It didn't make any sense. I found myself looking to the tree line, to the dark woods behind my house. Sometimes I felt something watching me from within those trees. I called DNR again. They told me bigger game wasn't common around here, maybe there was a squabble in the pack.

After days of watching the tree line, I started to think maybe it was over. Like whatever was there had moved on. Just as I started to put the nasty things behind me, I saw it. Deep in the trees, watching me. I don't know what it is. It has the head of a deer but the eyes bleed, and from the neck down its flesh turns to strands of something else. Something that doesn't make sense. Its body writhes in its confinement. I can't quite make it out from afar, but I swear... I swear it looks like spider legs. Tentacles. It watches me from the tree line, waiting. It's hungry.

I decided in the morning I will go into the woods. I'm taking the shotgun and plenty of gasoline. I'm gonna find whatever den it lies in and I'm gonna set it on fire, the whole woods if I have to. For my chickens, if anything. And if you find me dead, sell my property, and for the love of God, don't go past the tree line.

FOX

Lee buried the shovel in Rachelle's face, holding on with all his might as she thrashed around. Tears streamed from his eyes as she fell to the ground, and when he stomped on the spade to finish the job, he couldn't help but let out a cry of despair. In her final throes of death he sat next to her, sobbing uncontrollably. Shaking hands covered his face as he tried to hide from the atrocities around him. Next to them was the freshly filled grave of their son, Silas. I tiny wooden sign served as his gravestone, his stuffed bear sitting beside it. So much fear and pain in the last twenty-four hours, but it was over now. The monster was gone.

It all started with that damned fox. It first appeared when his son was playing in the yard, trotting up innocently like it was hoping for a scrap of food. Lee and his wife knew something was off immediately, be it the way it blankly stared around, or the way it would tilt its head like it was waiting patiently. Their son paid it no mind and tried to play with it, see if it would fetch a stick. But it would just sit there, looking at them.

When they took their son inside to get away from it, it started making that horrific sound foxes make. Like a family of rabbits through a wood chipper. That whining cackle went on for hours. When night had fallen it continued for a time, the frightening cry ringing in the night. It was maddening, such a twisted and horrible squeal. No amount of noise in the house could drown it out.

When it abruptly stopped, they assumed it had given up, maybe lost interest. They tucked in their son, assuring him the horror was over. He nodded silently and drifted off to sleep, snuggling into his covers like nothing ever happened. Mentally haggard, the parents went to bed, hoping to God the disturbance was over. All was quiet, aside from the chirp of crickets.

After they went to bed, Silas woke in the middle of the night and let it in. They woke to the screeching again, much louder and crackling this time. The noise pierced their ears until they ached, a sonic cry that could wake the dead. In a fit of desperation, Lee killed it with a steak knife and threw it outside. They spent hours trying to calm Silas down, and he seemed inconsolable. They tempted him with the TV, video games, even sweets. Nothing seemed to calm the child down.

At first Silas started acting weird, standing silently and moping around. Then he got frustrated, angry. What started as a tantrum bloomed into something violent, and soon Lee and Rachelle had to run from their own child. He grabbed anything sharp he could find in the kitchen: blades, corkscrews, the meat tenderizer. Anything he could use to break the door down and hurt them. They tried to reason, and when that failed, they tried to call the police, but their son collected their phones while they slept and fed them to the garbage disposal. After he cut the landline, there was no one to reach out to.

When they finally tried to subdue him, Silas knocked his head fatally in the struggle. A broken, swelling hole in his skull seeping profusely. They ferried him to the car, but something had been tampered with. A pop of the hood shed light on cut electrical, frayed wires poking awkwardly from its usual domain. With dawn breaking over the horizon and their minds broken, they buried their son. As the last shovel-scoop topped off the earth, Lee patted the loose dirt mound with the shovel. Before he could even set the tool down, Rachelle accused him of the same madness, and they turned on each other.

Lee sobbed until his eyes were puffy and dry. He was alone now, and as he wallowed in his tragic misery, the tortured cackle rang through the forest once more. He looked up to see the fox, its head cocked to the side. It sat there, watching him and his dead family with its blank, sagging eyes. Lee thought of the shovel and trying to chase it down. He knew he couldn't catch it; the game would only exhaust him further. He was done now. He had nothing left.

"What... What are you?" he asked weakly, eyes miserable and bloodshot.

The fox opened its mouth like it was starting to yawn, a gagging emanating from its fuzzy mouth. Its cheeks ripped apart with strands of sinew as the mouth opened too wide, tearing the flesh that held its head together. A pink, hairy mass birthed from its throat, sliding out with jerky thrashes and twists. Protruding from the gaping throat was the face of a man, a face he knew instantly as himself. The clone pushed out of the fox's destroyed mouth, staring as it wormed its human body out of the deflated fox carcass. It stood in front of him, tall and steaming, stretching popping limbs as it looked down at him. Fleshy strands glistened on otherwise clean skin.

"Now I'm you," was all it said, and without another word it left him there. It walked away slowly, hanging around long enough to hear Lee scream. As the nude man disappeared into the woodland thick, Lee looked at the upturned blade of the spade. With a last look at the corpse and grave, he positioned the spade pointing up and threw his neck upon it.

RAILS

Liam walked to the edge of the platform, his shoes crossing the yellow caution paint as he looked down. The subway tracks below were dark and rusted, like a long stretch of robotic teeth that ran infinitely. He closed his eyes and took a deep breath, exhaling slowly as he tried to calm the noise in his mind. He could hear the distant cry of the train still far away, and now that he was hearing it, he was sure his decision was final. He opened his eyes with bittersweet clarity and followed the tracks into the tunnel, where the headlights of the train were just coming into view. That was it, the train that would end his life. It wouldn't be long now.

Feeling anxious, he looked around the metro, and at 2 a.m. there wasn't a soul in sight. That was good, he thought to himself. Less people to see the mess, at least. Listening to the train grind closer, he loosened his tie and set his suitcase down, his toes still touching the edge of the platform. He took out his phone, wallet, and keys and set them gently on top of the suitcase. This way they wouldn't have trouble identifying him and the process would be a little easier on them. It was the least he could do. He closed his eyes again and breathed deeply. It was all he had left to do before the jump.

"Sir! Sir! Excuse me sir!" a voice was shouting, and Liam couldn't help but feel an immediate irritation. He looked to see a businessman like himself running toward the platform, coffee in one hand, suitcase in the other. Liam's eyes darted around briefly, hoping there was someone else here. But it was just him, unfortunately. The man arrived quickly; his wing-tipped shoes squeaking to a stop. He stopped next to Liam, immediately holding out his coffee and suitcase.

"Excuse me. Sorry to be a bother. Could you hold these for a moment?" he asked. His gelled hair was a little frantic from his run.

"*Pardon?* I'm a little busy,"Liam asked, clearly annoyed, glancing toward the train.

"It'll just take a second, I promise. *Please,*" he asked, with a cool smile. Liam sighed heavily and obliged, keeping his focus on the train.

The man thanked him and pulled a comb from his suit. With delicate precision he ran the comb through his hair, collecting the gelled strands with quick swipes until it was just right. Then he straightened his tie and smoothed the wrinkles from his suit. Seeming satisfied, he turned to Liam and stood straight. The train was almost here.

"Well, how do I look?" he asked, taking his belongings back.

"Good," offered Liam as he turned back to the train.

"Wonderful. I'm deeply sorry, friend. I had to make sure nobody took my day from me," he said, and to Liam's horror, he jumped down onto the tracks.

THE PUMPKIN PATCH

The rickety tractor slowed to a stop in the middle of the pumpkin fields. Crows circled above rows upon rows of decaying vegetables, each of them mushy and buzzing with flies. The farmer killed the engine and looked around, almost as if he was mourning for the rows of rotting pumpkins. He turned his attention to the hay-ride passengers, which consisted of three people: a husband, wife, and their little girl. He scratched his head and motioned to the field.

"Well folks, I'm sad to say that's the best of 'em. Weather didn't quite cooperate this year. This year's harvest was a bit of a wash."

Despite the field full of rotten vegetables, Brittney seemed ecstatic. She bounced on her hay bale, eager to find the perfect pumpkin. Her parents looked at her, then to the field, before exchanging mutual looks of disappointment. Brittney reminded them she was turning six this year, and she wanted to be a big girl and pick out a pumpkin all by herself. Reluctantly they let her go, deciding they would watch from the hay wagon. She squealed with excitement and took off, running and leaping over rows to find the perfect one.

"Don't go too far! Stay where we can see you!" her father called, but she was so focused on scanning the rotten pumpkins she didn't acknowledge them.

In Brittney's determined search, she encountered a rabbit. It was an adorable little thing, and at the sight of it she seemed to forget about all about her hunt. She was transfixed by the rabbit, with its fluffy fur and marble-like eyes. When it noticed her presence it scurried away, dashing through the patch in a white blur.

Brittney gave chase. Her pink rubber boots sloshed in the mud with every step. She weaved between caved-in husks and vines, hardly noticing the stray feathers and half eaten mice. Her boots stepped over bird carcasses and little piles of bones; little masses that seemed to be covered in dried yellow slime. When she finally found the rabbit, it was fidgeting nervously, its back against one of the better colored pumpkins. She reached a hand towards it and tried to beckon it, looking into the sweet little eyes of the rabbit. By the time she noticed the gaping jaws it was too late.

In a flash of orange and red the rabbit was consumed, hundreds of wicked teeth mincing the rabbit with a crunch. The large pumpkin looked at her with boil-like eyes, glowing pupils staring as its crooked maw gnashed the rabbit into paste. When all Brittney could do was watch in horror, the pumpkin paused for a moment, and opened its mouth to show the slimy, bloody contents.

A scream rang through the field, and her parents came running. She didn't want these pumpkins, was all she said. Her parents shrugged and took her home.

On the way, they stopped at the store to cheer her up. Later that night, a watermelon was carved.

THE SHEEPDOG

I go all out on Halloween. Every year in mid-September, I scout the decorations of every superstore and annual spooky shop alike, in search of the latest and greatest decorations for the holiday season. I spend weeks transforming my house into an icon for Halloween, so people from all over town and even the town over can drive down the block with their families, eyes wide at my collection of decorations. Lights, inflatables, fog, and creepy music. There's an abandoned house on my street and a few others don't decorate, so I like to go the extra mile. We set up a security camera on the doorstep to document all of the costumes and call out the best on social media. It's a hit every year. I've seen masks, makeup, and costumes of all kinds. However, I saw something last night that makes me question if I will ever decorate my house again.

We were in the final throes of trick-or-treating. There was only a handful of kids left, the crowds drifting away. My Husband and daughter had returned from their own route while I passed out candy; they were now sorting through her haul on the living room floor. I was trying to empty my bowl so I could end the night. I could see the last of the kids down the road, the only ones that hadn't come to my house yet. Two animatronics walking together, followed by a skeleton teenager who looked too old to be going door to door. After aweing at my spectacle, they came my way, pointing at my hanging skeletons and creepy window decals. They held out their bags with toothy grins, and I loaded the kids up with everything I had. I reminded them to avoid all fresh food and opened packages, and pointed to the camera so they could pose. They thanked me and skipped away, with the teenager saying something rude as they passed. When the skeleton teenager arrived, I showed him my empty bowl, and he said some words I'd rather not say. I shrugged him off.

"Better luck next year!" I said, and he followed the boys, after giving the finger.

As they left, I saw a figure across the street, standing in the artificial fog. It looked like a kid in a fuzzy costume, although what exactly I couldn't see. I smiled and waved them over, pulling an unopened bag from behind the door. They just stood there for a while, and I coaxed them over by opening the bag. They shivered and crossed the street, other kids paying them no mind. They moved slowly, creeping inches at a time. They left tracks behind them, muddy scuffs on the sidewalk. Like their shoes were caked in mud.

I couldn't tell who the costume was concealing, but I was patient with them. It looked like there was something wrong with their legs the way they shuffled, and the mask made them look straight ahead. When I got a better look at what they were wearing, I was impressed and unsettled at the same time. The kid was dressed as a sheepdog, but the costume looked very old. It was dirty, but I couldn't deny how good it looked otherwise. Like it had been pulled straight from the TV set in the 90s.

"Oh my gosh, I LOVE your costume! Did your parents get that for you?" I asked, motioning for them to come closer. I had a handful of candy ready for them. The sheepdog stood frozen. They just stared.

"What are you supposed to be this year, hmm? A puppy?" I asked cheerfully, keeping the awkwardness at bay.

They were looking past me, inside the house. I shook the handful of candy to get their attention.

"Don't say much, do you? That's alright. Happy Halloween," I said.

They stayed put but held out a crumpled paper bag. I brought it to them, unsure if there was a disability of some sort that I couldn't see. Closer now I could see the dirt in the fur of the costume, and there was a smell, an awful, piercing stench. I pushed it off, thinking maybe the kid was going through a tough time at home. As I filled the kid's bag I looked into their eyes, which were now very sharp and staring up at me.

"Are you alone?" They said, but the voice wasn't like a child's. It was deep and raspy, like an old man. I jumped, but tried to play it off. The eyes studied my movements, looking me up and down.

"What's that, hun?" I said, leaning closer. Goosebumps covered my skin.

"Who's in there?" They said, their deep groan of a voice giving me chills. Their large eyes looked past me again, then back up at me. This was a prank. Had to be. But the way it talked, the way it *wheezed*, it was too real to replicate.

"Excuse me?" I stiffened and backed away, blocking their view. Behind the mask, around the eyes, it was dark red. Like there was no skin.

"Are you scared?" They asked. I called for my husband.

"You should be going," I said. Down the road I saw porch lights go out. I decided it was time to do the same.

"Why? I'll have to come back." There was a beastly groan behind the mask. It sounded agitated, the mask shaking from the noise.

"Have a good night," I said, shutting the door and killing the light. I waited a moment before looking out, holding my breath while I tried to listen for movement. When I finally checked, the sheepdog was nowhere to be seen. My husband walked up, mouth full of candy, asking what I wanted. I went to explain but, in the end, I just shrugged and brushed it off. It had to just be some unsettling prank. Had to be.

The next morning, I checked the tapes. Everything was fine, kids coming up and down the sidewalk giddily for most of the night. Each of them was normal. There was nothing unusual. Until the Sheepdog kid. It was all distorted and grainy, several breaks in the screen's footage where the kid stood. When I went frame by frame, I could see it through the glitches. The old dirty costume, the skinned figure underneath. Fast forwarding a single frame with each tap of a key, the large eyes behind the mask took turns looking at me on the porch, then directly at the camera. Like it *knew*.

But as the night went on after I went inside, the kid blinked in and out of view, hourly through the night. Every time they would just stand there silently, eyes locked on the camera for minutes at a time. Sometimes they were at the front door. Other times, they were lingering across the street in the bushes. Towards the end, they were standing outside the front windows, trying to peek in. They shifted in and out of view all night, their last pose holding a stare at the porch camera, for over an hour. They stood there until the sun came up. As rays of light started poking through the trees, they just blinked away.

After watching it over a few times, I opened the front door and looked outside to make sure they weren't around. There was nothing aside from the candy wrappers from the kids the night before. Heading back inside, my foot scuffed a cluster of dried mud. The footprints were everywhere, shoe treads marked all over the place. Several of them littering the welcome mat. Near the footprints, I caught a whiff of that same unpleasant odor. That same rotting smell, radiating from where they stood.

RED LIGHT

Bob sat at a red light, cigarette softly burning as he tiredly waited for the color to change. Another late night, another long night shift. He took a slow puff, feeling a silent joy as the green glow illuminated his cab. Easing off the brake, Bob felt suddenly startled as a pair of headlights overtook him, coming out of nowhere and cutting him off before he could take his turn in the intersection. The stranger's sedan drove wildly, honking and spinning tires as they turned, and Bob could see the faint look of a woman's face as the driver. Anger enveloped him as she sped off, and only a second passed before he felt his foot mash the pedal to the floor. So many nights taking the same route, and so many rude drivers choosing their needs over his. He squealed into the intersection and pursued.

This bitch was getting a piece of his mind.

Traffics lines blurred in the night sky. Bob tossed his cigarette to the wind and white knuckled after her. Half a minute passed he caught up to her, her car idling at yet another red light. Fuming, he lowered his windows as he pulled up to her driver's side, insults loaded and ready to fly off his tongue. But looking through the red glow he found the car to be empty. The woman was gone, dome light on and the passenger door open.

"What the..." he trailed off, looking everywhere around him to see where she had gone. After a moment, he unbuckled and stepped out of the car. He walked around, looking into the car with frightened confusion. As he opened the sedan's door, his heart leapt in his chest. Grisly spatters of blood riddled the front seat, fresh on the cushions, dash, and steering wheel. Peering to the other side, he could faintly see a trail splashed over the road and into the rustled weeds. Police. He had to call the police.

Bob hurried to his car, the traffic light turning as he fumbled for his phone and started to dial. He got back in and shut the door behind him, holding the phone to his ear. His dome light shut off and he listened to the drum of the dial tone, heart racing as he frantically looked at the road ahead. Before he could shift from park there was a soft click, and his dome light came back on.

THE SKIN SUIT

Lindsey could barely see the road through the crowd of flakes. They seemed eager to clutter, rather *swarm*, the beams of her headlights as she navigated the terrain of the routine back road on her commute home.

With three hours of heavy snow and drifts clogging the wheel wells, she'd sworn she was on an alien planet. A drive that would usually have her attention spent on monitoring her Spotify playlist and catching up on the backlog of texts received while she was at work. But now the lines in the road were invisible, the signs spackled with white. As the minutes ticked away, she almost wondered if she had gotten lost.

Lindsey was more focused on the ache in her ankle—tediously working the gas pedal so she wouldn't spin out—when she saw it. The strange shape laying over the snow, a beige-pink sprawl amongst the universe of black and white. Her first thought was that it was a person, and she found herself braking immediately.

The wheels stopped, but the vehicle listed lazily, smearing slowly across the cluttered road in an awkward turn. Lindsey squeezed the wheel and felt the car rock as it found purchase on the road and was left looking at the mysterious shape in the snow.

It looked like a scarf or clothing, but there was an undeniable humanoid shape to it. It almost looked like someone had fallen while crossing the road.

She looked at it for a while before deciding to get out, squinting against the wild flurry as the headlights pointed through the downfall. She wanted to drive away, but couldn't help but think if it was her in the snow, would somebody help her?

Lindsey sighed and threw open the door, pulling her hood up against the elements. The wind was strong and tore at her clothing, and the snow shifted under her feet. She kept her eyes on it as she approached—the shape taking form with an unsettling realization that didn't peak until it was at her feet, limp in the snow.

Until she felt the clammy texture with her fingers, and the red residue that came off of it.

It was a suit of human skin, like it had been perfectly removed from a living person. It looked up at her with blank eyeholes, its deflated nose fluttering in the wind.

Lindsey decided to calmly walk back to her car and call the police, the unexplainable sight shaking her to the core. She tapped the screen on her phone, her thumbs slick with a slimy residue.

The wind was so loud, she couldn't hear it get up. Couldn't hear its awkward, floppy strides. The wheeze of its labored breathing when it quickened its pace.

As the deflated limbs wrapped around her, the phone fell softly to the snow.

When the operator answered, Lindsey's scream melted into the wind as the shape drug her away, the violent struggle fading once it was out of the headlight's reach.

FAILURE

Cal looked up at the clock at the top of the wall. It was 10:01 p.m. Six hours and fifty-nine minutes. He regulated his breathing, a trickle of sweat sliding down his temple. It seemed to crawl like a snail, creeping down the landscape that was his skin without even the slightest hurry. His intense focus on something such as a drop of sweat felt excruciating. He tried to blink hard and shake it off, but it stopped, almost as if in spite. Above him an old ceiling fan spun with a rhythmic creak, its axis a little off every time it completed a rotation. It was something he meant to fix, but he just never seemed to get around to it. He watched it go around and around, the creak almost hypnotizing him. After about a dozen turns he forced himself to look away, and when the dizziness faded from his vision, his eyes drifted back up to the clock. The minute hand was still ticking away, but not nearly as fast as he thought it was.

Cal was the head of maintenance for Dyer Falls High School. He had worked there for twelve years and counting, watching students come and go through time like they came off an assembly line. No matter how many kids grew and graduated, these halls always stayed the same, save for a replacement poster here and there. All that time fixing desks, wrenching on bleachers, and rehanging lockers, he stuck to his routine. In at noon, and out at nine. He worked like this for years, all the while keeping the school standing tall like it was his life's work. This all changed, however, when a few months ago, Coach Snyder gave him some friendly advice. Snyder was an athletic man, still maintaining a nice physique despite closing in on his fifties.

"You should start lifting a little. You lock the building up at night, you could get some time in and have the equipment to yourself. Just start slow, don't do anything I wouldn't do."

Cal started slowly at first, lighter dumbbells and cable machines. He built muscle quicker than he thought, and soon he started to feel a little more confident walking the halls of the school. It became a routine. As the nights went by, he upped the weight a little more and tried new things to expand his horizon of fitness. The more he pushed, the better he started to feel. Looking at the clock now, he heard Snyder's voice ringing in his head.

"Don't do anything I wouldn't do."

With the bar pinned to his neck, all alone, Cal could only look up at the clock helplessly. He breathed slowly, fighting against the guillotine with crushed hands as he stared at the clock. Coach Snyder would be in at five to kick off wrestling practice. He was always the first to get in. The minute hand had just completed a rotation. Six hours and fifty-eight minutes.

PIGS

Gerald awoke to the faint sound of squealing. The snout was snorting inches from his face, and when he sat up he was startled, unsure of where he was and how he got there. Above a red light swayed, casting a moving glow as it dangled on its cord. After looking around for a moment, he realized where he was and wiped his eyes in confusion. He was in his barn, but why exactly he wasn't sure. He recognized the red glow of the heat lamp above, something he had put in the keep it warmer inside for the winter months. When he looked around him, his confusion gave way to unsettling discomfort. Around him the pigs sat, their soft pink skin illuminated by the crimson light above. He picked himself up and looked at each of them; he was laying in the center of them, on the dirty canvas of hay that was the barn floor. They looked at him with shining glossy eyes, with nothing but the occasional snort to be heard in the barn.

"What's going on here?" he asked with a smile, but when they just sat and stared, he felt it fade into a frown.

Gerald had raised these pigs with his wife. Not for slaughter, like most farmers, these pigs were bred and raised as show pigs; living fat and happy lives in the barn with nothing but the best of care. She was a vegetarian, and when she passed, Gerald adopted the same lifestyle to honor her memory. They were all shapes and sizes. Landraces, British lops, Cumberlands, all plump and all winners of trophies. He was famous in town for these pigs, and he loved them more than life itself. Out of all of them, it was the baby Welsh pig that spoke first. Gerald recoiled at the sound of pronounced words from the pig's vocal cords.

"Why did you do it?" The baby pig asked.

"Do what? I didn't do anything to you," he pleaded.

Looking sad, the baby Welsh trotted away and nestled next to its mother. The other pigs squealed in disappointment, different pitches of cries forming an absolute hammer of screeching.

"He lies," they squealed. The red light swayed above, shining on every pig. They creeped towards him.

"Lie about what? I love you all. I always have," he tried to reason, backing away.

"You promised!" They squealed, tightening the circle.

"Please, I swear! I did nothing wrong." He put his hands out to make them listen.

Today was Gerald's fiftieth birthday. After the morning ritual of feeding the swine, he headed into town for breakfast with friends. It was nothing out of the ordinary to provoke such an unrest. But then he remembered, a tiny detail so miniscule yet devastating. The tears welled in his eyes. No one could save him. It was then he heard their prized Vietnamese Pot Belly lumbering behind him, each breath coarse and labored.

"The bacon. We can still smell the bacon," it wheezed, and Gerald's screams weren't loud enough to hear. Not over the squeals.

PULLED OVER

The brown sedan stopped on the side of the road, yielding to the strobe of the squad car behind it. On a ghostly back road in the middle of nowhere, a veteran officer was walking a rookie through his first night of rounds, and his first possible traffic citation. This car was going twenty under, making it an easy target.

"See? Now that we've run the plate number, the driver should be Fred Halls, adult male. White. Brown hair, brown eyes. You're up, kid. Just take it slow, license and registration. That's all you need to get. Get those and come back, I'll walk you through the rest," Jane told the rookie, trying to be as encouraging as possible. He looked nervous but determined.

"I got this," he said, and with a deep breath, stepped out of the car.

Jane watched from the passenger side, grinning a little. She remembered her first night, pulling over strangers in the dark. She watched the kid shine his flashlight in, chest puffed out. He spoke briefly, then shined his light on the back seat, then back at the driver. The driver turned his head slowly and spoke a little. Her grin started to fade, however. The rookie was walking back, empty handed.

He pulled open the door and sat quickly, his face drained of color.

"What are you doing, kid? Where's his papers?" She barked at him, but he didn't even look at her.

"We should go. Now," was all he said, his face frozen ahead in fear.

"What are you talking about? We can't just go. We're the *police*. What's going on? What's got you spooked?"

The kid said nothing. She looked at the car ahead, the driver was just sitting there.

"Fine. I'll take this one, just breathe, kid." She sighed and stepped out. She shined her own flashlight and walked to the driver's side, where the window was still rolled down. She put the beam on the driver, and said assertively: "License and Registration, please."

The man who turned his head slowly appeared to match the description of Fred Halls, brown hair, brown eyes. But the rest of him was wrong. His eyes were bloodshot to the point of bursting. His skin looked like plastic; his mouth cut on each side to outline his jaw. His hands were stuck to the steering wheel, bright reflective piano wire working severed digits that tapped at the wheel.

"What the hell?" she said.

"What seems to be the problem, officer?" said Fred, his jaw clacking every syllable. The piano wire coming from the back of his head jerked, like a fish on a line. She followed the line to see hundreds in the backseat, all leading to the trunk.

Panning light drew her attention, and she looked to see the squad car turning around. In disbelief, she watched the car speed off without her. She drew her gun.

Behind her the car door opened.

"What seems to be the problem, officer?"

FOUR-WHEELER

Morgan pulled into the driveway, his headlights casting a glow over his friend's house in the country. He had just finished his night shift and was doing a courtesy check for his buddy who was out of town. He needed to swing by and let his dog out, and make sure it had food and water before he went back home. For the most part, he was doing his friend a solid, but he had been slightly bribed into the chore. As he stepped out of his car, he heard his friend's voice replay in his head:

"Let Booker out for a few minutes after work and make sure his bowls are filled. You can hit the trail with the quad for a little night drive if you want, just gas it up and put it back in the garage when you're done. And be careful on the trails when it's dark."

He planned on doing just that. When he unlocked the door, Booker the Bullmastiff greeted him cheerily, and he quickly let him outside. He filled his large bowls with food and water, then eagerly made his way to the garage. The overhead door was still sliding up when he fired the quad up. He revved it excitedly and turned on the headlights, coasting out of the garage until he hit gravel. With a hefty crank he sped off, making his way for the forest trail he had set up behind his house. He saw Booker trotting around the yard as he disappeared into the trees.

The beaten path was dark and winding, little sugar maples keeping the trail narrow as he sped around. He ran the circuit during the day in the past, but the laps were short, so he figured he'd be okay in the dark. The maples blurred past as he climbed gears, the engine echoing into the night. The surroundings were spookier now, but it only fueled his adrenaline and made him go faster. Towards the end of his first lap, he saw something out of the corner of his eye. He swore it was an arm, but way too long. Had to be a branch, a trick of the light. He concluded the lap and decided he would go once more before putting it away.

Morgan shifted higher once more to make it a quick pass. He hot rodded down the trail faster this time, his eyes scanning the trees as he tore down the course. He thought of the arm branch and laughed. Surely, he was being paranoid.

Halfway through the dark course Morgan cranked the throttle, but it started to sputter. The ATV coughed and chugged to a creep before stopping dead on the trail. Before he could check the fuel gauge, something moving caught his eye. In the headlights something was watching, its bark-like skin blending in with the tree it hid behind. With a lanky finger it pointed to the four-wheeler, and the lights started to flicker. Through the strobe it emerged from the trees, limbs impossibly long and lanky. When the lights went out, Morgan turned to run and stumbled in the grass. He felt for something to help him but found nothing but grass and leaves. Left in darkness, Morgan could only listen as the slow footsteps drew near.

DUMPSTER DIVE

Pete was taking the garbage out late at night. His wife was in the apartment getting their daughter ready for bed, and he wanted to get the trash out so it wouldn't smell in the morning. The dumpster was in the back lot behind the apartment, and he walked to it to enjoy the cool fall air. When he reached the dumpster, he carefully hefted the bag so it didn't rip mid-swing. He heard the bag land amongst other discarded waste, and as he walked away, he heard a strange mechanical *whirr* echo from within. It sounded like a broken toy, and he curiously stopped to peek inside.

Looking over the brim, he could see a blue backpack shifting in the dark. He looked at it for a moment, and then looked around. He hadn't been in a dumpster since he was a kid, and for some reason he felt the old thrill nagging at him. He could check it out, it would be quick. After seeing no one around, he climbed inside. Trashed squished under his shoes as he grabbed the pack, and he unzipped it quickly.

It was an old robotic rabbit. It was old and dirty with solid, staring black pupils. It was stuck skipping in a hugging motion, joints clicking again and again. On its stomach was a little speaker.

"Hey there, little fella," Pete said. It felt very nostalgic,

"S-s-sing, w-w-w-ith m-e-e-e" All the while failing its hug motion. Pete sighed and went to set it down, suddenly feeling foolish for jumping in. He went to set it down.

"S-s-s-sing, w-w-w-ith, *who's watching the children?*" Pete stopped, and turned the rabbit around. It stared off, and the hugging ceased.

"What?" Pete said.

"*There's danger everywhere. Lo-o-ook both ways, b-b-efore crossing the s-street.*" The rabbit tripped.

"Oh. Huh," Pete sighed with relief.

"*Lock your doors, so they can't get in.*" Pete's hair stood up as he looked at the rabbit. It was looking back at him.

"*If the door is locked, try the windows,*" it said.

"What the hell?" Said Pete. He flipped it over. The battery tray was empty and clogged with dirt.

"*Hide under the bed until they sleep. We're patient.*"

"What are you?" Pete said, feeling small under the rabbit's gaze.

"*Who's watching the children, Peter?*"

"Fuck you."

"*The knife is sharp; the flesh is so—*"

Pete tossed against the dumpster wall. It bounced and started half-hugging again. Pete jumped over and stomped it over and over until it broke to pieces. He gathered the pieces up, stuffed them in the pack, and covered it with other trash bags. He hefted himself out and went back inside to find his wife and kid as he left them.

The next morning, the garbage truck came. The forks lifted the container and dumped its contents into its exposed top, every bag and pizza box falling to be compressed. Everything except a little blue backpack that bounced off the rim.

RUNNING

Jacob twisted the key, locking up the theatre for the night. The theatre was old and dingy but just closed on a fairly successful marathon of classic slasher films for Halloween. Every customer and employee alike were gone, leaving him with a dark theatre, and an even darker parking lot. He sighed. He was used to locking up at night, but it always gave him the chills. Like someone was watching.

He headed to his car, the only vehicle in the barren lot. He was halfway to it when he heard a noise, a sound coming from behind him. Someone was looking at the posters on the front of the building, the films coming soon. They had their head tilted to the side, like they didn't know what they were looking at. They were dragging something down the plastic frame of the pictures, but whatever it was Jacob couldn't see.

"Hey, buddy! We're closed for the night!" he yelled, feeling uneasy with the loiterer. Maybe they were drunk, or perhaps lost. Jacob stopped, his car only a few feet away.

"Hey, man, you hear what I said? We're *closed.* You gotta get out of here," he said, and suddenly the man turned. Jacob felt the stab of fear like ice in his veins, and his legs felt weak.

The man's bottom jaw was missing, the horrible mass that was his tongue swaying as he turned. His nose and eyes were also gone, bloody pits residing in their place. He held up a hatchet, its blade catching the light. That was when he started running.

Jacob panicked and bolted for his car, fumbling for his keys in terror. The sounds of shoes hitting the pavement echoed behind him, and he couldn't help but frantically look in the direction of his pursuer. The man's tongue wagged as he ran straight at him, closing the distance with an alarming speed. Jacob looked away and focused on the keys. The footsteps closed in, and he could hear the moaning now, a pained groan of a man without a jaw.

Jacob unlocked the door and scrambled in, thrusting the key in the ignition and starting the car. The man hit the passenger side with a loud thud, his horrible face pressed against the glass. The free-floating tongue lolled against the window, dragging slowly across. Jacob floored it and peeled out of the empty lot, leaving the running man behind. As he drove away he watched the man chase him, running as hard as he could. He watched him get smaller and smaller until he was gone. He sped all the way home, periodically checking the rear-view mirror.

Pulling into the drive, Jacob anxiously looked around. He contemplated calling the police, but he thought if he could just get inside the house, he would be alright. The face smear of blood and drool on the window served as a reminder of the close call. Jacob killed the engine and walked to his front door, crickets chirping in the eerily quiet night. He readied his key, went to insert it, then paused. He held it inches from the lock, hearing something through the haze of crickets. It was a rapid scuff, echoing in the distance. Pounding footsteps. He looked down the street, into the darkness past the lamp posts. It looked like someone running.

THE LOOKING GLASS

The long-haired woman slammed the bathroom door shut. She turned the rickety nob lock and threw her back against the door, looking around the shitty bathroom frantically as she reinforced the door with her body. She looked terrified but oddly focused, eyes darting desperately around the room as if the answer to her troubles was hiding somewhere in plain sight. There wasn't much to the bathroom; the walls naked aside from speckles of mold, a tiny dripping sink and mirror jutting from the wall, a dirty toilet tucked in the corner, and a bathtub complete with a shower curtain and rod. The bathtub was filling on its own, murky water bubbling in the tub so high it threatened to spill over the side. The woman was breathing hard, and for a second she closed her eyes and rubbed her temples, as if coping with a migraine.

The door behind her shook from a heavy *thud*, and the door rattled on its hinges. The impact startled her, and she faltered for a moment, throwing herself back against the door with a look of pure panic. Her bare feet slid on the grimy floor as she leaned as hard as she could. The monstrous *thud* pounded the door again, and the lock held with its last breath of life. The woman brushed the matted hair and looked above the tub to the shower curtain, and her eyes lingered there for a moment, the gears turning in her head as lip quivered in fear. She continued her stare while bracing for the impact, the brewing storm on the other side of the door calming. She tried to listen for booted steps, for heavy breathing, but there was nothing. Leaning on one shoulder she put her ear to the door, and the seconds ticked by in uneventful misery. All that followed was a series of chugs, and behind the door a chainsaw screamed to life.

A gasp couldn't help but escape her lips. She leapt from the door and snatched at the shower curtain, yanking it down with the rod in tow. As soon as her shoulder left the door, the rusty blade of the saw ate its way through, chewing through the wood like a million termites. The woman twisted handfuls of the plastic curtain and pulled, her bare foot holding the rod to the floor. As the linkage on the curtain broke one by one, the chainsaw blade angled through the door, coughing splinters as it worked. She pulled and pulled, the *tink-tink-tink* of broken rings getting closer and closer to an end. As the last one gave, she stumbled back on the sink, busting her elbow when she tried to stabilize herself. There was no time for pain. She let out a weak wail and flung the curtain like she was opening a trash bag. The wrinkles smoothed, and she held it up like a loose blanket. Beside her the tub began to overflow, the dirty water mixing with the wood shavings that were spraying in. The chainsaw eased, and the blade wiggled back out, retreating through the jagged scar it left in the door. With tears welling in her eyes, she squeezed the curtain in her hands and waited.

The bathroom door exploded. A bulky man in a metal mask and long ratty hair burst through, his shoulder leading the charge, with the chainsaw *chugging* beside him. The mask was of an expressionless face with closed eyes, like an iron cemetery statue. He was donned in a large black apron, rubber gloves that reached past his elbows, a dirty shirt and heavy boots. The blank metal face looked right at her, and without a word the saw was screaming and flying toward her. The woman ducked and threw the curtain in its path, the wicked teeth sucking up the plastic immediately.

The chain jammed suddenly and continued its swing, shattering the mirror above her. The masked man made an annoyed growl, and she crawled away, snatching the curtain rod before she got to her feet. Her pursuer ignored her. He just stared at the jammed chainsaw like he didn't understand. The woman gripped the rod like a bat and started swinging.

The rings jingled as the rod made contact again and again. The ribs, shoulder, and neck. Each time fiercer than the last, the rod denting every time it welted his mangy skin. The man seemed unphased by her effort but she pressed on, leaning into every strike until it ultimately broke across his temple. The metal mask turned to her once more, and an animalistic growl was muffled into the air. In one quick movement he let the saw go and threw a large fist toward her before it clattered to the ground. She barely moved in time, the gloved knuckles whisking her hair before it buried into the wall behind her. Rubble rained down as he cast a shadow over her, and she looked up just to see a raised boot coming down. She leapt away, sliding across the slick floor as his sole shattered to porcelain like a dropping hammer. She could do this. She was faster than him. With his hand stuck in the wall, she raised the mangled remainder of the shower curtain and stabbed him right behind the collarbone, driving it deep in a bloody spurt.

The monstrous man took a knee, a tortured groan escaped behind the ominous mask. His stuck hand still held by the wall, his other hand reached for the oozing rod above his chest. The woman felt relief to see him pained, and she tried formulating her next action. With the doorway behind her open and his saw immobile, she could make a run for it, surely it would take him time to...

In a blur, the chainsaw man ripped his hand from the wall. Before she could move, his gloved fingers covered her eyes and grabbed her by the face. The giant hand left her in complete darkness, and as she punched and scratched blindly he lifted her off the ground with his single hand. She kicked and tried to yell, but she could do nothing but flail at the air. In one broad swing, he spun her around like a doll and slammed her head into the wall above the tub. Her skull crashed into the tile and her arms went limp. The chainsaw man tilted his head to the side slowly and dropped her like a broken toy. The woman collapsed into the tub, water gushing over the side like a waterfall. The water washed over his giant boots as he looked down on her, completely and utterly defeated. Her nose broken, her eyes unfocused. A red trickle behind her head drizzled down the tub surround as her hands sunk into the water as she was submerged up to her stomach.

The man grabbed the chainsaw from the flooded floor and ripped the blockage from the chain catcher and guide bar. The mangled plastic came out in strands, and he took his time. The woman hunched forward and tried to move, but her head only lolled in response. The only thing she could do to stay above water was prop herself on her elbow, but it was no use. Her eyes couldn't focus, and they were starting to get heavy. The man cleared most of the plastic and tried the rip cord. It sputtered as it cleared the last of the plastic, then chugged to a stop. Another strong pull and it roared to life, ghastly exhaust clouding the small room. The masked man put a large boot on her shoulder and kicked her into the water, the foot riding all the way down until it held her under. She weakly protested, hands grasping at the leg of his pants. He ran the throttle hard and thrust the blade into the water where her face would be. With a terrible grind of bone and gore, the red water sprayed upwards like a geyser. The woman's hands contorted violently before falling back into the water. The saw continued to run, spraying the blank mask in an endless stream of...

Daniel pulled himself free from the viewing machine and the assistants steadied him and he slouched distraught in his chair. Back in the white room. He looked around in confusion, his vision fading between doubles and singles. Being here and not. He swatted at the men defensively, like he could feel the blood spray his clothes. But there was no blood, no water, no *chainsaw.*

Slowly he started to recognize the people around. The viewing technician was the same Asian lady in red lipstick. The athletic men and women in scrubs that held him still. Then he saw Winston, the handsome mad scientist guy. He adjusted his thick-framed glasses, and the staff seemed to relax as he drew closer. He held his clipboard in the crook of his arm, his other hand twirling a pen like a magician. The technician stood and handed some papers to Winston, which he looked over intently. He motioned for the staff to leave, and after some looks amongst themselves, they stepped out. Winston flipped through the charts silently while Daniel gathered himself. What was that? Was it real? What did it mean?

"Magnificent. Must've seen some wild shit in there. And still, you held in for a while. You could've pulled away at any time," Winston said and sat down.

"It was just so…" Daniel started, but Winston held up a hand in protest.

"I'm not worried about any of that. All I need to know is this: Will you be taking the next step forward, Mr. Brennan?" Winston asked, offering him the clipboard. Daniel looked away, thinking of the woman, the chainsaw, that evil mask. Even now the details were fading, but he couldn't shake the icy hand that seemed to be clutching his heart.

"Where do I sign?"

MIAMI NIGHT

Kimmy arrived at the hotel door, only to find it locked. She tried the knob several times but got nothing; only the soulless lack of turning in the humid summer night. A faint gust blew down the midnight street, rustling her sun dress. Through the neon glow of the surf shop behind her, she was able to see the printed instructions of the self-serve hotel.

CHECK YOU EMAIL FOR YOUR DIGITAL CHECK-IN. YOUR CODE WILL BE TEXTED IN TIME FOR YOUR ARRIVAL.

She didn't know when booking from the Midwest that her Miami hotel would have a digital check-in. No clerk, no human interaction, nothing. She cursed at her cell that was struggling to hold a signal. Each call to the support number ceased to the drifting dead zones, and each frequent glance at the empty streets surrounding her seemed to heighten her anxiety. A sports car quietly passed, the faint engine chugging as she pleaded for her phone to work. The support line rang indefinitely again, and she hung up frustrated. What a getaway this turned out to be.

She checked both ways, at the sidewalks covered in blackened chewed gum. The pictures online painted a different sort of scene, and she felt foolish for expecting better without seeing it in person.

Now she was stranded in a state she'd never been in, locked out of her own hotel like a typical tourist. She felt foolish and scared. If only she could get into the room and lock the door, everything would be alright.

She decided to take a walk, maybe get something to eat. The streets were shady and shadowy at night, but the neon glow of 24/7 shops added a shred of comfort. She walked down Ocean Drive, with a plethora of restaurants with dining extended into a once heavily trafficked street. She bumped into a man who grunted, his face mostly disguised by a Panama hat and designer sunglasses. He slurped at what looked like a street dish in a paper boat, shoulders hunched and seizing with every bite. Only when she got closer did she realize it wasn't a to-go container, it was a face. And he was eating it.

The man's split jaw separated vertically and crunched on his meal, a guttural groan emanating from him. She froze, and he paused to look at her with his ghoulish eyes. He roared, and her stomach weakened as her whole body crumbled in fear. She ran back to the hotel, the only shred of familiarity serving as a beacon of salvation. Her flip-flops slapped with each step as she bounded forward, the growling growing behind her.

Ahead, the door waved open; a janitor with headphones leisurely taking out the trash... He saw her running and waved her in, eyes wide at the maniacal tourist ghoul. The door slammed just as he dove for her. As he mercilessly beat the door, her phone chimed.

YOUR DOOR CODE IS 7246. ENJOY YOUR STAY AT SUNSET HOTEL.

THE VENDING MACHINE

Dilan wanted a Kit-Kat. He was in the middle of his rounds after hours at an office building he patrolled as a security guard. It was an easy enough job and night shift only. The team consisted of just him and another guy that would take turns walking a route through the halls of the facility. Their post was strictly to deter late-night break-ins, as the day crew would wrap up production after 5pm and the place would be empty for the rest of the day. It had been an issue as of late, vandalization mostly. Since he started it had been quiet, nothing but empty halls to break up the monotony of bad jokes.

He checked his watch; he was a few minutes ahead of schedule. There was an old vending machine a little ways back, and he decided he would hit it for a late night snack. He walked briskly, keys jingling with every step as he trekked back. In under a minute he made it, and was rewarded with the dated line-up of chips and candy bars. An old bulb lit the selection, flickering faintly as he looked over the display. He had never bought from the machine before, but tonight his craving was a little too demanding to ignore. After a glance in the empty hall around him, he fished a bill from his wallet and fed it to the machine. With a *whir* it lapped it up, and he glanced at the number below the red wrapper before punching it in. A3.

Nothing.

Dilan looked at its little screen, where it showed the clear indication of $1.00 in currency. He hit the buttons again. A3. The candy remained frozen in place, the flickering light teasing him in the dark hall.

"Come on, you," he said under his breath, and hit the number again. The idle screen taunted him with little green letters at the lack of selection: Who's hungry?

"*Me.* I'm hungry." He scowled and tried again. A3, nothing. He mashed the buttons, alternated them with his fingers in frustration. Same response: Who's hungry?

Dilan glanced in the hall again both ways and gave the machine a loud smack on the side. The lights flicked off, and he felt foolish for being rash. To his relief it was short lived, and they flicked back on, the silver coil turning to drop his prize. At last the Kit-Kat fell, but got lodged above the receptacle. Dilan sighed and crouched to reach in to retrieve it. Just as his fingers grazed the wrapper the light shut off again, leaving him indisposed in the darkness of the hall. He went to move, only to find his hand stuck.

The lights flicked loudly, and Dilan was met with a twisted face. Contorted in anger, the face stared at him, the attached body mangled and squeezed behind the glass. A bony hand was latched onto his wrist. It moaned two hoarse words, and Dilan started to scream.

Who's hungry?

FACES

"Can we stop? I need to rest. Just for a minute," she said, exhausted.

"Ok, but we don't have much time. We're almost out of light," he said, reluctantly.

"I'm so tired. I just need a minute," she said, sitting behind the large fallen tree.

"I know. I know. I am too." He sat next to her. They were ducked behind the remnants of a once gigantic pine, one that had long since fallen victim to gravity. He hoped it would keep them hidden.

"It hurts, babe. I just need to get the weight off of it." She sighed, rubbing her ankle. It was swollen, a maroonish tint enveloping the joint under her sock.

"I know. It'll be alright. You'll be ok. We got this." The pistol sat in his lap, his chin resting on her forehead.

"How much longer do we have? It's been *days*. How much farther do we have to go?"

"I don't know."

"We've been going in circles."

"We got this. We'll get out of here."

"It won't stop. Why won't it stop?"

"We'll outrun it."

"With this?" She rubbed her ankle.

"It's no big deal. We can do it."

"It got the others, Jim."

"I know."

"There were ten of us. *Ten.*"

"We'll be ok. We'll get out of here."

"It took their faces, babe. While they were *alive.* What kind of thing does that?"

A twig snapped in the distance, and they were silent. The whistling wind blew through the barren forest that seemed devoid of all life. Bare, twisted branches for as far as the eye could see. Above the trees, the sun was starting to descend.

"I miss home, babe," she said, her eyes heavy. Her head resting on his chest.

"Me too. We'll be there soon."

"I'm just so tired."

"We'll rest a minute. We'll be ok."

"Ok. Just a minute. Then we'll go."

The wind blew, and the branches knocked. In the distance, leaves rustled.

"I'm sorry. I'm weighing us down."

"No, you're not. We're sticking together. No matter what."

"I'm sorry, babe. I didn't see the log."

"Don't be sorry. It's fine. We'll be fine."

Behind him leaves crunched, just loud enough to hear. She was almost asleep.

"Babe?" she asked.

"Yeah, babe."

"I love you."

"I love you too." He kissed the top of her head. Behind them another branch broke, and a whisper carried on the wind. She didn't hear, for she was thankfully snoring, softly and peacefully. She wouldn't hear the gunshot either.

The loud crack echoed in the dead woods, and the deep groan immediately followed. The sob left his lips against his will, but it didn't matter now. He was allowed to grieve.

He saw the arm first, long and slender, reaching over the fallen tree to hoist itself up. The shifting body of necks and heads came next, garbed in the faces of his friends. It could have his face. He didn't care. The last bullet kept hers from joining theirs.

THE SNOWMAN

I pour a generous splash of whiskey into the half full mug of hot chocolate. I watch it mix together, a bitter concoction of sedation and holiday cheer mingling terribly in the mug. I know it won't taste good, yet I bring the mug to my lips and tilt it back. I take it all in one mouthful and swallow quickly, trying to get it all down my throat before the bite hits. I swallow and wince as it catches up, sighing as the warmth burns its way down. I set the mug down sloppily and wipe my mouth.

The living room plays the same old shit, Frosty and Rudolf going to the ends of the earth to make Christmas possible. My glazed eyes watch the TV as I fumble for the end table, to the open pack of cigarettes. I knock my phone over in the process, but I find them, fishing one out and tucking one in my lips. I'm drunk already, a little sooner than I anticipated. I step into my slippers and yank open the slider to the patio, my movements exaggerated, exhausting. The night air chills my skin. I close the door behind me a little too hard, and the knock echoes into the night. I gather myself and light my cigarette on the third try. The cherry glows as I suck in, and as I exhale, I stare directly at the silhouette in the apartment yard. They built another one, it seems.

The snowman stands idly in the dark, its blank face mocking me. There's no coal or rocks for eyes, no corn-cob pipe. No arms either, just the regular three-ball stack of white packed snow. Even without eyes and a mouth it mocks me. Taking another drag, I stare hatefully at it. I know it's the inebriation clouding me, but even that doesn't keep the faces out of my head. I see them tonight just as clearly as they were twenty years ago. Flesh frozen solid, eyes perpetually staring forward. I wasn't there to hear their screams, but I hear them now, fabricated in my head to torment me. I dig my hand inside my pocket to feel the bulky plastic of the flare gun.

I look into the blank face of the snowman, itching to crush it to pieces. There's no way it comes back now, after all this time. A part of me thinks I lost it long ago, that I'm just a puppet waddling around on the strings of the past trauma. But when the flakes start to fall, and the children roll the mounds into his shape again, I think of Braxton the Snowman, and his deep predatory growl.

I flick my cigarette to the wind and it sparks against the molded body of the sculpture. It doesn't react, only stands quietly in the dark flurry. With a last taunting look at the snowman and head inside, hearing the screams of the past fade as I slam the slider behind me.

A LIFE THAT FITS

Somewhere along the way, my husband and I had lost our spark. We couldn't quite place why and we didn't talk about it. We just idly watched it slip away. Like an out-of-control car heading to a lake, I watched my husband sink into depression. At first, I took the initiative to try and make him feel better. I signed up for the gym and encouraged him to go with. I tried cooking his favorite meals to surprise him. I even tried to spice things up in the bedroom, but nothing seemed to work. Several times I asked him what the matter was, or if there was something I could do. Each time he shrugged and only offered the same words.

"I feel like my life doesn't fit me anymore."

Over time, we talked less and less about it. Looking back, maybe things would've ended better if we tried. But in the back of my mind I felt the same. Perhaps that's why I watched it burn out. I doubted myself at first, but that changed the day I met Julia.

Julia was bubbly, athletic, full of life. I saw a beauty in her I had never seen in a woman before, and in time, it was all I could think about. It was innocent at first. A lunch date here. Running together after work. My husband seemed to notice my new enthusiasm, and it only seemed to drive him down more.

As I spent more time with Julia, he got worse. Whereas I started running and feeling better, he stopped eating and talking almost altogether. He grew thinner as my infatuation with Julia grew, and before I knew it, she took me on a date. My spark had returned, but for someone else. It was something I would have to come clean about soon.

We met at a bar on the outskirts of town, a little place called The Sixth Shot. It was there my husband and I had first met; a place we hadn't been since our rut had begun. Julia and I shared a table, and in time, we shared drinks and the feelings we felt for each other. Later that night, we shared a bed.

I enjoyed it so much, we agreed to meet there again. I couldn't deny my guilt, but still I looked forward to it, more than anything I ever had before.

It was a few days before we met again, and when I saw her, she was beaming. She was at the same table we had before, but was sitting oddly different. Her shoulders seemed more hunched, and it's like her makeup wasn't right. The closer I got, the more apparent the changes became.

"I feel much better, thanks to you," she said, in a voice very unlike her own. The smile she gave was wrong, limp even.

I looked past the stretched skin, into the undeniable eyes and grinning teeth of my husband.

"Now that I have a life that fits."

LOOK AT ME

I see the image, and I scroll past it. I watched the NSFW tag drift up until it was gone, replaced by something I can view without needing to click past the blurred image. They always get you with it. Curiosity gets the better of you. If not this time, it'll get you when it comes back. The title doesn't really matter. But it's the lack of initial perception that drives you crazy. Something you could see if you would just pull back the curtain. When you can't see it, it's like a joke you haven't been let in on. Maybe it's nudity. Gore. Maybe some inappropriate words. But you don't know until you see it. You just have to let it sucker you first.

This isn't the first time I've seen it. I've already scrolled once. This time is the second. It's all blurred, like usual. The picture is distorted, and it looks like the silhouette of a person. Maybe it's a selfie. Maybe it's a girl, flashing her breasts. Maybe it's a guy, and his face is beaten up pretty badly. I don't know what it is. It could be anything. It could be nothing. The NSFW tag and the blurring doesn't betray itself. You can't see it unless you *want* to. Conscious effort must be put into it. Almost as if it's on purpose, the title of the post simply reads:
LOOK AT ME.

The post is fairly new. I saw it for the first time a couple hours ago. It's got some upvotes. It's getting traction. Whatever it is, it seems to interest enough people. But I just don't feel like I should. I read the title. It's bait. It's definitely bait. But there's something about this one that unsettles me. I don't know what it is. I can't explain it. Whatever is there, hiding until I give it permission, it must be there for a reason. Maybe the image is cursed. One of those things. They float around, give people sudden spooks. It's all a joke, really. A cheap thrill. Well, you know what? I don't feel like doing it. Not this time. I'm scrolling past it. I don't need to see what it is. It's not important. What could it really be, anyway?

A few hours later, I see it again. I'm on my phone in the bathroom, scrolling through bored. Just procrastinating getting up, really. The same title. The same tag. LOOK AT ME. Not safe for work. Again. This is the third time today. It's in "hot" now. Or trending, whatever you want to call it. I see it and I almost immediately scowl to myself. A few thousand upvotes. Almost a hundred comments. Whatever the post is, it's got people talking, that's for sure. But I'm not doing it. I'm sticking to my guns. It's not absolutely *necessary* that I view the post. I don't *have* to, and that's fine. It's annoying me now. You don't have to look at it. You don't. I won't. I'm off the app for today. I'm putting my foot down. Who had the last laugh now?

It's there again.

LOOK AT ME.

Just the sight of it pisses me off. I'm at work, getting changed. About to start my shift. I boot it up just to see what's going on in the world before I get to the grind. That's all. And what do you know? It's there. Waiting for me. Taunting me. It blew up overnight. This fuckin' thing. Same title, taunting me. The thumbnail is blurred, the same mystery picture or start of a video. There's no way of telling, but I'll tell you what. It's got over fifty thousand upvotes. Awards, stupid shit like that, keeping it IN MY FACE. Over a thousand comments. How does this happen? It makes me furious. I'm not doing it. I don't have to. Matter of fact, I blocked the post. I'll never see it again. Simple as that. Sucker someone else with your bullshit, cause it won't be me.

I don't understand. I'm off work now, finally get some time to go through my phone. And what do you know? It's there. LOOK AT ME, I'M NOT SAFE FOR WORK LOOK AT ME LOOK AT ME. It's ridiculous. Not only is the post I blocked still gone, it's like it multiplied in spite of me. Several different forums, over and over again. All "hot", top of the day, every single one of them. A hundred thousand upvotes on some, comments in the thousands. How can this be happening? What could be so *damn* captivating? What could it be? Why are you guys giving it the attention? You let it get like this. It's like you're not giving me a choice. Do you want me to look? Is that what it is? You know what? Forget about it. I can do whatever I want. I'm uninstalling the app off my phone. That way it'll be gone. It has a lot of trouble running my old desktop anyway. It wouldn't even be worth the effort. I'm gonna call some friends and see what they're up to. Later.

I looked. I didn't want to, I just sort of did. I don't know what came over me. I called my friends, to see if they wanna hop online and play something. And you wouldn't believe what they were going on about. That damn post. They're raving about it, it's all they're talking about. It's bullshit.

"You gotta look, man, just check it out. You gotta see it. Check it out and get back to me or something. It's insane. Then they hop offline without another word. All of them. Three of them, in a row. I didn't really have anything else to do. I booted it up on my computer. And sure as shit. It doesn't take long to find. It's at the top of every sub it gets posted in. It can't be stopped, it's everywhere. I can't escape it. I clicked on it. I didn't know what else to do. I figured if I just looked, it would go away. Right? The page loaded painfully on my old desktop. Turns out it's a video of a guy. Nothing special. He's just a guy, nothing special about him.

But the video's still buffering, so I skim the comments to try and get the scoop before.

"Yo, what the fuck?"

"Is this shit real?"

"Who is this? Anybody now him?"

"Dude, why? I can't unsee that."

"Sick, really. What's wrong with you?"

"That's enough internet for today."

"I think I can see what he's looking at. It's hard to see though."

"What is he looking at?"

"Is this fake? It doesn't look like it. I think I'm gonna be sick."

"This is metal A.F."

"I CAN SEE IT."

"Oh god, I looked and I can't unsee it."

"Why is this shit everywhere?"

"DUDE, I CAN SEE IT TOO. I'M GONNA TRY TO GET A CLOSER LOOK."

"Why the fuck did you have to share this with me?!? Now I can't stop thinking about it. Glad I already brushed my teeth for the night. Still..."

The post finally loads, and the video starts playing. The guy is just looking at his webcam, and just the video itself makes me uncomfortable. He's using a little handheld mirror, trying to see into his mouth. He looks frustrated. He tries a few times with it, but whatever he's trying to do he can't make it work. He's mumbling, but it's hard to make out what he's saying. Something like:

"I can almost see it, I just can't get far enough." Something like that. He glances periodically at the webcam, like someone is watching him. I don't know if it's a stream or what, but the whole thing gives me knots in my stomach. Like I need to click off it. But I can't, I'm already invested. It's like I don't have a choice. I need to see what happens.

The guy tries the little mirror one more time and shakes his head. He looks back at his screen, and you see his eyes tracking something from his monitor. He's reading a message, from the looks of it. He reads the words and nods. Mumbling in agreement.

"Yeah, I think you're right, I need to open wider."

Without warning, the guy grabs his top and bottom jaw and starts to force them open. I cringe immediately. That's when he turns completely toward the webcam and starts screaming. You can see the strain of physical pain, but he doesn't stop, and I couldn't bring myself to look away. He gets closer slowly, the screaming getting louder. You see his jaw break, and the corners of his mouth start to rip. It's horrible. It's the worst thing I've ever seen. His mouth splits faster than you would think, but it's so terrible I don't know how to describe it. I panicked and tried to click off, but the video froze. My cursor froze. After what seemed like an eternity of me looking at this frozen screen, the window minimized itself and I got a pop-up about how the specific program stopped responding.

I was left in traumatized silence once it was over. It didn't make any sense. It looked too real. There was something nagging at me though. Something aside from the trauma of the video. It was at the very end when I saw it, right before the window crashed. Deep down in the darkness of the guy's throat, I saw *something*. Something looking at me.

I don't know what it was. Sometimes I think it was an eye, other times I think it was a face. Every time I seem to recall it, it's like my brain conjures up something new. I'm not really sure what to think, but one thing is for certain: I can't stop thinking about it.

I relaunched the website and tried to find the post. But all I found was more confusion. The videos were gone. All of them. Not a single one remained. I checked every sub, even ones where I knew for sure I had seen it posted. The video was gone.

LOOK AT ME was gone.

I tried finding it for days after that. The images are burned in my mind, and I think about it constantly. When it didn't turn up,

I started digging online. Every time I thought for sure I found the right link I would click on it, but it would only be a dead end. "This page cannot be found." Shit like that. I tried to get ahold of my friends, but none of them were getting back to me. They didn't check their texts. They didn't answer my calls. It's so strange. I have no one to share my experience with. Only you.

The strangest thing of all is I saw something the other day. I had just finished brushing my teeth, and I was flossing. My mouth was wide, and I was trying to really get in there with my hands. I just happened to look. There was something in there, deep down. I didn't know what it was. I only saw it for a second. I stood frozen in the mirror. I stood there for a while, trying to see it again. But there was nothing, just the back of my tongue and my tonsils. I know I saw something back there. I just need to get a closer look.

WINGS

Alan opened his eyes, straining against the brightness of his environment. He was lying face down, his cheek pressed against a sandy surface of ground he had never seen before. He lifted his head and felt the ground beneath him, parched lips gasping like it was his first breath. He rolled over and sat up, his eyes wandering in dismay as he failed to recognize his surroundings. Slowly he wiped his eyes, a heavy fog filling his brain as he tried to recollect something, anything. But there was nothing, and he could only look around in wonder at the ever-expanding world he found himself in. Surrounding him were miles and miles of what looked like fine sand, like pearls that had been crushed to dust.

He felt the grains between his fingers, watching them fall in silence. His eyes wandered to the almost indiscernible horizon, to the sky above that was identical to the ground on which he sat. There was no sun or source of natural light; this plane just simply seemed to be.

"Do not be afraid." Words rang in his mind, a chorus of toneless yet oppressive voices speaking through the haze in his head. Alan looked for the source, whirling around his blank purgatory with wild eyes and shaking hands. There was no one but himself, and at first, he thought someone had pulled some elaborate prank. Until he looked above.

The shape was menacing and absolute, something beyond his comprehension. It looked down at him with several eyes and writhed with the sound of twisting leather. It floated down from above, dwarfing him under what looked like thousands, *millions* of feathers. It was an amalgamation of wings that stretched in every direction, taking turns flapping softly as it made its silent descent to him. As the gears in his mind fought to identify it, he conjured the only term that would fit such a beautiful, horrifying creature.

It was an angel.

"What happened to me?" Alan asked, his voice dry and raspy.

"It would seem you perished," said the voices, its body coming to a stop just inches above the smooth earth.

Alan winced, a barrage of flashes strobing his mind. He could hear the squealing tires on repeat as the car crash looped in his mind, the wreck that crushed him into a tree. When the vision passed, he looked at the angel.

"I died," he said plainly. He looked down the never-ending plane, a whirlwind of sadness, regret, and longing aching within him.

"Yes. That fate has brought you here," said the Angel, drawing closer. The many feathers on its wings flexed as it came near, dozens of eyes narrowing on Alan.

"I see. Are you here to take me to Heaven?" asked Alan, looking up at the Angel. Its wings curved outward and around him. Alan looked at the feathers, and how the vanes melted together. It was then he realized they weren't feathers. They were teeth.

"There is no Heaven."

MIRAGE

Sally trudged through the sand, angling her sun hat down to keep the wind from blowing it in her eyes. It was much hotter and windier than she thought it would be. Sweat trickled down her back, and the breeze was more punishing than it was enjoyable. Just when she was starting to regret her little desert trip, she saw the faint blue light ahead. Quickening her pace, she forgot the wind and ran for it, holding on to her hat so it wouldn't blow away.

It looked like an orchid, sprouted from the sand like it had been placed there by magic. With its petals stark white and the stem vibrant and healthy, the mystic flower radiated with chilly blue light. It was beautiful; the way the petals moved with their own grace despite the harsh desert conditions. She sat and withdrew a sketchbook and charcoal pencil, stealing glances between quick strokes on the paper. It was perfect. *This* is what she came here for.

She was entranced by the flower. With the sapphire glow reflecting in her eyes, she sketched madly, each stroke purposeful and precise. The ethereal aura pulled her in like a caress on the cheek, beckoning her towards the cool light. A crisp bead of moisture rolled from a petal, and she watched it hang off the edge, holding her breath as the pencil replicated the moment in charcoal. Just as she was almost finished, something caught her eye, and she was pulled from her trance like a glass shattering.

Off on the horizon, through the shimmering waves of heat, was a squiggly line. It reminded her of an inchworm, the way it wiggled. It didn't look real, and at first she thought it just was a mirage. But when she squinted, it almost looked like it was coming closer. She tried to ignore it and finish the drawing, but when she heard the sound, she felt a pit in her stomach, like she was suddenly looking over a cliff. It was like the sound of a circular saw screaming through plywood.

"PULL ME OUT! PULL ME OUT, NOW!" she shouted, stuffing her things in her bag. In the distance, the inch worm was getting bigger and bigger. With each squiggly jump it dove into the sand and resurfaced, its size doubling so fast she couldn't breathe. The screaming worm was rocketing toward her, its gaping maw lined with serrated teeth and whipping tentacles.

Sally woke at the desk, hysterical and sobbing. She pulled the headset off with shaking hands and looked at the drawing. There was no flower, only erratic lines and smudges across crumpled paper. She didn't understand. She was so close. Behind her, a man garbed in full Kevlar armor approached, an assault rifle held limp. His face was nothing but her own reflection in his visor. He looked at the mess of scribbles and sighed.

"Disappointing," he said, and motioned to the guards behind her. They marched over immediately, each taking an arm. They yanked her out of the chair and started dragging her away.

"I'll get it right, I swear! Just me another chance—" she pleaded desperately as they hauled her off.

"There is only one chance. And you failed."

"Just one more chance! Please! *Please!*" She kicked at the guards, and they grunted with frustration. The man in the helmet stepped in and clocked her were with the stock of his gun. She went limp, her shoes squeaking on the tile as they carried her.

"Put her with the others. She's no good to us. Get me the next trending artist."

TO HAVE AND TO HOLD

She looked at the paring knife, hand trembling as her eyes followed the sharp edge of the blade. With a trembling hand she emptied her glass of wine, hoping it would give her the courage to do what she needed to. All of this because of an accident.

For better or worse.

She couldn't bear the pain and suffering any longer. She returned the knife to the block; a wedding present from what felt like another lifetime. She considered each of them, inspecting the steel as she refilled her glass. The filet knife was too thin. The bread knife too crude. She swallowed another mouthful, tears streaming involuntarily. The chef knife would do. At least she could put her weight behind it.

For richer, for poorer.

Pawned possessions, unrelenting bills piled high. Not enough money to buy out of the hole that had been dug. Knife in hand, she wiped her tears and left the kitchen, crossing the once furnished dream house stripped of all luxury to help stave off the debt.

Through sickness and in health.

Trips to the hospital, written prescriptions. So many drugs, steadily stronger as the tolerance built. Her husband's retching, and the sobbing apologies that followed. His desperate, slurred begging echoed in her mind every time she closed her eyes. Sleepless nights, and the constant reminder of what would never be again. These thoughts drove her up the stairs, validating every step. She gripped the knife as she ascended, holding on to it like it was the only thing she had left.

To love and to cherish.

She stood in the doorway like a ghost, her shadow from the hallway light casting a silhouette in the darkened room. There he lay, slightly propped, snoring softly in his constantly inebriated state. The drugs kept him out, but not for long. If she wanted it done, she would have to move quickly. She crept into the room and to his bedside, the sight of his face quivering her lip. Quietly she straddled him, holding the knife close as she maneuvered in the dark. With a groan he awoke, tired and sedated pupils confused. When they fell from her face to the knife they welled instantly; they know of what's to come. She kisses him and he returns it weakly.

"I'm so sorry for all of this. I love you." His words choked towards the end, and he's too tired to keep it together.

"It's not your fault. It never was. I love you too."

Until death do we part.

She leans into the blade and it cuts easily, severing the skin and tendons as she sawed across his throat with both hands. With his teary eyes squeezed shut, his broken spine and shattered legs kept him from resisting. As he gives his final throws, she sobs and looks to the nightstand at the numerous pill bottles covering its surface. Soon, the car accident that destroyed his life and spared hers would haunt them no longer. She could only hope there was enough to do the job for her.

DASHCAM FOOTAGE

*T**he following is being used as evidence for the disap-
pearance of missing person Blake Emmerson. If you
have any information pertaining to his whereabouts, please
contact Dyer Falls Police Station.***

Footage procured from vehicle plated under the name "Blake Emmerson" starts en route down a highway, time stamped 3:59p.m. Driver appears to be driving clean, staying in their lane at an appropriate speed. Video continues for several minutes without anything unordinary. Altercation appears to start at timestamp 4:04p.m.

START OF FOOTAGE

Driver suspected to be Emmerson is passed by another vehicle, a 1997-1999 Lincoln continental with no license plate. The overtake is quick and dangerous, the Lincoln effectively "cutting off" Emmerson without signaling to change lanes. Emmerson is seen braking immediately, almost rear-ending the Lincoln. The driver ahead speeds away, a red-gloved hand flipping the middle finger out the window. Emmerson is audibly heard inside his vehicle, sounding angry.

Emmerson hangs back and slowly changes to the left lane. Emmerson appears to speed up, presumably to get a look at the driver. Both cars accelerate past appropriate speeds. Approximately a car length away, the Lincoln continental changes lanes again, effectively cutting off Emmerson a second time. The Lincoln brake-checks, and Emmerson barely slows in time. The Lincoln swerves provocatively, and Emmerson can be heard swearing inside the vehicle. Somewhere in the car (presumably backseat) children are heard crying.

The Lincoln continues slowing down. Emmerson chooses to change lanes to avoid the aggressor. Midway through the lane change the Lincoln swerves again, cutting Emmerson off for a third time. Another brake check, inches from collision. Emmerson clearly audible inside the car, apparent distress, more swearing. The crying of children is also clear.

Ahead, the Lincoln puts on a signal and starts listing to the shoulder. Emmerson keeps straight, then at the last second follows, presumably heated and looking for confrontation. Emmerson's vehicle and the one ahead come to a complete stop on the shoulder.

Emmerson is heard briefly, and the car teeters as he exits the vehicle.

Ahead, the Lincoln sits for a moment. The driver is not visible.

Emmerson appears in view of the dashcam, wearing a gray t-shirt, tan cargo shorts, and a brown ball cap.

His hands are raised, gesturing aggressively to the driver, then points to his own car behind him.

Emmerson approaches the rear of the vehicle, fists clenched.

Driver door opens on the Lincoln. A second later, the trunk pops.

The driver of the Lincoln steps out, a foot taller than Emmerson. Suspect is dressed in fluffy but stained striped clothing with red gloves and boots, presumably a Halloween costume. Suspects hair is curly and red. Suspects face is painted like a clown.

Children audibly crying in the victim's car.

Trunk to the Lincoln opens slowly, an additional suspect crawls out, similarly dressed. Wielding a baseball bat.

Emmerson turns to run.

Accomplice from the trunk swings the bat.

Emerson falls, and together, they put him in the trunk.

Both clowns look back at Emmerson's vehicle.

Audible crying.

END OF FOOTAGE

TWO ENTER, TWO LEAVE

One hour. Two enter, two leave. The rules were simple, yet I couldn't help but feel the existential dread as I was seated at the table. The room was small and packed with a table and two wooden chairs. It was relatively empty save for a little red dot camera in the corner, a fire extinguisher, and some of the most obnoxious wallpaper I had ever seen. A timer sat on the table's surface, a big red 60:00 ready to count down. Across from me, an older man was sitting down.

"Oof," He said, shifting as soon as he sat down, "You'd think with the money they're advertising they could get some more comfortable seats."

I thought he was being dramatic. My chair wasn't *that* bad.

Behind us we heard a loud 'click' of the door locking. We both jumped; it was one of those hefty industrial locks. It reminded me of a bank vault.

The older gentleman continued to grimace over his chair, readjusting several times before settling in. It was quiet for a time, seconds passing awkwardly as hung out in the silence. We exchanged a nervous look as the timer started counting down, the sudden movement of the red digits raising the hairs on my neck. We looked from each other to the plain room, waiting for some announcement on the intercom there was nothing but us and the walls.

"Some ad, huh? 'Two enter, two leave'. Like a game show," I said, scratching my head.

The older man let out a chuckle. He uncrossed and recrossed his legs, sighing again over the chair. He looked at the walls, eyebrows fluttering in amusement.

"I know. They said it's a social experiment. But twelve grand for an hour? It's crazy. Fits right in with all the other rubbish in this town I suppose. Guess that explains all the paperwork," he said.

"No kidding. It's like the town is cursed."

"You know, you're right," he shifted in his chair, "that deal with the salesman's kid? And that guy getting burned alive? You remember that?" He leaned forward.

"Yeah, yeah. It was all over the news. My family talks about that shit all the time. They're always talking about that cat. And that *fucking shirt*. You ever see em?" I asked, looking at the timer. The digits were ticking down quicker than I thought.

We laughed, and the man perked up in his chair. "Nah. But the shirt! Dear god. I swear, once this is over, I'm buying one of those ridiculous things. Just to prove 'em wrong. It's a hoax. Gotta be. That is, if we get out of this alive." He winked.

We bullshit back and forth, talking about work, life, the weather. We even talked about the ridiculous wallpaper. Before we knew it the time was up, an eerie silence ending our conversation as it reached 00:00. We both raised our eyebrows. Nothing happened.

"Guess I'll knock and tell 'em it's over" I said with a sigh, getting up. The man looked suddenly worried as I went for the door.

"Did you hear that?" he asked, and he looked like someone had whispered something in his ear.

"Hear wh—"

With a scream the chair collapsed, taking the old man with. It happened so fast, pained screams and wet chomping echoing off the terrible wallpaper. Pulsating meat, like a hotdog turning inside out in a microwave. I looked around frantically to find something to help, but I knew deep down, whatever was happening was well beyond my control. The way it ingested him... it was instant. Beneath the table I watched it gestate, an ever-changing form of mutilation and wooden carapace. It shifted rapidly, expanding and compressing as it fed loudly. Whatever its form truly was, my mind couldn't make sense of it. I could only stare and listen, hoping to God it wouldn't come my way.

It started to shrink, the squelching slurps easing as the mass seemed to collect itself. Hesitantly I looked over the table, and it shimmered together, slowly calibrating back into a chair. The screams faded, and all I could hear was its breathing, a deep wheeze that seeped through the grain of the wood.

I jumped at the loud 'click'. The door was unlocked.

I made my exit quickly, my skin crawling even after I was out of the room. A rather disheveled scientist looking fellow pulled the door closed behind me. I scratched at my skin, feeling vulnerable and violated. I could still hear the slurps in my mind. I don't think I'll ever forget them.

The scientist handed me an envelope, and after staring at it stupidly, I realized it was the money.

I opened it up and looked at the stack of bills packed tightly within.

"It's all there. Twelve thousand," he said, looking me over then turning back to his clipboard.

"So... what now? I just leave?" I asked. I couldn't help but look at the door and wonder if the lock would really keep it in.

"I mean. You can go back in, if you want. But you'd have to give me back the money," he said, wearing an amused grin.

"No, no. God, no," I said, shoving the money in my pocket.

"That's what I thought. Well, you have a good night now. You find yourself hurtin' again, feel free to come back. Same rate, every time."

"Yeah, no thanks," I said, turning on my heel. I went to walk away but stopped, a nagging thought getting the better of me.

"Say, uh, what *are* you guys doing here, exactly? And you expect me to believe anyone *actually* comes back?" I asked, and his face was immediately serious.

"You know I can't tell you. You signed the forms. Besides the fact, you *don't* want to know. And to answer your second question, you'd be surprised," he said, waving me off before turning back to the clipboard.

I left him to it, trying to focus on the money instead of whether I'd ever be able to sit in a chair again.

MAKE THIS GO AWAY

"I just want to know what I did wrong. None of this makes any sense. We used to be so happy. You haven't been the same since you came home late that night. You don't even touch me anymore. I can't even get you to look at me. I even bought lingerie," she said, her eyes welling from pain and desperation.

The therapist looked at the wife and husband sitting across from him, one partner in shambles, the other apparently distant. The woman was weeping now, looking longingly at her partner who sat straight, his face blank. He looked oblivious, hands on his knees like this was all a misunderstanding.

The therapist scrawled in his notepad, erratic strokes scribbling the words: abstinent, disassociated, affair? He cleared his throat and uncrossed his legs, reaching for the tissue box as he leaned forward.

"Mrs. Stellar, would you mind if I spoke to your husband in private for just a moment?" he asked, offering her a tissue. She sniffled and nodded, taking a tissue as she sat up. With her heels clicking on the floor, the husband watched her go, eyes tracking her as he sat straight. Once the door closed behind her, he let out a breath and spoke curtly.

"Make this go away."

"I'm sorry, Mr. Stellar, but that's not how this works. In my counseling, I work to bring both sides together equally, so you two can reach an understanding, and hopefully repair your marriage."

The husband stared, leaning in slightly.

"Make. This. Go. Away," he said again, his words slow and cold.

"Burying the issue won't resolve anything. I need you to open up to me and to your wife, or we won't be able to move forward. Whatever the problem is, I promise you we can work through it. But until you show me what's really going on, we are anchored here," the therapist said, removing his glasses and setting the notepad down.

"You want me to show you?" the husband said, more a statement than a question.

"Yes. Once we know the root cause, we can focus on healing. I've helped many. I can help you too," the shrink said, making a bridge with his hands.

The husband nodded slowly, then without a word, he blinked. Hard. When he opened them, his eyes were unfocused, looking in two directions. With a loud wheeze his throat inflated, like a bellowing frog. His mouth opened unnaturally wide, and through the gaping tunnel that was his throat, arms protruded. Tiny and blood soaked, the arms pulled, hefting out the body of a disfigured fetus, a singular eye staring from its disfigured head. Its features were human, but unnaturally warped.

The therapist could only sit petrified as the husband rose and crossed the room, the little body commandeering until it was inches from his face. As the large eye narrowed, the husband spoke, drool spilling as it spoke slurred but understandable words:

"Make this go away. Or I'll wear you instead."

GROCERY STORE SURVEILLANCE

Grant tapped slowly on the keyboard, the screen switching to a different view of the store each time. Each feed showed a different aisle, and he inspected each grainy shot intently. Moms browsing many boxes of cereal, kids wide-eyed in the toys section, men silently contemplating in the liquor aisle. After several snippets of daily life, he stopped in the condiment section, his finger hovering above the key as he stared at the broken jar of banana peppers. He adjusted his glasses, swiveled in his chair and leaned in close, his hand reaching toward the phone receiver. After clearing his throat, he pushed the page button and spoke in a well-practiced voice:

"Clean-up on aisle eight. Clean-up, on aisle eight."

Grant moved on from the feed, cycling until he saw an employee. In the live recording, he watched them give an exaggerated sigh and make their way to one of the supply rooms. Leaning back in his chair, he removed his glasses and rubbed his eyes, feeling a slight headache forming from the monitor's glare. As he looked away, people came and went, pushing carts as their eyes looked from product to product. In his peripheral vision he saw someone stop, and the movement made him turn back to the screen. Standing completely still in the center of an empty aisle was a man, and he was looking directly at him.

"What the hell?" Grant said, resting his glasses back on the bridge of his nose.

The man was completely still, eyes locked on the camera, almost like it was looking at *him*. He had a slight grin on his face, but that wasn't what made him unsettling. Even through the grain on the old camera feed he didn't look right, like he had been cutout from a movie or something and placed there. Younger kids and adults looked at the cameras curiously all the time, but this was different. It was like his body was outlined in static. Grant reached for his radio but stopped. The man was walking now. Backwards.

With his eyes still on the camera, he moved, like someone was rewinding him in a movie. The steps were strange, jerky. When he reached the end of the aisle, he turned without looking, his stare remaining until he was out of sight. Nobody even noticed him.

Grant switched to the next feed, and there he was, walking backwards. It was a little faster now, and he was weaving through the boys' clothing section, the same rewound motion as before.

He switched feeds again, following him. Each time the speed increased, his backward jog heading somewhere without looking. Grant started to panic, his hands shaking on the keys. Pediatrics. Shoes. Electronics. The jog continued, just as the stare. Grant was holding his breath. He was getting closer. The smile growing. The last feed was a full backwards sprint through customer service to the back door. *His* door. He heard the glass break, and he covered his eyes.

THE MOUNTAIN GOAT

Quentin looked through the scope, keeping his arms steady despite how badly they burned. Through the glass of the optic was a gorgeous mountain goat, quietly standing in the breeze. The wind rustled its fur and the blades of grass around it, its solid black eyes pondering as it stood still. Part of Quentin wished he had a camera instead of a firearm, but after the purchasing of licenses and travel fare, it would be silly not to take the shot now. Despite his admiration for the beauty of the animal, Quentin disengaged the safety, and felt the crisp, cold steel of the trigger on his finger. Training the reticle behind its broad shoulder, he held his breath and started to squeeze.

Something wasn't right. He eased off the scope and looked with the naked eye, careful not to move too much despite his sore, aching limbs. Far away the goat remained still, and Quentin watched for a moment before returning to his looking glass. Through the magnification he ran the reticle over one of its horns, taking in the details until he saw what had stood out.

There was something hanging off one of the horns. A tag?

He backed off again, resting his sweaty forehead against the stock as his thoughts raced. Surely it wasn't part of some kind of reserve, was it? It didn't make sense. He bought the tags from the

DNR office specifically. He was allowed to hunt on this land. He was *sure* there was nothing to worry about. Even with his assurance, the thought persisted.

He looked again.

It swayed gently in the wind, almost blending in with the dark exterior of the horn it was attached to. Quentin was transfixed on it, despite his body's demand for a stretch. But there was something about that tag. It wasn't right, he just couldn't put a finger on it. He stared for what felt like minutes before it dawned on him. It wasn't a tag; it was a charm. But of what, he wasn't certain.

Quentin backed off the scope again and wiped the sweat from his eyes. The wind blew harder in the valley, tossing the grass around him and chilling his neck. He swallowed and settled back on the scope, his cheek pressing against the stock again. The sight picture showed nothing but the grass in the wind.

The goat was gone.

Quentin panned slightly, feeling foolish for missing such a perfect opportunity. He hoped to catch it trotting away, and he shifted his elbows to adjust directions. Quentin's elbow struck something solid, and goosebumps crawled over him like a wave. Hesitantly, he looked to see a hoof, its dark outer wall splitting and seeping under the bright white fur. His eyes trailed up, and the shadow of squirming, separating flesh cast over him.

Without even a scream, the gun fell to its side. The sounds of struggle were brief. When the wet ripping subsided, the grass danced peacefully in the wind.

EVERY NIGHT, I HEAR THAT SOUND

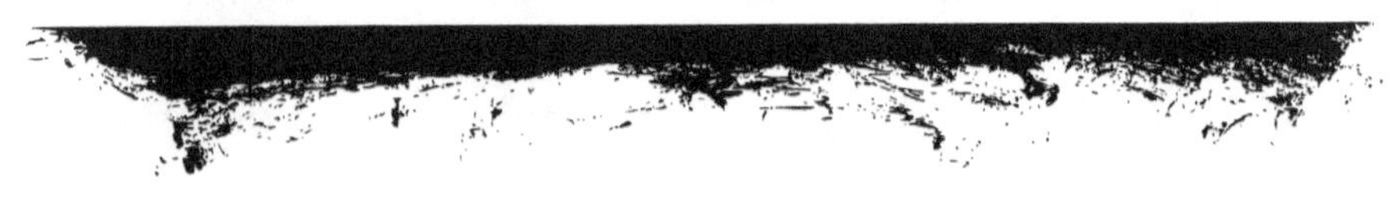

Every night, I hear that sound. Like a dry serpentine on a winter night, that squeal echoes off the trees like a dying rabbit on the wind. Every night I listen to it, my sanity breaking under the wheel of this isolation. I watch the trees sway in the breeze. I see the animals scurry. Scared, no doubt. Each time I wonder when it will be me who steps foot out there, in search of that god awful noise. It squeals every night, taunting me. I look out the window, trying to spot a difference in the same mundane landscape, wondering why I took this job in the first place.

Each morning I walk the premises. It's a few acres, nothing much. It feels like surveying most days. I walk the property, notepad in hand, jotting down every significant detail. Most days, it's the same. The same old pines, the same dead grass. I report my findings on a little corded phone, one that's screwed to the wall of my hut. Day in, day out. Despite the monotony of it all, I do it and I do it right. Every shrub, every dead log. The woods that surround this place, I don't know what's wrong with it, but I know it's watching. I know it feels me there, and I know it doesn't like it. Maybe that's why they pay so much. Maybe one day, *something* in this place will take me. I hope it's something new, at least. I grow tired of looking at the same shit. The fat wallet doesn't compensate for the *rotting* of my time. It doesn't pay for the wasting of my brain cells. Whatever it is they're guarding underneath this wooden shack, I hope it's worth it.

They said something broke out today. It's strange, really. No unordinary sounds, no sirens, nothing. I guess maybe it's so far underground I wouldn't hear it. Just the same shack and the same woods. I long for the change in scenery. Part of me wants to see what the hustle and bustle is about. Maybe it's something exciting.

Today, my little cordless phone rings nonstop. They want answers, they say. They want to know what's *changed*. I look through the little window, looking at the same trees and the same dead wilderness as the night before, and the night before that. Nothing unusual, I say. I look and I look, but they still persist. It doesn't make sense. I've seen it so much, surely I would spot the difference. Maybe if my word isn't good enough, they could do it themselves. I don't see them coming up from the underground. I don't see them risking their necks to find the "difference".

There's a willow in the yard today. I look at it, and I swear I've seen it before. It sways in the wind next to the other trees, like it's been there all this time. I swear it belongs, but in the back of my mind, I *feel* something isn't right. Its flexible limbs draped like a gorgeous head of hair in a summer breeze. Locks flowing, begging to be touched. The vines are a bright green, the leaves blood red. It's unlike anything I've seen before. I'm sure it's nothing, but I should go check it out. All I know is, that same sound, the same squealing, it's much louder now. Even when I cover my ears, it's so loud my ears ache.

They're bleeding now. I pick up the phone, but I can't hear what they say. Only ringing. I look at the willow, the graceful limbs beckoning. I want to touch it, but that damn sound. Why is it so loud? Make it stop. How do I make it stop?

PIZZA DELIVERY

There's a heavy knock at the door, three hard raps that echo in the apartment hall. Doug looks up from his book, an uneasiness washing over him as he looks at the door. He wasn't expecting company. He waits for a minute, staring at the door, worried eyes looking above his glasses. Maybe it was just a mistake.

The second set of knocks makes him jump, and he quietly closes his book. He declines his lazy chair, watching the door cautiously as he approaches.

"Pizza Delivery," says a young voice. It rings unusually loud in the hall.

Doug creeps to the peephole, taking a deep breath before looking through. On the other side of the door is a bubbly young man, patiently waiting with his red satchel in hand. Silently, Doug looks in the corner next to the door, to the loaded double barrel leaning against the wall. He didn't order pizza. He hasn't in a long time.

"Wrong house. Go Away," says Doug, looking through the peephole again. The young man looks confused. He shakes his head and reads the address out loud.

"That's you, right? Says here 'Large Bacon and Jalapeno'," he says, looking a little annoyed.

Doug shakes his head. It doesn't make any sense. He didn't order this pizza, but it *is* his favorite. He could smell the bubbling cheese, the savory scent of the bacon. It calls to him.

"There's been a mistake. Now leave," Doug commands. He walks back to his chair and returns to his book. The Pizza guy leaves.

The next day, he comes back. Three hard knocks.

"Pizza Delivery."

"Wrong house, again," says Doug, shotgun in hand. He breaks it open slowly, to make sure it's loaded. The brass blasting caps shine in both barrels.

Same address read, same toppings.

"Wrong. House. Don't come back," Doug says. He returns to his chair, taking the gun with him.

He returns the next day. And the day after that.

"Pizza Delivery."

"Pizza Delivery!"

"I brought your pizza, Doug."

"Open the fucking door, *old man*."

He doesn't knock anymore, he's just there, all hours of the day.

"I brought your favorite. Open up!"

"Pizza's here!"

"I brought two this time."

"Pizza Delivery, pizza deli—come on man, open up."

"*You can't hide forever.*"

"You fuckin' hungry or not? I got all day. I got *all fuckin' day, Doug.*"

Doug looks through the peephole, sweat dripping down. It's different every time. Sometimes he just stands there. Sometimes he crab-walks up the wall, backwards. Sometimes he's hanging there, swinging from a noose, *pizza delivery,* on repeat. Yesterday his eyes were closed, and when he opened them, they were mouths.

"Pizza Delivery."

"Pizza Delivery."

"You know who it is. Open up."

Doug sits against the door, the shotgun held close. The delivery guy isn't talking anymore, but he's always there. Sometimes, there's only growling.

Doug looks outside from the third-floor window to the burned-up cars and overgrown streets. He smells the cheese, the bacon. He's getting hungry.

WE WATCHED THE SUNSET

I watched my father struggle with the stone slab, wondering how he mustered the strength to keep going after all this time. He never gave up hope, even after the doctors exhausted every option to make my mother better. His resilience continued even after she succumbed to the illness, going out in the middle of the night in search of "trinkets" after we lowered her into the ground. Nights of endless research, looking through books and typing at his computer.

He shoved the slab aside, revealing a doorway into the crypt.

"Don't be afraid. We're almost there," he said, exhausted, wiping his brow and motioning to follow.

"You remember what I told you?" he asked, walking through the dark corridors, his lantern lighting the way.

"Yes. Keep my thoughts happy. No matter what happens," I said, solemnly.

"Good. That's my boy," he said with a smile, but I could tell it was breaking. He patted my shoulder and we walked together, the stairs growing darker the further we went.

The steps were crawling with bugs, skittering appendages squirming around. If you looked hard enough, the walls looked back at you, pulsing eyes following.

"Eyes forward. Stay focused," my father said, grabbing my hand.

As he guided me through, I thought of his instructions and tried my best to keep my thoughts happy. I thought of how we would go to the beach when my mother wasn't sick, splash in the water and build things in the sand.

The stairway opened to a massive derelict room. Things lurked in the shadows, watching and drooling. In the center stood a tall obelisk, accompanied by a stone statue. Groaning horrors of flesh watched curiously with grinding teeth.

I thought back to the beach, melting ice-cream cones, and flying kites so high they looked like specks in space.

At the obelisk, my father had me stand back. He laid the objects out, each trinket wicked and intimidating. The stone statue came to life, looking us over with an unblinking face. I held my breath as it approached my father, but he stood tall.

I thought of the hugs they would give me together, and the days we would go and just lay on the beach. Making shapes out of the dancing clouds.

My father and the statue exchanged words. Eventually the statue spoke, its voice deep and monotone.

"Very well. Every child needs its mother."

My father returned to me and knelt down, giving me a big hug. He fought back tears, but he was smiling.

"We did it. But I need you to be strong, understand? No matter what happens. I love you very much."

I nodded, unable to restrain the tears. He walked to the altar, hands at his sides. At the top of the obelisk a massive eye appeared and looked down at my father.

His screams came next, and I closed my eyes.

On the beach, we smiled. I rested my head on his lap, and we watched the sunset.

MIDNIGHT SMOKE

Connor kissed his daughter goodnight and followed his wife to the doorway of their child's bedroom. He stood by the light switch for a moment, letting her snuggle in.

"Goodnight, sweetie," they said, and he flicked off the light.

"Night Mommy. Night Daddy," she said, and they walked away, leaving the door cracked.

Connor followed his wife down the hall. When she turned to the bedroom, he brushed past her to the living room.

"You're not coming to bed?" she asked, and he scratched his head.

"I'm just gonna step outside really quick. Get some air," he said, already pulling on his coat.

"I thought you were *quitting," she said*, her scowl harsher than her words.

"I know. *I know.* I'm working on it. Just real quick before I lock up," he said shamefully. She eyed him for a moment, then waved him on.

Connor pulled open the slider to the balcony, shivering against the outside air before shutting it. This was winter's second coming in February, or third or fourth, it seemed.

Shrugging against the wind, Connor got out a smoke and lit it. His drag and exhale were slow, hoping to lift the weight that seemed to be bogging him down. Work. Bills. Car trouble. Stress in every imaginable form was trying a balancing act on his shoulders. He just wanted a minute of peace.

The snow was coming down. Connor looked at the flakes dancing around through the cherry's glow. Despite the harsh temperature, it comforted him. He stopped mid drag and coughed, noticing something in the whiteout across the road.

There was a man across the street, and he was watching him.

Connor rubbed his eyes and looked again. He had moved a little closer, like one leaping step.

Squinting, Connor waved at him as he tried to make out the details. People walked up and down this road all the time, but they never just *stopped*. He was just standing there, mouth slightly open.

Connor looked around in the heavy snow, but he was the only one on the balconies. He looked back and jumped. The man had crossed the street, head still angled up. Not moving at all.

"Can I help you?" He shouted down. No response.

What the fuck, he thought, turning to look inside. The living room was empty, his wife and child were still in their rooms.

He turned back, hoping it was just his imagination.

The man was in the front yard, the same frozen look of expectation.

"I *said,* can I help you?" Connor yelled. He dug out his phone to call the police. After dialing the digits, he checked on the stalker.

The man was outside the apartment door now, hand on the knob, looking straight up. Smiling.

He looked just like him. Before Connor could speak, the man winked.

Connor turned, reaching for the door. Pounding steps raced up the hallway stairs.

The slider was frozen shut.

Through the glass, he saw the front door open.

AN ORDINARY OIL CHANGE

Zach strained against the ratchet, putting all the force he could exert as he tried to remove the oil plug. The bolt started to turn, and he felt relief, praying it was the bolt coming loose and not him stripping it. It broke loose, and he worked the ratchet one quarter turn at a time as he freed it from its grave. With the sound of grinding sand, he turned it free, a horrid wafting scent stinging his nostrils as the seal was broken. It popped free and tumbled away, and he barely slid the drain pan in time to catch the mess.

What unleashed from the oil pan was a chunky, sloppy pour, carrying with it the scent of rotting flesh. Zach covered his mouth and gagged, wondering exactly how long this craigslist car had sat before he picked it up for cheap. The oil plug was caked with what looked like burnt oil, a batter-like substance packed in the threads. Whatever the previous owner added to it, it couldn't have been good. His only goal was to flush the fluids and flip it, send it on its way with a fresh battery and hopefully come out ahead a couple grand.

He shimmied under the car, hoping to get away from the awful stench as he felt for his chain wrench. As the last of the dregs drained from the pan, he looped the chain wrench around the filter and gave it a crank. To his luck, it twisted free, the same burnt texture breaking loose with a sharp *hiss*. This was almost burned on as well. The smell worsened as Zach spun it off, and a squirt of hot oil hit him in the face.

The thick fluid hit him between the eyes and traveled across his skin like skittering centipedes. He swatted and wiped his face, but the fluid was too quick. It burned worse than gasoline, and drug like it was full of gravel. The putrid ooze invaded his eyes and mouth and choked his throat as he tried to scream.

"Hey, I remember you from earlier. Oil change, right?" Said the auto store attendant.

Zach's eyes were irritated, and he wiped his face with a shop towel.

"Yeah. I grabbed the wrong oil. The high mileage was too thick. I must've made a mistake," he said with a sniffle.

"May I suggest full-synthetic? Although if the car's too old, the change in viscosity may cause leaks. You didn't have to bring the funnel back though."

"Oh, this? It's a little too wide. And sure. Mind grabbing it for me? I had a bad spill, got all over. Sinuses are killing me," Zach said, looking around the store.

"Sure thing, just a second and I'll grab that for ya."

A minute later, the clerk returned with a new five-quart jug, and Zach watched him approach with a blank face.

"Was that cash or caaAARGH!"

The attendant grabbed his throat as it gushed wildly. Zach dropped the knife and yanked the attendant's head back, holding a jug and funnel to his eviscerated neck. The dark blood spurted and sloshed on the floor, and he adjusted the angle to better catch the flow. Zach watched it trickle in, licking his lips as the jug grew heavy in his hand. Behind his eyes, the parasitic oil squirmed with hunger.

GATOR

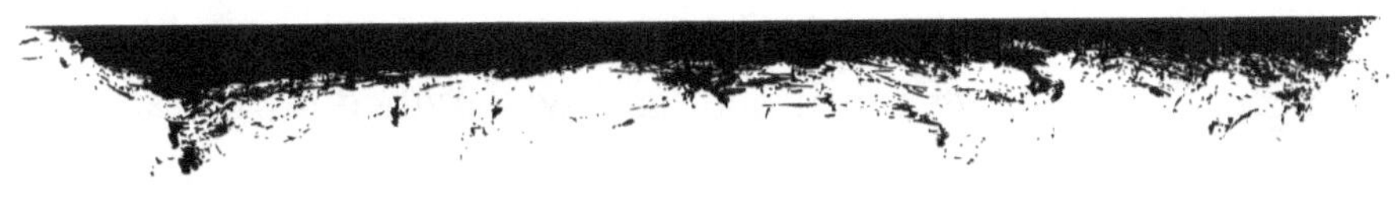

It was just a joke. It started at the mini-golf course, at the little kiosk where you get the tiny clubs and your ball to put. There were six of us total: Matt, Wyatt, Cory, Uzzi, Big Mike, and me. We were out trying to decompress after a stressful couple of weeks, an attempt to shake off the gloom we shared with some beer and effortless fun. We were just about to start the course when we noticed a ramp leading to a little platform, exotic yellow lettering on signs that read "Feed the Gators".

We spent a couple bucks buying pellets, and the six of us ascended the ramp to check it out. It was a little pond, crowded with tired-eyed alligators, each the size of a small cat. We tossed the pellets in, watching the lizards lazily eat as we finished our beers. When we exhausted the supply, we came back down the ramp, reading the many signs as we passed a couple of girls. After reading the signs out loud so many times, I turned to Matt, and accidentally called him "Gator".

"Wait, is your name really gator?" One of the girls said, and Matt stifled a laugh. I was just about to speak up when Uzzi stepped in, putting an arm around Matt's shoulder.

"*Why yes,* his name *is* Gator," Uzzi said, patting him on the back.

"No, my name's not really—" Matt started.

"Wow, that's *sooo* cool. Gator, what a wild name," they said, laughing as they walked away.

Matt rolled his eyes as we laughed. I wish I could say it was just a onetime deal, but the forced nickname continued for the rest of the put-put course. He laughed along with it for a few holes, but by the time we reached the end of the course he had thoroughly had enough. The *gatoring* continued, and we laughed at his expense until our sides hurt and we wiped away tears.

"Gator!"

"Get it Gator!"

"Matt—sorry I mean Gator."

When the fun was over, we all parted ways. Each of us got into our own car and drove off; Matt, Uzzi, and Cory were driving to Ohio for a five-day SCA event while Wyatt, Big Mike, and I had to work during the week. We agreed to hop online and play video games when they got back the next weekend.

I got through another grueling week of work, catching Snapchats from the three at their event. It looked like a blast, lots of badass armor and homemade weapons, complete with hot elf cosplayers. I tapped through their stories as the days passed, living vicariously through them to drag myself through the grind. However, as the week progressed, I noticed something peculiar about the snaps they were sending me. By Wednesday, Matt had stopped sending altogether. The others continued until the end of the week, but every group picture they took started to have the same similarity. In each time photo, Matt was looking less and less enthusiastic. With his lips pressed tight and his brow furrowed, he looked angrier as the days went on. On the last one, he looked absolutely furious, like he was boiling over.

I imagined the heat had gotten the best of him, or perhaps he had forgotten to bring the portable camping fan he used to help him sleep at night. Either way, he looked like he wasn't having a good time. I figured I would hear about it when they returned.

Friday evening Uzzi hopped online, and I took that as the cue that they had come home. One by one we each grabbed a headset and sat in front of our computers, joining the same chat room to bullshit now that the week was done. Everyone showed, except Matt.

"He said he's not feeling well. He's probably burned out. God knows I am," Uzzi explained through the mic.

"Yeah, I'm sure the Gator thing didn't help though," Cory said.

"What *Gator* thing? Uzzi, what's going on here?" Big Mike said, audibly popping a beer in the background.

We thought of the mini golf the week prior, and we started laughing. Uzzi and Cory did not.

"Yeah. The Gator nickname thing got a little out of control. Eventually, the whole camp had chimed in. I don't think he cared *that* much, but it went on a little longer than it should. It just... happened. People thought it was hilarious, so we kept the bit going."

"Yeah. He didn't say much on the ride home though. Hope he's not too mad," Cory added.

"I'm sure he'll be alright. Probably just cranky from all the driving," I assured, but the whole thing felt a little off.

"Should I pay him a *visit?* That outta cheer him up," said Wyatt, who had a knack for ending conversations with sexual innuendos, usually butt stuff.

"Oof."

That night we went on without him, dicking around on a "Souls" game until we were too tired to continue. Uzzi and Cory called it early as they were bogged down from the trip, and we agreed to call it a night. Work had kicked our asses as well.

The next night, Cory didn't make it online. Neither did Matt.

I gave him a call, listening to the dial tone ring on repeat. I hoped he was alright. He *did* enjoy his solidarity and would usually reach out when he was ready.

That night, we got a call from Cory's mother. He had been attacked in his sleep and bled out during the night. I tried to get more details, but she was hysterical, saying a bear had mauled him, something like that.

We were devastated by Cory's loss. The whole thing was strange though. We didn't have bears around here.

It was like a shadow had been cast over the friend group. We didn't really chat or talk about playing. It didn't feel right. Nobody really knew what to say, so we didn't talk about it.

Big Mike was found next. His spouse found him in the basement, at his little bench where he painted miniatures. His throat had been annihilated by large gashes. There was blood everywhere, a trail of footprints leading up the stairs and through the backyard. Forensic analysis said the footprints weren't human. Matter of fact, they said the prints didn't make sense at all. Whatever had made the prints didn't exist.

I tried ringing Matt several times, but each time it went to voicemail. I stopped by his house, but his truck was gone. The front door was unlocked, so I let myself in. His house was pretty normal, aside from the layer of dust that had accumulated. It was like he had been home, but not actually living there. I searched the whole house, finding nothing but long dirtied dishes and old pizza boxes. There was no sign of him anywhere.

I was just about to leave when something caught my eye: a little light shining under the door of his computer room. I opened it, hoping to find him in there, maybe sitting at his desk.

His computer was smashed, both monitor and tower ripped apart and strewn all over the room. The computer case had been gutted, frayed wires sticking from the crater that had been left behind. The floor was covered in little steel cutouts and shavings, scattered about like a scrap yard. It was his SCA armor. It didn't make sense. The gear had cost a fortune.

I left the house in a hurry, deciding to personally check in on Wyatt and Uzzi. If I could just get to them first, maybe we could run and get help.

When I was a block away, I could already see the cherries and berries flickering in the distance. I idled past, afraid of what I would see. In the back of my mind, I already knew.

Wyatt was disemboweled, strung up on his balcony from his own intestines. I wanted to stop and help, but I had to help Uzzi. Pulling the car onto the highway, I rang Uzzi and was relieved when he picked up.

"Waddup," he said, sounding tipsy.

"He got Wyatt," I said, my foot burying the pedal.

"Oh god, no. I was hoping we'd be wrong."

"What do we do?" I asked.

"Alright. I have a plan. First, I'll... hang on a second. I think I hear something," he said, sounding distracted.

"No, wait, get out of there!" I yelled into the phone. On the other end, there was silence.

When I finally heard something, it was faint, like Uzzi had set the phone down.

"Matty?" I heard him call, followed by the undeniable racking of a pump shotgun.

There was silence for a minute. Eerie, lingering silence. Then a deafening gunshot. Screaming, loud and torturing. Another gunshot, then silence.

I hung up the phone and u-turned home, pissing off every driver as I swerved into the oncoming lanes. I sped home, running through red lights and stop signs until I made it home. I needed to get home and warn my family.

The radio was buzzing with the onslaught, witnesses reporting a wide string of creature attacks. Some say it's a bear or a lion. Other sources say it's just a man wearing a metal costume, or a robot breaking into homes and committing the murders. People all over town reported their sightings, each with something new.

Some said it's like a suit of knight armor with cut out teeth and modified boots. Others say he has deadly claws; a pair of gauntlets fashioned with many kitchen knives. Others say he has a tail of wires and computer parts. Some swear it's actually a reptile that can drive.

I made it home in record time and ushered them out of the house to somewhere safer. I would have to handle this alone. My family would stay at her grandparents' house, and I would call when everything was over. Watching the car pull out of the driveway, I had a sinking feeling I wouldn't be calling. I hope I'm wrong.

It was just a joke. I'm recording this now just in case I don't make it through this. Hopefully someone can piece this together. I hope they don't have to; I hope I can...

He's here. He's getting out of the truck now; I can see him underneath all of it. It's hard to see, but I know it's him. I'm scared, but maybe I can talk him down. I hope I can. If I don't succeed, tell my family... tell them I love them.

"Matt? What have you done?"

"You must have me confused with someone else. My name is *Gator*."

THE CHAIR ALWAYS WINS

I t was just an ordinary chair. Old, hand carved oak coated in a long-scuffed varnish. Somehow it was still standing the test of time, in the middle of the little white room, as if out of spite. In the eerie silence of the room, a patient sat watching, sitting on a cot next to it. Outside, men in white coats waited, looking through the glass in the door.

Maxwell stared at it like a live bomb.

Sitting there in his gown, he lifted his gaze from the old wooden chair to the doctors outside, and they encouraged him with a nod. Swallowing, Maxwell stood from his cot and cautiously approached it.

The test, or game, if you will, was simple. Maxwell reciting the doctor's words in his mind, like trying to find some deeper meaning.

Get out of this room, and you are free. But keep in mind, the chair won't let you. The chair always wins.

Dyer Falls Penitentiary was known for its unorthodox reintegration programs. It was reserved for only the most "troubled" individuals, but promised either total rehabilitation or death. Twenty-six forms required a signature to be admitted, and only one required to get out.

Maxwell looked at the chair, then looked around the room. With only his cot, the small window and the door, there was nothing to it. The door was locked, a full security team on standby while the doctors observed. The window was locked as well, trying to open it yielded nothing but jotted notes from the doctors. No bookcases, no end tables, no ceiling fan. Everyone even waited outside. There was nothing stopping him, nothing to be afraid of... except the chair.

All he could do was stare as it sat there, taunting him. He couldn't help but be apprehensive about it, the way they broke it in, garbed in full hazmat suits. It didn't make any sense. Would they *really* just let him walk if he could get out?

Hesitantly he held his breath and touched the chair. Just a few fingers on the seat, but he prepared himself for a shock or needle prick. Nothing. He grabbed it, held it up, and looked at it. The wood was worn and cracked with age, but that was about it. It was just an ordinary chair after all. He looked at the doctors, who were scribbling away.

He hefted it over his shoulder and smashed the window.

With a loud crash the pane shattered, large shards breaking on the ground. Maxwell tossed the chair aside, a grin on his face as he started climbing from the window. One leg out, he stopped suddenly, and slowly retreated back in. He looked at the glass, how it glittered in the sunlight, and then back at the chair that had somehow landed straight up.

Then he turned back to the glass and thought about how easily it would cut open his flesh.

The doctors watched from the other side of the door as Maxwell carved into himself, jotting down notes as he scored his flesh with the largest shard on the floor. They scribbled intently, even as the patient collapsed to the floor, sawing through veins until his last breath. As the lifeless body lay in the growing pool, they finished their notes and clicked their pens. Their last look was not aimed at the expired patient, however, but at the simple wooden chair.

It was facing them now. As the doctors walked away, the pool from Maxwell rippled, sentient streams breaking away and traveling across the tile.

A WORK OF ART

Vera looked at the job description again, reading it over for the fiftieth time. At the top, the post read simply:

"Looking for a grotesque wall of flesh and eyes"

She looked at her prototype, sketched stitches and eyes filling the screen. It looked like the kind of wallpaper they put on the walls in hell. She reviewed it again, looking over every tortured eye and wicked tooth. It looked perfect. With a deep breath and crossed fingers, she emailed the buyer, attaching the picture with it.

Once sent, she stood from her desk and walked away, her cat trailing behind her. She wasn't even out of the room when a reply chimed on her computer. She sat back down, opened it, and felt digitally slapped. Her piece had been rejected. Large, almost angry capital letters read loud and clear:

REJECTED. NOT REAL ENOUGH. FIX IT.

The note from the buyer hurt. It was the first time she had a client turn it down immediately. Her cat sat on her lap and purred, almost sensing her unease.

Vera sent a reply in apology, and swore to make it right. She started from scratch, trying to add more detail. Each desired feature was redone with more detail, ramping up the menacing pain expressed in the art. She worked diligently, trying her best to deliver the goriest piece yet. This time when she pressed "send", she was sure they would be satisfied. Exhausted, Vera rested her head on her desk, and her cat comforted her once more.

The reply came quicker than the last one. The capital letters yelling once more:

IS THIS A JOKE? I SAID *REAL*. FIX IT.

She cried at her desk, the weight of failure looming over like a dark cloud. She was upset but angry and found herself going over the piece again. It didn't make sense; it looked visceral enough. How could it not be good enough?

She wanted to send a nasty email but decided against it. With trembling fingers she typed another apology, then decided she would do everything in her power to satiate the customer's deranged request. She was a *damn* good artist, and she would show them.

In the days that followed, she didn't leave the studio. She blacked out the windows and shut off her phone to avoid distraction. She spent hours staring at her computer, searching the darkest depths of the web, looking at some of the most harrowing images she had ever seen. She took in every gunshot, every live flaying. Her mind twisted as she found the perfect layout for the grotesque flesh and eyes. She didn't sleep. She didn't eat. The images teared her eyes and made her vomit, but she kept on, every stroke bringing together a terrifying spread of gut-wrenching horror. When the digital brush was finally lifted, she sent the copy and wept at her desk.

Her cat jumped in her lap, and as it purred softly, the emailed responses chimed in. The sound made her flinch, and she was so anxious she didn't even want to open it. After a few minutes, she wiped her eyes and gathered the courage to look. Reading the text aloud, she felt the world shatter around her.

"NOT. GOOD. ENOUGH. DO IT RIGHT, OR I'LL FIND SOMEONE BETTER."

Vera broke down again. She couldn't do it. She couldn't look at any more body horror. She couldn't make it any more realistic than it already was, it just wasn't possible. Weak and defeated, she went to type her final apology, then stopped. Her hollow eyes fell on her cat, who was looking up curiously. It was then it hit her. It wasn't real enough. It never was.

Vera pet the cat slowly, a single tear falling as she crushed its neck. Her next attempt would be her best yet.

Starting with a large blank canvas, Vera sewed the flayed pet in, feline teeth and eyes frozen in petrified anguish. It was magnificent; a true display of agony so real it couldn't be mimicked by any pencil or brush. The work was difficult and messy. When she finished the application, she stepped back to admire. It was fantastic, but the joy was temporary. Even after using every bit she could, it still only covered a quarter of the canvas. She would need more.

The mailman would be next. She had seen him dozens of times, walking down the sidewalk to deliver every package and bill. His striking blue eyes always stood out, the color of a beautiful summer sky. He suspected nothing when she lured him in, the knife in the back giving her the upper hand she needed. Even caught off guard he was a struggle, and one of the pretty blue eyes had to be sacrificed in order to maintain the new supplies. Luckily, she was able to salvage the other, the vibrant color forever preserved for the commission.

To add local flavor, Vera visited a local farm in the middle of the night. She found a young black goat to be a perfect fit, another addition to the collection of eyes. As the piece was near completion, her acts had made the news. She needed just a little bit more, but it was too risky to leave the house.

Vera found solace in her off-hand. Surely, she could live without it. Ignoring the flies and smell that had accumulated in the house, she lopped it off, cleaning the bone to display her own signature at the end.

The last of the sewing was difficult with one hand, but she pressed on. She filled in the gaps with a large brush; her coagulating paint caking the visible canvas that poked through. With the last of her energy, she weakly aimed the camera, and the flash lit the finished product in all its glory.

Sirens blared outside, and she could see the glimmering strobe through the darkened windows. She fumbled the drive into the computer and transferred the file, shouts echoing in the street. She attached it to the email and sent it to the buyer.

Police kicked down the door, guns drawn as light spilled into the darkened house. Flashlights shined, illuminating the horrors of her artistic process. As they burst into the studio, a final email chimed. They surrounded the artist, only to find her deceased. Expired from blood loss, Vera was left a statue at her desk, her frozen hand still hovering over the mouse. On the screen was an email of an accepted payment, and a message that simply read:

PERFECT. A WORK OF ART, *TRULY*.

A HORSE WALKS INTO A BAR

A horse walks into a bar... and nobody looks.

The routine is the same each time; ever since the day he first showed up, eight months ago.

They focus on their drinks, ignoring the clumsy clopping of hooves as they slowly and heavily draw near. Some swallow hard, others start to sweat. They hear him reach the bar and they don't dare look.

They don't acknowledge his upright posture, and how he struggles with each step.

They don't acknowledge his three-piece suit, the crude and custom stitches barely stretching over nearly a ton of meat.

They don't acknowledge his butchered forelegs, lopped off at the bend and replaced with human hands.

They only stare at their drinks, hoping to God he doesn't come talk to them. Praying.

He scoots next to a stool and sits on the floor in front of the bar, meeting the harrowed gaze of the bartender as his suit fails to contain his frame. The horse sounds restless, agitated. His breathing is ragged. He stares at the bartender with its massive black eyes, and when he speaks, it sounds like an old man being held underwater.

"The usual," the horse says.

The bartender reluctantly nods, grabbing a polished glass from the bar and reaching for the top shelf whiskey. The horse looks around at the other patrons, who are still avoiding his presence with all their energy. They dare not look at his wispy, splotchy mane, or his horrible, scarred hide. They only want to go unnoticed until he leaves.

The bartender shakily pours two inches of whiskey and sets the glass in front of him. The horse eyes him for a moment, leaning over the counter slowly. The horse bares his teeth, large and yellowed incisors grinding together amidst a scoff of hot breath. He keeps leaning until one of his void-like eyes is an inch from his face. The next words spoken by the horse are whispered in a sinister tone, but everyone manages to hear.

"How. Many. Weeks?" His tortured voice groans, and the bartender freezes.

Everyone, including the bartender, shifts uncomfortably. He chews his lip for a moment, unsure of what to say. His pupils slowly dilate, and he answers on command.

"Four," the bartender says, tears streaming down both cheeks.

"Good. Very good," the horse seethes, before picking up his glass of whiskey.

The horse's pale, stapled-on hands touch the glass fondly, caressing it like a sacred chalice. The bartender returns to normal, and everyone grimaces at what's about to come.

The horse puts the cup in his mouth and chews, an explosion of whiskey and glass grinding against his oversized teeth. They flinch as he works his jaw, the sound of the glass shredding his gums and grinding into powder like nails on a rusted chalkboard.

Without a word the horse leaves, and the awkward silence slowly turns back like nothing happened. Everyone looks happy.

Everyone except the bartender, who thinks of his wife at home. Thirty-six weeks pregnant.

THE BUTCHER

The Wanderer stood atop the crumbling cliff, eyeing the shadowy landscape below. The tall grass quaked at his feet, every blade shivering away from the soles of his worn rubber boots. The wind was fierce at such a height, the pinnacle of tortured moans tossed his clumped hair and whipped at his apron. The chainsaw felt heavy in his hand, his fingers frozen around the grip in a painful inability to let go. Occasionally he squeezed them around the deteriorated foam handle, feeling every digit pop in its restless embrace. He could feel the aura of power calling to him, an intoxicating tether reeling him to the next worthy soul that could feed the teeth of his saw.

Far below the rocky cliff was a rundown house, one that was built along the edge of a quarry. It looked like it was barely standing near the edge, ready to cave at any second. The sinister presence seemed to radiate deep within the walls of the shoddy structure. The chainsaw man felt the overwhelming sensation of bloodlust boiling in his fuel-festering veins, a feeling that the tall grass seemed to respond to. The blades flattened against the ground and shook in fear as the boiling rose throughout the Wanderer, a feeling the masked man himself had trouble keeping under control. The mask on his face shook, vibrating so fast the outer rim was a blur. The man squeezed his fist and forced the adrenaline to subside, promising that soon it would be able to take the reins and swing the saw to its heart's content. Inside the beaten home was an enemy much stronger than the previous. One so strong he could feel its aura bleed out through the siding.

The Wanderer took a step forward and free-fell, letting his arms out to embrace the cool wind. The sudden rush of air whipped his wild hair as he watched himself plummet, feeling nothing but the thrill of the impending massacre. Even as he fell, he held his gaze to the house, feeling the demonic aura like an echoing heartbeat. It *called* to him, a song of anguish luring him in with a gentle, caressing hand. The ground rapidly approached, and the air whistled in the Wanderer's ears. Holding his lusting stare, he positioned his feet at the last second, his boots meeting the earth so hard the ground shook in protest. The bones in his legs shifted, a temporary inconvenience that would sort itself out before he even made it to the front porch of the gloomy destination.

There was a sort of gravel driveway leading to the building, thousands of human teeth crunching under his boots where gravel would be appropriate. There were no roads connecting to the driveway, only the rocky wall in which the Wanderer had just descended. It was almost like it was paved there just for him. The crackling mixture of molars and canines shifted under the weight of each step; the grinding sound was pleasant to him. It would've taken hundreds of victims to make such a thing, and the power of the individual responsible would be something worth seeing. The wind sang across the valley, wind that seemed to come from the direction of the run-down house.

The Wanderer marched up the drive, the crunching teeth getting louder the closer he got to the porch. There were glinting beads watching him from under the steps, two little glassy eyes shining in the darkness behind the steps. The Wanderer continued his pace and watched the eyes without the faintest feeling of interest.

Each step closer showed more of its appearance, cheeks and ears becoming visible until the entire face revealed itself.

It was the head of a child, only a few years old. It looked to be floating in place, holding itself up with thin jellyfish-like tentacles.

Its mouth was open blankly, and its eyes tracked The Wanderer as he drew close. He stopped and watched the face silently, feeling a trickle of power seep from under the shadows of the porch. The floating head looked like it wanted to say something, but the only sound to escape its lips was a repetitive gasp. Other orbs began to materialize around the child's head, little specks of neon pink blinking to life in sets. Two, then four, a dozen—two dozen. The sense of power grew as the orbs surrounded the floating head. Then, in an instant, the head was gone. Hundreds of pointed teeth snapped down and devoured it, suddenly turning it into digestible pieces.

The many eyes drew closer, followed by the skittering body of an oily spider abomination. It had too many legs to count, and they twitched in all directions, each appendage barbed like a scorpion's stinger. It hissed defiantly, as if to warn The Wanderer to back off. The Wanderer simply stared at the arachnid hybrid, even as it revealed two crab-like pincers dripping with poison. The rusted iron mask strapped to the Wanderer's face just looked at it unamused, its closed eyes and emotionless visor offering nothing at its aggression. The chainsaw remained limp at his side.

The spider hissed once more, then retreated to an unseen hiding spot under the house. The Wanderer said nothing and climbed the steps, each board aching under his weight as he worked his way to the front door. All the windows were boarded up, and there was no way to see inside. The Wanderer tried the knob and was surprised to find it unlocked.

Inside, the house was derelict. A thick haze of dust wafted through the abode like a cloud, the heavy particles catching cracks of light through the slits in the windows. It looked abandoned, plain living room furnishing staged and unused like a forgotten movie set. Old rags and illegible newspapers littered the floor, along with random discarded trash. The garbage itself didn't make any sense, like it was someone's inclination of what garbage *should* look like.

At first glance, it looked like nobody was home. The Wanderer took a step in and panned his head across the room. His body was stiff; in need of a kill, and the effort it would require from his body. Stagnant veins begged for stimulation, and the rusted blade felt empty in his hand. He moved through the house autonomously, determined to find the reason he was drawn here. There *would* be sufficient sustenance here, he wouldn't settle for otherwise.

In the living room, there was nothing. When the empty kitchen failed him as well, he took down the hall to the bedroom, which produced only a heavily stained mattress and more boarded windows. The Wanderer looked around slowly, trying to pinpoint the heart of what had called him there. Outside, the wind assaulted the house, whistling cool air fighting its way through the siding to produce a draft. The air howled its tortured groan, the same tune the Wanderer had heard hundreds of times on his possessed search for challenge.

But still, he craned his head. There was something *off* about this particular tune, an additional pain that sounded too close to him to be a part of the chorus. It was a *moan,* a tired bleating of weakness, and it was *close.* The Wanderer looked at the floorboards beneath his feet and tightened his grip on the chainsaw.

Below, the hunchback waddled leisurely amongst the chained stock. A single lightbulb hung from above, swaying in the draft from the wind outside. Men and women of every age surrounded him in the dingy basement. Those who couldn't hide in the dark simply covered their faces and whimpered. With their hope long lost, their only choice was to huddle obediently on the filthy concrete. Most were beaten and starved, stripped of their clothing, and forced to wait in the perpetual line that led to the large wooden door. It was locked at all times, and only opened when the master required it to.

The hunchback, his shrunken and malformed body garbed in a cloak stitched from the skin of many who had been processed, narrowed his eyes on a young woman. She was shivering and hugging herself, looking up at him with a single good eye, the other heavily bruised and swollen. He lurked toward her like a goblin, every two steps followed by a slap to the floor to keep from falling over. His other hand dearly held the key around his neck, one made of shiny brass. The young woman wanted to turn away but was too weak to do so, only capable of helplessly watching as he shuffled over to her.

The hunchback caressed her thigh with a bony finger, running the digit along the outline of ribs and the flutter of her stomach as she whimpered. He dug into his cloak with a giggle and produced a sharp boning knife, one that he used to gently carve into the flesh of her abdomen. Her pain was hushed and disassociated, but he still found pleasure in it.

The way her flesh cut easily, tender and lean. She would be a perfect next choice.

Above, the ceiling exploded, followed by the heavy impact of a large, broad form. The hunchback wiped debris and dust from his face in time to see the solid bulk of The Wanderer crouched before him. From behind a false metal face, the intruder was looking silently at the ground, where his knee had completely obliterated the young girl's face, her head along with it. He was already climbing to his feet, leaning on the blade of a rusted chainsaw to help himself up. His joints cracked as he stood tall, and the other cattle shrugged away from him, clawing and thrashing at each other to hide in the dark.

Flustered and angry, the hunchback shouted at him. Incoherent syllables meant for an insult, falling on deaf ears. The Wanderer shrugged him off and looked at the large wooden door—the master's room. There was no way he'd be allowed such entry, it was forbidden.

With a scowl, the hunchback threw the boning knife at him to get his attention. The handle bounced off The Wanderer's face-mask harmlessly, then disappeared into the darkness of the damp dungeon. The Wanderer stopped and looked at the hunchback, his rusted face of closed eyes and mouth staring blankly in annoyance. He could hear the intruder squeezing the handle of the chainsaw, the twist of leather in his elbow-length gloves.

The hunchback teased and dangled the key out to him, the only means of opening the door to the master's room. Its polished brass finish shined in the overhead light, catching The Wanderer's attention. The chainsaw wielding man looked from the large wooden door to the key and reached out a hand to take it.

In a swift movement, the hunchback laughed and tore the key from his neck, promptly swallowing it. The Wanderer watched the cold iron work down the hunchback's wrinkly neck, already working its way to his stomach. The Wanderer watched him for a moment, before looking at the door again.

The sounds of wet chopping echoed off the walls as The Butcher cleaved the arm from its shoulder. Heavy, precise swings made quick work of it, and soon the limb came free in a gush of blood. Spatter drizzled down The Butcher's face, the burlap sack sewn permanently as a second skin with crudely cut eyeholes. The man the arm belonged to—long dead and decayed, stared up at him with lifeless eyes. He returned the stare from the darkness of his mask, obscured eyes portraying no emotion for the massacring that had taken place. The Butcher buried his cleaver in the corpse's forehead and let its dead weight hit the table and tossed the severed arm into a bucket.

The room was dim, scattered beams of gray light from the gloomy sky outside shining in through a single egress window. The light was enough to illuminate his workspace, the same dull glow painting the importances of the room. The wooden table and chopping block. The wall of hung butcher's cleavers and knives. The many, many meat hooks dangled from above from their grimy chains. There wasn't a single inch of the room not covered in arterial spray; the room looked more like a hollowed-out cave than a workshop.

The Butcher rolled his shoulder, stretching stiff and rippling muscle that pulsed against the straps of his apron. Now that it was cleared of limbs, he grabbed the torso and held it up to the many jingling chains hanging above. Links and hooks sticky with blood and gore, all stemming from a grand spiderweb of them several feet above. With practiced delicacy, he pierced the torso and let it hang, taking pride as it joined the sway of the dozens before it. He admired his work, each victim dismembered uniquely to be on display with their special hook.

On the other side of the door, The Butcher heard a ruckus. One of the cattle must've gotten out of line. He paid it no mind, pulling the cleaver free from the freshly hanging torso and returning it to the wall. He looked over the blades—each dull and caked in blood, but still worthy enough of use.

Behind him, something slammed against the large wooden door. The force was enough to rattle the hinges, kicking up dust in the dimly lit room. A cry from the hunchback rang loud, a sound most curious in the redundant routine he was accustomed to. He felt his blood boil at the disturbance, unseen eyes immediately searching for the right tool to deliver punishment. He scoured the wall of cleavers, taking note of the different shapes of blades and the types of cuts they would provide.

Something slammed the door again, harder this time. The hunchback was silent this time, something unusual for the pesky beast. The Butcher looked at the wooden door expectantly, his large hands cracking knuckles as they curled into fists. He hadn't had a visitor in quite some time.

The Butcher watched as the door exploded, splintering chunks of wood breaking away from the hinges like a bomb had detonated. The deadbolt tore a portion of the wall with it, clearly unable to contain what wanted in. The Butcher watched the doorway, wondering what was causing such noise.

The heavyset visitor stepped in, and The Butcher noticed two things immediately: the rusted chainsaw held at one side, the bleeding remnants of the hunchback in the other. Holding him by his caved skull, the visitor tossed the body of the hunchback at The Butcher's feet, before looking up expectantly through a metal mask.

The Wanderer had found his adversary. He was bigger than he expected, nearly seven feet of stacked muscle held back by an apron quite like his own, his face hidden by a burlap sack. His legs were the size of telephone poles, the stretch of canvas pants barely containing his bulk. The Wanderer looked upon the giant of a man and readied the chainsaw in both hands. Behind him, the many prisoners fought to escape from the hole in the ceiling, frantically climbing over each other in hopes of a better life.

The Butcher looked at the body of the hunchback, his face caved to a pulp like a broken pumpkin. His only form of mourning was a labored exhale, before immediately turning to the wall of cleavers to his right. He reached up with both colossal arms and selected a cleaver from the very top, one with a foot-wide blade and a handle to accommodate its size. The Butcher returned with his weapon of choice, brandishing it with a flex of his forearms.

The pull of a ripcord, the scream of the saw. The Wanderer's blade roared to life, thick black smoke erupting from the machine as he bellowed a battle cry. With abnormal speed, he crossed the room with a leap, swinging down vertically with his weight behind it. The Butcher raised the cleaver in defense, a flurry of sparks grinding off his blade as the teeth bit angrily. He held the cleaver firm, pushing against the momentum of the Wanderer as he bounced back from his assault. Veins ran taut in his arms as he steadied the cleaver, face-to-face with the metal mask that invaded his home. Muscles flexed and the Butcher thwarted his strike, then the Wanderer immediately came down with another.

As the chainsaw's blade blurred inches from his burlap sack, The Butcher side-stepped and grabbed The Wanderer by the back of the neck and slammed him into the table. The surface erupted into broken lumber as the Wanderer crashed into the floor; the impact jarring his limbs as he was met with solid concrete.

Before he could toss the rubble off of him, The Wanderer looked to see the heavy weight of The Butcher's boot immediately following his head. He rolled to the side, barely missing the stomp, and a spiderweb of cracks formed where his skull had been. The Wanderer slashed upward with the chainsaw as he climbed to his feet, knocking the cleaver away before coming down once more. The Butcher was surprisingly fast for his size, bobbing and weaving away from the screaming blade before retaliating with his own. Sparks flew, and every clash lit up the room, and the scent of the black smoke mixed with the rot and decay in the room.

The Wanderer swung wildly, a maniacal cry growing behind the mask with every deflected strike. In between slashes, The Wanderer connected a solid backhand, one The Butcher shrugged off like it was nothing. He raised the large cleaver and brought it down harder, forcing the Wanderer to take a knee and brace against it. Even as The Wanderer folded under the strength of The Butcher, he relished in the sickly sweet taste of the power he held, one that seemed to grow the longer the fight went on. It radiated off of him like a bloody fog.

The Wanderer braced for the next slash, only to feel the unexpected grasp of The Butcher grabbing him by the throat. The headbutt he received was hard enough to shake the house. The Wanderer felt the metal mask crush everything behind it, shattering his nose and blacking both eyes. Before he could recover, the uppercut that followed hit harder, sending him sprawling across the floor like he had been hit by a truck. He rolled to a stop next to the deceased hunchback, still clutching the rumbling saw.

Blood pooled from behind the mask, trickling onto the concrete as he picked himself off the ground. The Wanderer's rusted false face started to vibrate intensely, the edges of metal falling out of focus as it shook. He looked to see The Butcher momentarily flex to taunt him, massive shoulders popping as he squeezed the cleaver's handle. He rushed in again, leaping across the room with the crude blade held high. He brought it down with a shout, watching the blade separate flesh and guts in a powerful sweep. The damage was overwhelming, so distractingly so The Butcher didn't realize he had cleaved the body of the hunchback down the middle.

Lurching through the entrails of the human shield, The Wanderer wrapped his arms around the waist of The Butcher and suplexed him with inhuman speed. The concrete floor burst under the combined weight, the shoulders and head of The Butcher smashing chunks into powder as his neck broke sideways. As The Butcher thrashed weakly, The Wanderer elbowed him in the temple, sending him sprawling awkwardly. The Wanderer grunted and snaked his arms around his legs and twisted his body, pulling his heavy opponent into a spinning lift. The Butcher clawed through the rubble as he was swung into motion, whipping through the air like a pendulum. After three rotations of momentum, The Wanderer let him fly, and The Butcher catapulted into the wall of cleavers like a missile. Bones and concrete alike shattered as his body caved in the wall, blades of every size raining down and clattering to the floor.

The Wanderer dashed forward instantly, the chainsaw screaming as he brought it down on The Butcher's shoulder, cutting diagonally as his head lolled. The jagged teeth ate greedily, buzzing through flesh and bone until it tasted intestines. The Wanderer stared into the burlap sack, which frothed red through the fabric. The Butcher parted down the middle, peeling apart in a spray that coated the entire room. The engine gorged on the fluid, chugging along as the plume of smoke exhaled like a freight train. The Wanderer's hands jolted as the saw jammed, sputtering to a stop as the teeth bit into The Butcher's pelvis.

Flayed almost in two, the hulking Butcher went limp, his head resting against the broken wall. The Wanderer wheezed behind the mask, each breath heaving through bubbling blood as he admired his work, and the devastation caused by his oil-burning companion. Relishing his victory, he placed a boot on his enemy's chest and started to pull the blade free.

An explosion of energy erupted from The Butcher's body, and a burst of hot air hit The Wanderer like a wall. The limp Butcher's hands sprang to life, one grabbing the Wanderer by the hair while the other drove a meat hook under his chin. The hook punctured until it stuck into the inside of the metal mask, and as his vision suddenly clouded and felt the tight wrap of a chain around his neck.

With an angry pull of a chain, The Wanderer was lifted off the ground, kicking his feet as each consecutive pull brought him closer to the ceiling. The Wanderer caught glimpses of the scene before him in dizzy passes, his dead weight spinning as he dangled helplessly.

The Butcher stood awkwardly, his separated body pulsing as it freed the chainsaw from his midsection. The power tool fell amongst the other weapons, and as The Wanderer tried and failed to free himself, The Butcher gathered another chain from the floor. He looped it around his body several times and pulled it tight, groaning painfully as his body rejoined itself. Every breath from behind the bloodstained sack came in a cloud of steam, and the aura of power emanating from him was deafening.

In his blind desperation The Wanderer felt for the chainsaw, an invisible tether reaching for the tool as The Butcher tied a loose knot in the chains. He rigged it in place with a metal spike, and the coil of links stretched taut against his bleeding mass. The Wanderer called for the chainsaw again, and as he contorted his fingers, the saw started to shake. The Butcher reached up and felt for his head, seething with anger as he worked to reset his broken neck.

The chainsaw skittered across the floor and bounced toward The Wanderer's outstretched hand. Hanging helplessly, he pulled on the ripcord until it sputtered to life, then held it up to saw at the chains constricting him.

The Butcher rolled his adjusted neck, tendons and vertebrae impossibly recovering from his previous annihilation. He worked his shoulders against the chains and tested his movement as sparks showered The Wanderer, a guttural roar radiating from his lips. Just as the saw was almost through the chain, The Butcher bounded after him, each step angrier than the last. The chain snapped, and The Wanderer fell free, just as The Butcher slammed into him. The saw buried into The Butcher's face as he tackled him into the wall. Together they punched through the wall of the basement and the earth behind it.

In a rush of flailing limbs they burst through the side of the quarry, exchanging blows as they tumbled over layers of steep rock. The gloomy wind tossed at their clothes and blood painted the air, each punch and chainsaw slash sending a spatter to a growing avalanche. The Butcher threw jabs and hooks with every topple, and the chainsaw nicked at his chains and scored his flesh. Even with the hook still stuck in his jaw, The Wanderer fought back ruthlessly, rending in weak spots until the momentum was too much to work the saw. The Butcher wrapped both hands around his throat, shoving the meat hook further as The Wanderer dug a thumb in his eye.

Like a boulder rolling down a mountain, they bounced in unison down multiple cliffs of rock. Each impact tried to force them apart, but their deathroll resumed each time they hit air. The world blurred around them in a barrage of kicks, punches, and knees. Just as it felt like they would fall forever, a sudden stop came in the form of mud and standing water. The splash was tremendous; disfigured creatures scurried away from the pit in fear of the screaming saw.

The Butcher was up in an instant, mounting the submersed Wanderer and pummeling with such rage. He didn't stop even as the chainsaw bit into his stomach. The blade spun furiously, spraying a bloody geyser out his back as he held his enemy underwater. Through a murky film, The Wanderer watched him rain down punches, driving his head further into the sucking mud as he held onto the saw for dear life. Turning entrails to mush, the chainsaw kept working until there was nothing left to eat. Chains split and bones shaved away, but still The Butcher pummeled away. With a defeated sputter the chainsaw succumbed to lack of fuel, coming to a silent halt in the ruined torso.

The Wanderer battered and clawed his attacker, fingers coming back wet with strips of gore and burlap. He punctured eyes and dug into open wounds, but nothing would stop the punishment from The Butcher. Water filled his lungs, the world started to fade, and The Wanderer felt for any attempt to gain ground. The chained vessel simply would not stop, even as knuckles broke against the mask and fingernails came free. Just when The Wanderer felt himself slipping away, he felt the meat hook in his jaw.

The hook came free in a rip of flesh, and The Wanderer shoved it upward as hard as he could. As the hook pierced through The Butcher's eye socket, he felt a brief pause in the brutal beating.

A second was all it took.

In the flash of an eye, The Wanderer wormed out from underneath the crushing weight of The Butcher, and wrapped the hook's chain around his neck just as he did moments ago. He hurdled over the confused Butcher, pulling the chain hard with both hands. The Butcher tried to fight, but the hook ripped violently, making his body obey with every tug. The Wanderer stomped him and planted a heavy boot on his back, and put his whole body into a final, devastating pull.

The chain worked as both a noose and a guillotine, and with a loud *rrrip* The Butcher's head came free from his body, bringing his spine along with it.

Alas, The Butcher fell silent.

The Wanderer stood victorious, letting the beheading chain fall with a splash. Thunder rumbled, and a crackle of lightning forked across the sky. With heavy, wheezing breaths, The Wanderer looked above, just as the patter of rain started to hit the metal mask. He let out a battle cry as the rush faded, and in the smear of muddy water, it almost looked as if the face was trying to move.

Slow and exhausted, the chainsaw man rolled the headless corpse over and grabbed the saw. The handle was hot to the touch, and it came free with a squelch.

In the shadows of the pit, a wicked creature watched with frightened interest: a man that walked on his hands, pulling a tail of twisted entrails behind him. He watched the masked man from a distance, his upside-down face observing with long ago gouged out eyes. The viscera merman shuddered as the masked man unscrewed the fuel cap of the chainsaw and tilted back his metal face, right before vomiting violently into the reservoir. The burning scent of gasoline carried on the wind, and with a few pulls of the ripcord, the chainsaw came to life once more.

Without as much as a word, The Wanderer left his adversary behind, sauntering through the mud almost like he was disappointed. Above the pit, the merman watched as the butcher's house started to fade away, dissolving like sand in a box. Shingles, siding, and boards fluttered away like ashen butterflies on the wind.

When the merman looked back at The Wanderer, he was gone.

As if nothing ever happened.

AGGRAVATED FLESH

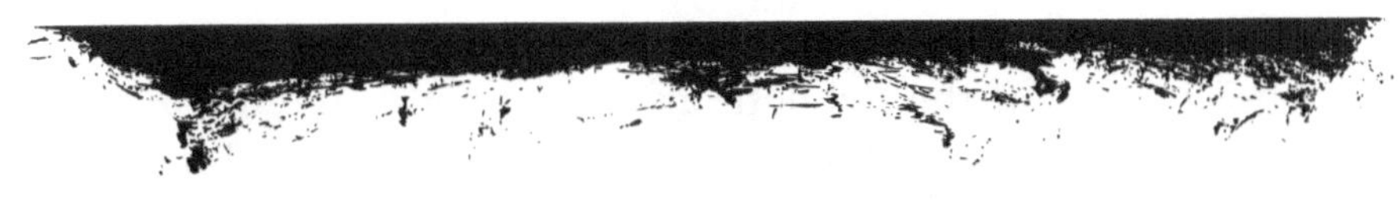

Going out for a late night drive, I find myself at a red light. The weather was nice, and I didn't have anywhere to be, so a nice little cruise to clear my head seemed like the right thing to do. I've had a lot on my mind lately, and a nighttime cruise sounded mentally satisfying.

After all, I've been doing *so good*. No reason not to.

Ahead the traffic lantern sways in the breeze, the red glow beaming through its weathered lens. There's no one else at the intersection, and the empty streets start to make me feel antsy. My palms start to sweat, and I readjust my grip on the wheel as I look around.

To my left, there's a gas station. An old mom and pop looking place, with a single duo of pumps standing under a flickering light. When I look through the window, there doesn't seem to be anyone working behind the counter. Maybe they're taking out the trash?

To my right, there seems to be a bar that's closed up for the night. The parking lot is empty, and their neon sign is shut off. I try to make out the name, but it's too dark. The sixth something. Maybe I'd have to come back some other time in the daylight and check it out.

The light ahead remains red. No matter, I'm not in a hurry.

I crack my knuckles nervously and turn on the radio. Some soothing music will do the trick. I tune the dial to find a station, watching the needle move on the dash as I navigate the static. The walls are meat. The needle wobbles back and forth, but nothing can really come through. I must be too far from the local stations. Something about the aggravated static makes me uneasy, and I feel myself start to sweat.

I got to look at the red light again and get distracted. Across the street there's a fox walking in the grass, one that's pulling a tiny leash behind it. It stops and looks at me momentarily, tilting its head in interest. Something about it makes me uncomfortable, and I feel the condensation of sweat on my brow.

I rub my eyes, feeling the glimmer of a migraine behind it. It passes, and when I look down, I see a relief to the unending static on the radio.

Sitting in the cup holder is a cassette tape. It seems too good to be true.

I grab the tape and look at it. It's an old tape, one that looks like it's seen much use. Celine Dion's "Falling Into You" album. Perfect.

I look around the intersection, and see it's still empty. I have time to put it in. At last, some kind of reassurance for this damn red light. I check both ways again and lean over to put the tape in. The rectangular plastic of the cassette is satisfying. The crisp drag of it entering the deck is satisfying.

I'm satisfied.

As the tape plays over the speakers, I feel myself relax. I've been doing so good. It's better now. *I'm* better now.

I sink into my seat as the piano intro starts, and I feel like I can breathe again. The music calms the buzzing in my head, and my nerves start to calm. Now if only the light would change, and I could get on with my peaceful drive.

Across the street, the Fox continues to look at me. I pay it no mind and place my hands back on the steering wheel. It's nice out tonight. Through the haze of the windshield, I look up at the red light. I don't know why it refuses to change, but I'm patient. It'll get there. It's fine. Everything's fine. I glance at all lanes of the intersection, thinking maybe a car is coming and I didn't see it. That's why it's taking so long.

The streets are empty.

The streets are empty.

The streets are empty.

I look nervously at the gas station to my left, expecting it to be empty, and it's *not*. Something is standing behind the register. It looks like a man in a metal suit—like knight's armor, horribly modified with a tail made of wires and computer parts—

"No," I whisper to myself, looking away. I've been doing so good. There's no way it's gotten away from me. It's not really there, I know it's not, so I look to the right and make sure—

The parking lot to the closed bar is no longer empty. Something stands tall amongst the rows of painted lines. A large horse in a suit, human hands stapled where the front hooves should be—

"*No,*" I say again, feeling a rush of bile in my throat. I swallow and keep it down, along with the murmur of the migraine that begs to return.

I've been doing good, really. It's fine, everything's fine. It's been fine for a while. Really.

The familiar cold sweat returns, hands clammy on the wheel. The song rises over the speakers of the playing tape, and I plead for it to comfort me as I look desperately at the red light.

Why won't it change?

Why won't it just change?

I don't want to do this; I *can't* do this.

Above, the red light mocks me. Across the street, the fox mocks me. It looks at me in judgment, its face twisting as it looks like it's trying to gag. Something behind it stirs in the trees, and I can faintly make out the outline of a large rack of antlers, and a writhing mass of slick tentacles—

"Please! *Please!*" I beat my hands on the steering wheel, feeling myself crumble under the weight of it all.

Above, the light is red. Behind me, I see headlights for another car. I watch them in the rearview mirror, and I feel the welling of tears in my eyes. The hair on my neck stands straight. My armpits are moist, a stream of sweat drizzles down my temple. I want to feel for my phone, but I don't think I have it. I don't think I've had it for a while.

Behind me the car slows for the red light, then pulls in the lane next to me. The car stops, the groan of another engine idling threatening my music. I don't want to look at them, so I don't. I don't care who it is. I try to focus on the music but it's hard to hear it.

I decide I'm going to run the red light. I mash the pedal to the floor, but the car doesn't move. I try again, and again, each time harder than the last. I look at the fuel gauge... and see I have no gas. Every warning light on the dash is on now, a collection of symbols telling me I'm not going anywhere soon.

Deep breaths. You can do this, deep breaths. *Breathe.* You've being doing good, you been—

Across the street, the fox is vomiting what looks like a man. Tearing fur makes way for a head and naked body, a slimy face with eyes that open in time to look at me.

"Please," I say again, looking away from the oral birth to the car next to me. The window rolls down, revealing two men in suits and close-cropped hair. They watch me wordlessly, eyes shielded behind sunglasses and a film of cigarette smoke that billows out. They say nothing, only watch, as the sound of my music fades away to nothing.

No—nonono*nonononono*—

I try to turn the volume down, but the radio explodes with noise. The sounds of a hundred screams fill my ears. So loud it hurts. I scream against the noise, but it doesn't stop. I hit the "stop" button, try to eject the tape—anything. The screams become too much, and I find myself tearing off my seatbelt and fleeing the car.

Outside of the car, it is silent again. A fog is rolling in, one that wafts over the intersection until it's consumed by it.

I look to the gas station for help, only to see the inside of it painted red. Inside the station a man in a hardhat is getting mutilated, watching me with a smile as a metal-alligator-human tears through his guts with gloves made of knives. The alloy abomination snarls and stomps the man on the ground, crushing both his skull and the hardhat with a large steel boot. Outside, a garbage truck rumbles to life at the gas-pump.

Please.

Over the crisp night air, I hear the *neigh* of the horse man. He's closer now, standing on the side of the road. He downs what looks like a glass of whiskey, before squeezing it in his hand so hard it shatters. His unnatural hand runs the thumb over its fingers, shards of glass serrating the pale digits.

Across the street, the fox completes its purge. The naked man rises from the fetal position in the grass, standing tall and awkwardly with a face and eyes that look just like mine. Behind him, the deer monstrosity emerges from the woods, a portrait of animal gore of all kinds shifting under a hundred reaching feelers. I turn to get away, to get back into the car, but when I turn around—

My car is gone. The men in sunglasses watch without emotion, their eyes bleeding from behind the sunglasses. After staring at me for a moment, they turn their heads in unison to face the intersection. The trunk of their car pops, and a clown climbs out with a wooden bat in his hands. He points past me with the club, in the same direction the men in sunglasses are looking.

"Please, help me—"

My voice chokes when I follow their gaze, and I want to cover my eyes as the fog retreats in fast-forward.

In the intersection, there is no red light. The pavement has crumbled in on itself, forming a crater where the street used to be.

I don't want to see it, but I have too—I can't look away. My feet move on their own, and I ignore the abominations as I focus on the gaping hole. It calls to me, and I can't seem to resist its voice.

I look down in the pit, wishing I could stop even as I lower myself to climb in. There's something down there, and I need to see it. I make my descent, hands and shoes navigating the jagged concrete and twisted rebar as I blink away tears. As I near the bottom, the things from above gather around, each silently observing as I go deeper and deeper. I don't want to go, but I don't know how to stop. I scream at them for help, and they ignore me. I curse at them angrily, shouting and pleading until I feel the purchase of flat ground beneath my feet. My breath shudders as I turn, but my body continues on autopilot to the center.

Laying on the ground, is a Hawaiian shirt. The fabric is frayed and dirty, the floral pattern torn in multiple places. I reach down to grab it but it ignites into a ball of fire, stitches withering and turning black against the flame. Through the smoke of the smoldering shirt, a door materializes in the wall of rock. I don't understand. I don't *want* to.

I want to cry, but the tears won't come. I look above for guidance and see the rim of the pit is outlined with a silent audience.

The naked man that looks like me. The standing horse in a suit, with stapled on hands. The men in sunglasses, bleeding from their eyes. The horror with the head of a deer. The metal alligator monster.

In unison, they point to the door. I don't want to go, but I know I must. I need to see what they want to show me. Reluctantly, I head to the door. I hear the screams trying to get out, a chorus of pain and death and fear, all welcoming and warning. I feel an angry heat the closer I get, and the knob is hot to the touch. When I open the door, it feels like my skull is breaking in two. I step in and the door slams behind me, a momentary darkness transitioning to a single flickering light.

Behind the door, the walls are meat. Gestating, *aggravated* flesh. They squirm and wiggle, arms reaching and eyes staring as I break before them. I shiver and hug myself as it all comes back to me, like a bomb detonating in the calm ocean that was my brain. I want to say I've been doing good, but I know it's a *lie.*

I recognize the laundromat, even in its appalling state. Washing machines thrash on each side, the clanging of metal boxes squelching in the gore that has replaced the tiled floor. In the center of the room stands an old television on a cart, overgrown by tendons and sprouting teeth.

Around me, everything screams. I look behind the glass of every agitating machine, and all I see is a mass of pounding limbs fighting to get out. Fingers and toes kicking and screaming, digits breaking against the glass. I want to be far away from here, back in the car on the open road.

Behind me the door is gone, replaced by a stretch of skin and veins. The light goes out, and all I can hear is the convulsing of the meat, and the banging of the broken machines. In the darkness, the walls come for me, and I can only cower and sob as they draw near.

In the dark, the television blinks to life. Even as I watch, the walls close in and the writhing corridor narrows around me. The picture is old and grainy, but I recognize the scene, like it's a movie I saw long ago. A man in a straight jacket, kicking against men in white coats. The man thrashes inconsolably, even as they stick a needle in his arm. His eyes are bloodshot and dart around, and his hair is tossed and missing in places. But there's an undeniable, sickening familiarity to him.

He shouts the same things over and over, and it all comes back to me as I make out the words. I mouth the words myself; the syllables feeling natural even as I sob.

I seem to have misplaced my pills.
Somebody help me.
Help me.
Please.

ONE NIGHT STAND

I woke face-down in the pillow, my entire body screaming as I tried to roll and sit up. My bones ached and my joints felt like they were scraping together, each movement punished by the weight of gravity as I tried to untangle myself from the sheets. I squinted around the room against the pain of the light, two details coming front and center in my slog to sit up in bed.

I was naked and hadn't bothered to try to cover up in my sleep.

I was alone.

What the fuck happened last night?

Glances around the room brought memories of the night before, glimpses trying to poke through the fog that smothered my brain.

A used condom on the bed.

Two empty wine bottles.

My phone halfway off the nightstand, next to what I recognized as *my* panties.

The most unnerving detail of all wasn't just one thing but a unity of them, and I found myself looking around with an unsettling audience of foreboding. It wasn't the state of my room that unsettled me, but the... *recent redecoration.*

Every mirror in the house had been brought into the bedroom, all positioned to capture angles towards the bed.

Towards *me*.

A dozen of my bewildered looks. A dozen motions of me suddenly covering my breasts. Dozens of me looking at me.

What the fuck?

Amongst the many questions, I focused on the ones that counted.

1. What the fuck happened last night?
2. Are there any notifications on my phone?
3. Is the door locked?

I forced myself to stand, every muscle in my hungover existence protested movement in the slightest. My whole body felt bruised, most importantly my jaw. I was into the rough shit—quite a bit, frankly—but something felt wrong. I didn't *do* this kind of shit, even when I hit rock bottom.

My clothes scattered the floor like I had exploded out of them. I pulled on my blouse, shoulders feeling broken as I reached through the sleeves. The soles of my feet felt like nails had been driven through them.

Slow, swaying steps towards the door. I had to lean against it to gather myself when I realized it was, in fact, locked.

My brain rammed against the inside of my skull with every beat of my heart.

It took me forever, but I made it back to my phone. I needed to check it. I obviously had a partner last night. Hopefully just one.

Ten percent battery. One notification.

I unlocked my phone and read it desperately, hoping for a piece of the puzzle. The contact was saved simply as: HIM.

A single text, seven words.

"I had a good time last night."

I texted back hesitantly, standing quietly in the hall. The mirrors wigged me out.

"What happened?"

They started typing back immediately.

"You don't remember? You were wild."

I started to feel sick and asked again.

"What happened? I can't remember."

Typing again, and I rubbed my arm anxiously while I waited. It brought horrible pain, and the scrawling bloom of a bruise started to spread beneath.

I looked at the bedroom, a scene that started to look worse the longer I looked at it. Clothes everywhere. *Two more* wine empties had been kicked under the bed. I rubbed my jaw, feeling like I had been slugged over and over.

"You wanted to see. The pictures turned out great."

I held back the bile churning in my throat.

"What pictures?" I texted, my arms feeling like they were tied to weights.

"You'll see."

"See what!?"

"Everything."

I looked into the bedroom, where a stray mirror had caught my reflection. My eyes looked sunken; my nose looked wrong. My jaw didn't look set right.

My phone chimed over and over, each time a new image replacing the last. I couldn't breathe. My fingertips hurt.

Each picture was of me in bed, but the more I scrolled the worse it got. I was slumped in different poses, each time looking rougher, *beaten.* Slowly my limbs started to contort, angles pushed to their limits until the bones ruptured from beneath. My eyes bled and my flesh parted, but through every picture, I held the same uncomfortable smile. The mirrors multiplied the angles to capture every bruise, every cut.

Even the last picture, where my body was a pile of gore, my faceless skull looking at the camera, jaw broken to the side.

I dropped my phone, distracted by the spreading rash of bruising.

I looked to the bedroom, where the red started running over the sheets. The faceless me in the mirror looked at me and worked the ruined jaw. I started to cry.

My phone went off again, and my legs almost crumbled as I picked it up.

It was HIM.

"Same time tonight, right? You *promised.*"

NINETY-NINE BOTTLES

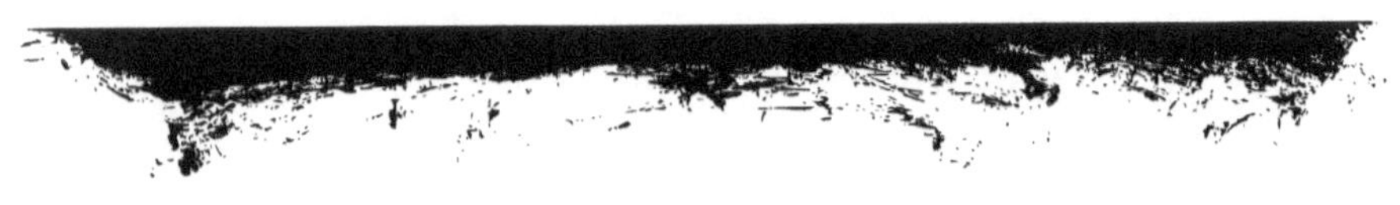

Ninety-nine bottles of beer on the wall, ninety-nine bottles of beer...

My therapist says humming or thinking of a little jingle in my head will help distract me and make the time move easier. Something catchy, something easy to remember.

Take one down, pass it around...

They say it will help ease my heart rate and calm me in severe stress, help me keep my bearings when things seem like they're going to go over the edge. Like being conscious for a seizure and waiting for it to pass.

Ninety-nine bottles of beer on the wall.

They reassure me it's not real. I look into the eyes and the tightly pressed lips. Skin the color of white yogurt. They say it happens to *so* many people. I look into its feminine face, somehow malicious despite there being no facial expression whatsoever. It's usually much further away from this. It's only watched in the past. My mental voice takes liberties, changing the pitch and tone of the song to try and calm me down. Comical as it is, I'm sweating bullets and terrified.

Ninety-nine bottles of beer on the wall...

Hypnagogic Hallucination. Or as the internet prefers: Sleep Paralysis. The hallucination, or "demon" part, is sworn to be purely fictional, just a fabrication of the human mind as the gears shift from wakefulness to slumber.

Ninety-nine bottles of beer...

They swear it's not real. Pure harmless imagination. Like that sensation of falling, or a bicycle throwing you over the handlebars. *Whatever you see, it can't hurt you*, they tell me over and over. Melatonin, Benadryl, none of it is strong enough to keep me out for the night. Sometimes she starts in the closet, other times outside the window. Always hunched over, arms dangling. But she never comes this close.

Take one down...

One of her thin legs swings up and around, planting unnaturally on the bed. The way she moves, it doesn't make sense. It's impossible. In my stasis, I look at her foot, eyes painfully straining to see it on the quilt I'm sweating under. If it isn't real, why does the mattress cave under her weight?

Pass it around...

Sing or hum your tune and calmly wait for it to pass. It *will* pass. It's just a dream. You're just recalibrating to be awake. Their words of comfort jumble with the panicked scream echoing in my musical monologue. The climb and mount is almost instantaneous. Somehow I missed it, even without the ability to blink.

Ninety-nine. Bottles. Of. Beer. On. The. Wall.

Her eyes stare into mine. Black, soulless. For the first time since her visits, she smiles. The hair caresses my face. I hear her breathing. My tune is a dying whisper, barely audible. The eyes roll back, like a shark. The mouth opens impossibly wide, her throat a dark tunnel to nothing. I feel my body lift upside-down, pulled in bursts, like a bird with a worm.

Ninety-nine bottles of beer on the wall...

POSSUM

It all changed the night a possum got into the chicken coop. The frightened squawking from the chickens woke us in the middle of the night, my wife and I scrambling for a flashlight and a gun, fearing the worst as we went out to investigate. Frazzled and half asleep, my wife stayed behind with the flashlight, aiming the beam ahead while I held the shotgun close, waiting to see a pair of eyes reflect off the light. There was no coyote in the yard, no raccoon making a break for it. Whatever had spooked them was still in the coop.

Together we lifted the hatch where they nested and shined the light in.

Inside, terrorizing the chickens, was a possum. With black eyes and spikey teeth, it nipped at the chickens, making them flutter their wings erratically to escape. It saw the light and looked at us, spikey teeth bared as it started to hiss. I was already aiming the barrel of the gun in there, ready to blast it away. I thought it was my husbandly duty to protect the animals on your property; I was ready to shoot it on principle alone.

Despite my conflicted gut, my finger reached for the trigger. My wife begged me to stop, insisting it wasn't a predator, it had just found its way in there by mistake. When I looked into the marble eyes of the hideous varmint, something changed in me. This possum *was* just lost. It's not its fault it's hideous.

I lowered the gun, and together we shooed it out of the coop. It took the better part of an hour, but as I watched it shamble away in the grass, I felt a relieved peace, almost having turned it into hamburger. We locked the coop up for the night, and in the morning, we reinforced any weak point it could've used to get in.

I work late, most nights coming home just before midnight. Through the long hours of my night shifts, my wife has been texting me, saying the possum has come back. She said she's fed it a couple times, even cutting up bananas and laying them out so it can enjoy a treat. She sends me videos of the little monstrosity chomping away at it. It's cute in its own little way. I think of its whiskers and its little pink nose, and I feel bad for almost shooting it.

Last night I saw it for the first time since it got in the coop.

It scared the hell out of me, its little head peeking through the window, its pink nose touching the glass.

It bares its little dagger teeth, its mouth opening wide, like it's angry.

It opens until its maw is like a Venus flytrap, a sharp drooling stretch that it presses against the glass. It holds it there, long enough to make sure I see. Like a *warning*. Then it shambles away, slinking off into the night.

WORMS

We don't know where it came from. The plague swept through our village seemingly overnight, turning our smiling abode into a basin of frightened tears and paranoia. Half of the homes are burned down now, the other half standing like skeletons under the black smoke.

When the elderly fell, we questioned the livestock. We checked them all, even butchered them out of desperation. We found nothing in the meat, no signs of the infestation.

But the worms would only show near the end; it was impossible to see symptoms until it was too late.

Our treatments provided no relief. Stricken with exhaustion until it burrowed from their skin, we had no choice but to let the grandparents perish alone. We couldn't risk spreading it, however it was managing. We sent brave souls to accompanying villages for help and better medicine. Those who didn't return tired and empty handed didn't come back at all.

When the children fell sick, we questioned the water. We were unable to discern a difference between boiled and not, and despite our efforts we couldn't find a way to halt the progression. There were no eggs, no signs to show how it bred. It just showed up, feeding off their insides until they had nowhere to go. The eyes were the most common exit, a wriggling you couldn't even feel until someone pointed it out. The once soothing salty breeze from the coast is now a constant reminder of how alone we are.

When we burned the bodies, we questioned ourselves. Pyres in the thoroughfare, stacked high and smoldering with thick smoke. Watching it shrivel and pop in the fire is the only sure way to know it's gone. We wore masks and heavy skins in fear of the smoke spreading it, stoking and shoveling in shifts to make sure it was eradicated. Even in our sacrifice the worms still persist, squirming and festering from within even though we don't eat and drink. The raging flames secrete the ghastly groans of the departed, and the loud suffering of those not yet expired. Those who couldn't work ended their lives, or the lives of others out of fear.

I am the last one left.

I do not know why I still tend to the fires, stoking the beacon of rot that is now our home. My shovel is my only companion, scooping the ash and breaking the bones to make room for another familiar face.

The fire is hot, and it bakes me under the mask. I think after tonight, I will let it go out. I've fed it for days now, but I'm growing too tired, and the shovel is breaking.

The water is cool on my face. I sit on the shore, gazing into a reflection I no longer recognize.

I can see the worms.

The worst part is, it's not the sight that disturbs me.

Alone on the beach, I wonder if there's no scourge at all. Maybe they've been there all along.

THE SUNROOF

Chanice squinted at the trees, her pounding head pushing her vision in and out of focus. Her late-night drive had taken a sudden turn from the highway to the desolate darkness of the woods off the shoulder. Despite feeling lucky to be alive, she couldn't help but feel a looming danger remaining. It wasn't the shock of the accident, or the fact she knew her hazard lights weren't visible from the road. Something was scurrying around her vehicle.

From her automotive prison she had only caught glimpses of it. It was humanoid and moved too quickly for her concussed brain to make sense of it, and it seemed to cautiously avoid the glow of her one remaining headlight. She could hear it trying to get in, rocking the car as it tested the walls of her confinement. Last she heard it; it had crawled under the car.

A tree pinned the driver's side, and a hill seemed to block the passenger. With the seatbelt acting as a vice against her chest and her phone lost somewhere in the void that was the floor, she could only silently hope whatever was out there would lose interest and leave her alone.

Chanice looked in the rear-view mirror at the lights of the highway. If she could just make it there, maybe she could flag down someone to help. Her arm was broken, and she suspected a broken rib, but if she could just get out of the car, she thought she would stand a chance.

Just as she was about to give up, she found a shred of hope above: the sunroof. She was small enough to fit through, and even as beat up as she was sure she could climb out.

Weak and shaking, she managed to unbuckle and shrug off the deflated airbag.

There was no noise, nothing in the view of the headlights.

Quietly she reached for the sunroof cover and slid it open.

A face was pressed against the glass above, eyes wild and menacing. Its skin was gritty and the color of bark, lips peeled back—eyelids gone. When she screamed it opened its mouth, chattering dull, too-long teeth. She jolted back to her seat, the chatter so loud she could hear it through the glass.

When she looked ahead, she froze.

There was a silhouette with a rock the size of a melon hefted above its head, ready to swing at her only remaining headlight.

It never occurred to her that there had been more than one.

NO HOPE

A single tear emits from a haggard eye as the strained finger misses its mark. As the tip graced the panel instead of the heavily worn button, a squealing of struggling machinery wailed in the dusty rafters of the warehouse.

The sound that followed could be mistaken for a bomb going off.

Emergency stop. The machine powers down, and all is quiet for a moment, save for a low chorus of labored breathing and groans.

A door opens and slams shut, and a purposeful rhythm of footsteps approaches.

"Damn it. *God damn it.* Again?"

A phone receiver is lifted, and four buttons are pressed.

"Maintenance to line two. Maintenance, to line two."

A tall man with a stark white hard hat taps his foot impatiently as two men approach leisurely with a squeaky cart. A trembling hand reaches for the tall man, and he leans just out of its reach with a scowl.

"Take your fuckin' time, why don't you? Do you know how much the backlog is? We need to *run.*" His face turning red as he seethed.

"Relax. We're here, aren't we? Needed to make sure we had the right tools. What happened?"

"Missed a cut. Crashed the machine. Do you think maybe the legs could use a bit of work?"

The haggard eyes watched them converse as if they were invisible.

Lights clicked on and they examined the legs.

"Please... help me..."

The mechanics sighed in annoyance.

"The tendons are severing. It's a wonder it's still standing... but we can do it. Y'know, if you don't want the downtime, you could always fix it right."

"Let me go... please..."

"Nonsense. You know how hard it is to find ones like this? They're expensive. Besides, this one's still good."

"You're the boss." They shrugged,

"No... don't."

The muffled screams were covered by the sounds of searing flesh and sizzling metal. The maintenance team worked quickly, fusing flesh and steel to ensure the limbs wouldn't be able to give out again. The bright arcs shed light on the broken equipment, withered skeletal structure patched with metal rods and plates. They kept fusing all the way up the thigh, connecting it to an already heavily modded lower back.

"Should be good now. Baby it this time, will ya?" One of the maintenance guys said as they wheeled the squeaky cart away.

"I've *been* babying it," the boss said, and turned the machine back on. The line roared to life, illuminating the barely conscious, wild-eyed operator.

The boss looked at it for a second, went to walk away, then stopped himself. He cleared his throat and leaned in close. The operator flinched against the harness that kept him attached to the control box. His finger trembled, aimed at the worn button once more.

"If you don't run this line, who's going to pay off your credit debt? Hmm? And smile, will ya? It's Friday."

TO MAKE A WISH

Monica looked at the cascading water in the fountain, to the shining coins below. Pennies, nickels, and quarters rested at the bottom, all spotless from the constant churning in the chlorinated water. She stared deeply at them, trying to ignore the giggles and lips smacking next to her.

Her older sister Lisa and her boyfriend Pat sat on the edge of the fountain, taking a break to make out for the third time. Monica looked at them in annoyance, watching their tongues explore each other's mouths. Pat opened an eye and looked at Monica, and started pulling away from Lisa, suddenly looking embarrassed.

"Hey, I got an idea! Let's make a wish," he said, digging into his pockets for change while nonchalantly trying to readjust his arousal.

"Wow, fun," Lisa said sarcastically, flicking her hair and throwing an annoyed glance at Monica. The only way their mother allowed her to go to the mall with her boyfriend was to bring her younger sister along, and Lisa was making it a point to remind her constantly.

"Here, we each get one." He handed out the coins. Lisa sighed and took hers. Monica took hers quietly, and Pat kept one for himself. He cupped his hands together and breathed on it, shaking it like he was about to roll dice. Monica looked at the coin in her palm, watching it catch the light.

Pat tossed his in, as did Lisa, each coin hitting the water with a little *plip*. Monica curled her fingers around the quarter and closed her eyes thoughtfully. After a moment, she turned her hand and held it above the water, letting it fall in.

"What did you wish for?" Pat asked Monica.

"Probably to have you all to herself," Lisa teased, and they laughed.

"Well, I *did* wish to get lucky tonight," Pat said, and Lisa hit his arm. A second later, his phone chimed. Pat dug it out of his pocket and checked it.

"Huh," Pat said, eyebrows raised, "my dad just texted to say he's working a double. He'll be home late."

"No way," said Lisa, and he showed her the proof.

In the mall lobby, an employee hurried past, pushing a big cart of luxurious boots, coats and coach bags. One of the bags fell off the cart, and he kept on without noticing.

"There's no way," Lisa said, snatching it up, "I wished for a new pur—" she stopped suddenly, and felt her stomach.

Suddenly Lisa coughed and hacked, convulsing so hard she dropped the purse.

"Ohmygod, Lisa! Are you okay?" Pat tried to steady her, but she got worse. Something gargled in her throat, and she wretched a violent stream of red onto the tile. Blood splashed all over the purse and her knees buckled.

"Help! Somebody help!" Pat shouted, his voice echoing in the lobby.

He looked desperately at Monica and was surprised to see her smiling.

"Jesus, Monica, what did *you* wish for?"

DRIVE-THRU

Henry pulled into the drive-thru and looked at the large, illuminated menu. He was tired and hungry, and this was the only place open at this time of night. After looking at all the professionally photographed shots of food, he decided what he wanted.

He looked at the speaker expectantly and got nothing.

Henry looked around the parking lot. Perhaps he had made a mistake, and the place was closed after all.

There were a handful of cars, and the lights were on inside.

"Hello?" he said, feeling a little weird for speaking first.

Nothing but silence. There were no cars ahead of him, and nobody waiting behind him.

He continued to wait, getting anxious. If he didn't get something from here, he would have to go home empty-handed. He didn't have any food at the house. Just as he considered driving off, he heard something in the speaker. It sounded like someone slamming cabinets shut. Were they just ignoring him?

"Can I get some service or what? Come on, I'm fuckin' hungry," Henry said, his face feeling hot.

There was rustling in the speaker, like someone was adjusting a headset. The voice that came through sounded like a young man, and he sounded amused by his anger.

"*So* sorry about that wait, sir. What can we get you today?" Said the voice on the other side, like they were trying to keep from laughing.

"You think this is a joke, kid? You know how long I've been sitting here?" Said Henry, hanging out his window.

"Sorry about that, sir. We had some *complications* in the kitchen. All straightened up now," said the young man.

Henry sighed and ordered his food.

"Will that be all?" Said the kid.

"Yeah."

"Pull forward."

"Wait, how much is the total?" Henry asked.

Nothing, just the same muffled noises as before, accompanied by the sound of the guy breathing into the mic.

Henry groaned and pulled around. Arriving at the window, he could see the young man with the headset, and nobody else. Henry felt a twinge of guilt; they were short-staffed all along.

The young man had his back turned at the bagging station, furiously shoving things into a paper sack. He hurried over and threw open the window. A rancid smell wafted from inside, like something had been horribly burned. The employee wore a heavily stained shirt and a tired smile.

Henry went to offer his debit card, but the young man shoved the food toward him. The bag was soaked and dripping with grease, like a bunch of fresh fries had been dumped in.

"Alright man, shit." He took the bag hesitantly, and when he tried to hand in the payment, the young man slammed the window shut, bolting back into the kitchen.

Confused, Henry turned on the cab light to check the order.

Behind the restaurant, he heard the back door shove open, and the scuff of sneakers on pavement.

The bag was filled with sizzling body parts.

KISS ON A SWING SET

"Hey. Sorry it took so long. I got here as fast as I could."

"No, it's ok. Sorry I texted so late. Did I wake you up?"

"It's cool. I was just hanging out anyway, no biggie. So... what's up? Everything alright?"

"No... not really. I just didn't want to be home. Just wanted some company, you know? I didn't want to be alone. I know this isn't the most ideal meeting place. I just didn't want to be seen."

"Are you serious? This is great. You know how long it's been since I went to a playground? Been on a *swing?* This is cool, actually."

"Oh. Ok. Cool."

"It is kinda creepy though... being here so late. With the fog and all."

"Yeah... yeah it is."

"I'm sorry you're having a rough time at home. Anything I can do to help?"

"Just you being here is good enough for me. Thank you."

"Hey, no problem. Least I can do. You couldn't have picked a shadier spot to meet though."

"Yeah, I know. Creepy right? Did you tell anyone you were coming out here?"

"Nah. I snuck out..."

"Oh. I'm sorry..."

"No, no, it's cool, seriously. Besides, who would leave someone so pretty to swing by themselves? Uh... heh. Sorry, that was... dumb."

"No. That's pretty sweet of you."

"I've actually wanted to say that for a while."

"What took you so long?"

"I don't know. Scared, I guess. Didn't know if you wanted to be just friends. I didn't want to be weird."

"Oh... well, maybe after this you won't have to be."

...

"Wow. Heh, sorry."

"No, it's alright."

"That was... actually my first kiss."

"Really?"

"... yeah."

"Well. It was a good kiss."

"You're just so beautiful... I didn't think I ever stood a ch—... wait... do you see that?"

"See what?"

"*That.* Over there!"

"What is it?"

"Some guy, I guess. Walking like he's drunk."

"..."

"Hey! We don't want any trouble! Just leave us alone."

"..."

"Why is he... what the fuck? What's wrong with its... what's wrong with his face? We should go."

"I can't."

"What? Why? We need to get out of here."

"I can't. I'm sorry."

"Sorry for what? *Oh god...* what's wrong with its face? It's like it's... rearranged. Why is it... walking like that—April, we gotta go, c'mon!"

"He said it doesn't hurt. It should be quick. *I'm sorry.*"

"*What?*"

"I didn't know what else to do."

"What do you mean? This doesn't make any sense!"

"I'm sorry... It was the only way to make him go away."

"What the fuck... get away from me. I said GET BACK!"

"Oh god, you brought a gun?"

"..."

"You can't! Please, he won't stop—"

"I said get—"

"..."

"God... *oh god no... April...*"

you killed her

"I didn't... I didn't mean... it was an accident."

she offered you to save herself

"From what?"

~~me~~

"FUCK YOU!"

i'm afraid that won't work

"What do you want from me?"

everything

"No... let me go..."

you should've saved one for yourself

THE APPLE

My Pa used to take me shooting. It was his favorite thing. We'd always go to this clearing on the property and set up an apple twenty yards from a bench we would sit on. It wasn't a matter of sighting it in, as I would always see him *plink* the apple effortlessly every time we started. He would take the first shot, reset the apple, and hand the rifle to me.

I wasn't really a tomboy, and the activity brought me no pleasure. But I didn't want to let him down, and it seemed to be the only way we could connect over the years. I didn't have any friends; we lived so far away from town it was all I really knew. When he handed me that rifle, I wanted to make him proud, and I would try my best every time to bullseye the shot.

I would hear his words before he spoke them, as he would repeat them methodically.

"Keep your finger off the trigger until you're ready to shoot."

"Hold it tight to your shoulder."

"Rest your cheek on the stock."

"Look through the scope, but not too close. It'll bite ya."

"Find your target."

"Once you have it, steady your aim."

"Take a deep breath and pull the trigger."

Each weekend we would go to the clearing. Over time, my aim improved, but the shot wasn't always easy. Sometimes my heart just wasn't in it. Sometimes the apple would fall. Most times I would hit the apple. Other times I would miss. My Pa didn't scold me when it happened, he would just tell me to focus. If the apple didn't fall, I was to try again, racking the old bolt and sending the old brass to the wind. I would try harder, and on the times I got it right, he would smile at me, and take us home and have ice cream.

When I started making the shot consistently, his smile would falter. No 'that's my girl', or 'excellent shot', nothing. His face slowly turned to stone until the smile was no more than a tight-lipped line. By the time I didn't miss anymore, we didn't speak at all. No cheery ride home along the long dirt path, no ice cream at home. Just straight into the house and into my room for the rest of the night.

The next week, I wasn't allowed out of my room. The time passed dreadfully, thinking of nothing but the next shot, and hoping I could do it better so he would be proud again. When the next weekend came, things changed.

It was my sister's turn to shoot. Even after begging for one last turn, he *still* handed the gun to her. She wasn't calling him Pa yet. Looking at her trembling hands made it harder to keep the apple steady.

"Keep your finger off the trigger until you're ready to shoot."

BREAKROOM MICROWAVE

Jay pushed through the break room door, keeping his eyes on the refrigerator as he walked towards it. He yanked it open, looking over the several grocery bags of containers and wrapped leftovers. Wedged rudely between forgotten Styrofoam husks was his lunch, a sight that always granted an audible sigh. He pulled it from the graveyard so he could feed it to the microwave.

The crackling Tupperware top, and the *beep-beep-beep* of a long-worn interface.

One minute, thirty seconds.

Pork tenderloin and rice spun weakly behind the glass, and Jay chanced a look at his phone to kill the time. He had only scrolled through his feed for a second before his attention was pulled abruptly.

The movement was quick, just a blur in the corner of his peripheral. So easy to miss. But he saw it, nonetheless.

Jay took a deep breath and focused on his heating lunch. Rice turning molten on the outside as it worked its way to the cold pork. He didn't see it move again, but he *felt* it, the out-of-sight scurrying making him shudder.

One minute, fifteen seconds.

Jay kept his eyes forward, but the presence continued to grow behind him. It enlarged slowly, reducing the cool air in the room, as well as the space between them.

Fifty-nine seconds.

As the pork began to sizzle, Jay mentally urged it to go faster. He could almost hear it slinking behind him, disguised under the struggling *whir* of the microwave's plate. The scraping of nails against tile as it moved closer to him. It's almost done, just a little longer.

Thirty seconds.

"C'mon..." Jay says, both hands fidgeting at his sides.

Breath, quick and raspy on the nape of his neck. Chills run down his back, and he resists the urge to bolt out of the lunchroom. He feels the hands rest on his shoulders. The fingers are long and dirty, twitching as they grace the fabric of his uniform. Filth caked under its nails. At his feet, a naked tail unwinds. A trickle of sweat runs down his temple.

Ten seconds.

The smell wafts over him, blocking the pork and rice until only the diseased odor remains. The teeth grind in Jay's ear, two pronounced incisors sawing back and forth as the hissing—

Jay mashes the button and the microwave door pops. A waft of steam hits him and the stench fades away, but he's not thinking of what's behind him anymore. He grabs it from the bottom, feeling the scorch on his fingertips as his free hand maneuvers the door open.

Out in the open air of the warehouse, the weight lifts. He breathes a sigh of relief, only for the sickening realization to cut it short.

Jay looks back as the door swings back, catching the beady eyes staring as it closes.

He forgot to grab a fork.

THE RAILGUN

The creature that flew over the Pacific was the exact kind of threat we built the gun for. It was mammoth in proportion, wider than San Francisco, with a length impossible to estimate. Its long body slithered across the sky, looming in the distance like a living storm. Widespread panic began upon the sight of it, and officials frantically pleaded for assistance. From the government. From the world. Even from God.

Nuking so close to American soil was out of the question, and its size too grand to be affected by aerial strikes. It was the exact opportunity we needed to demonstrate its power and show the world what we had produced in secret. *To make them fall in line.*

Immediate evacuation, minimum ten miles from the coast.

Enough to dampen the casualties of the inevitable tsunami that would follow the creatures' collapse once we felled it. It was a small price to pay compared to the risk of radiation, or the devastation the large creature would inflict if it was allowed to touch land.

The evacuation was slow, people panicking as they scrambled to get away from what looked to be floating death. Panicking so much they failed to see the mountains part in Death Valley. As the artificial summits shifted, camouflage doors gave way to a black pit, and from the darkness a rapidly ascending machine.

It towered into the sky like a reaching hand, standing tall for the world to see. Once high enough it started changing shape, billions of black-budget dollars coming to fruition as its perfect design took shape. Under its large shadow, the world watched as The Railgun took form, something so magnificent even the cameras turned from the leviathan to marvel at its configuration.

Evacuation complete. Estimated time to charge: 60 seconds.

Estimated cost: temporary rolling blackouts for the state of California, 48 hours maximum.

The gun began to charge, a gathering of brilliance that made the lights flicker statewide. The country watched it in the setting sun, panic and dread lost under the hope of the technology wiping the giant creature from existence.

Charge complete. Fire when ready.

As state-of-the-art calibration zeroed in on the floating threat, sirens wailed through the sky. The beam of light erupted from the hollow barrel and raced toward the creature, nearly cutting it in half with what could only be described as pure light.

As it went down, the creature seemed to frown, even as it descended towards the water.

The ground quaked, and the gun powered down. Immediately followed by the state of California, and every other state in America.

Blackout. Nationwide.

As the sun set, everyone watched in confusion as the lights didn't come back on.

Watched as the creature didn't make a splash, but merely dissolved soundlessly into the Pacific.

Watched in darkness as the ocean began to churn violently.

Then listened hopelessly, as they heard the tsunami rumbling toward them.

Made not of water, but skittering legs.

STOMACH PAINS

I feel the pinch in my stomach, but I refuse to look down. The pain is duller than a knife but still punctures, a prodding and burrowing that waters my eyes as it burrows past my skin. I focus on the walls, trying to distract myself from the erupting pain that begs for my attention. I look at the serenity of the white paint, hoping to hypnotize myself as I feel the tiny barbs tearing through my abdomen.

The prodding gives way to tearing, and my hand grips the countertop to steady myself. I blink and the tears stream, drops that are dwarfed by the spattering I hear hitting the floor. I don't dare look. I'm scared to. If I can just keep looking forward, maybe I'll close my eyes and it'll be over. It'll fade away, and the wet ripping won't matter anymore.

As the hole in my stomach widens, my gaze falters from the wall. I look at the tile in desperation, feeling weak as the electrical stabbing fades to a deeper discomfort that surpasses the sensation of pain.

It's rooting around my insides.

My eyes keep drifting, even after I feel teeth clamp down on something within. The pristine white tile gains speckles of red, until the splatters grow into the pool soaking my feet. When I finally look down, the sight is devastating.

The sudden evacuation of my guts weakens me, and my intestines flee like a spool of stained yarn. I watch them unravel, following the lead until I rest my eyes on the culprit. At the end of the purple rope is my dog, Maxwell.

A spine of raised hair trails down his back, and even with his mouth full, I see the damage his canines cause. His jaws snap on the leash, choking it down inch by inch as it swallows it like human pasta. In my fading consciousness, I don't question why. I only hope it is enough to take care of him after I am gone. The white of the kitchen fades to black, and I am left with the repetitive gnashing of his teeth on my insides.

I wake in my bed, tired and weary. The reflecting sun stings my eyes, and through my squinting I can see the tubes and bag of the IV. I am reminded of my illness.

I hear the claws on the hardwood floor. A moment later, the licking of my hand. My only remaining comfort, in a world of burned-out families and a tide of medical bills.

I look into his eyes, trying to express as much love as possible.

"I had the craziest dream, Max. I dreamt you ate me. But you'd never do that, would you?"

His cheery panting ceases, and his ears flutter. When I ask again, he looks away.

SLEEPING BLINDFOLDED

The blindfold is one of those with padding for the bridge of your nose. It shuts out the light and the shield over my eyes provides a sense of comfort that I didn't know I needed. I started using one after the accident, once I had to use the adjustable bed.

I didn't have a choice when Susan showed up.

My bed faces the doorway of my bedroom, and it's where Susan started to appear. She just showed up as I was trying to sleep during the day. Her haunted, ghastly face. Her wispy, white hair. Her lack of eyelids.

Since the accident, I have spent most of my days propped up, trying to sleep through the discomfort. Every day she shows up, rounding the corner and stopping in the doorway like she's lost. She looks around the room, and when her bulging eyes fall on me, they stay there. She never comes any closer.

It doesn't matter when I lay down. She'll always show up.

In the middle of the day.

During the night.

She stands there every time I try to sleep, her lips parted slightly like she wishes to say something. At first I would just stare back, unsure exactly what the fuck was happening. I thought maybe it was sleep paralysis. But I'm wide awake. I've called the cops, and when they show, she just turns and walks out of the doorway. I don't know where she even goes.

When the cops grew tired of taking my calls, I had to do something. So I bought the blindfold.

I wondered how she would respond at first. I didn't know if her staring was a game or a curse. The first time I put it on, I did it slowly, almost worried I would upset her. I pulled the soft shield over my eyes. Forcing my eyes to close, as hers were incapable of closing. I checked a few times to see if it triggered some kind of response, raising it slightly to see if she was still there.

She would always be there. Eyes staring, lips slightly parted. Her lower jaw working ever so softly. Like she's chewing.

I started sleeping soundly. When I wake and raise the blindfold, she is gone.

But she always returns when I'm off to sleep. Before I lower the blindfold, I'll see her turn the corner.

She never used to leave the doorway... until last night.

I woke up in the middle of the night. I couldn't take the blindfold off. She wouldn't let me.

I felt the wispy strands of her hair on my face.

The sounds of grinding teeth in my ear.

With her finger, she prodded the blindfold from the outside, feeling the depressions where my eyes were.

Today when I laid down, she didn't show. Something's not right, I can feel it.

I keep waiting, but she's not showing up.

I'm afraid to put the blindfold on.

I can hear her waiting around the corner.

WEEDS

*A*ll roadkill on Hitchcock St. must be incinerated within forty-eight hours.

Chaz recited the words in his head as he shouldered the utility truck. He left the vehicle running, almost humming the words in a tune as he stepped out and flipped open the diamond-plate box on the truck's bed. After looking thoughtfully at his recently pressure-washed tools, he took a moment to glance at the deceased rodent sprawled between the lanes.

A large raccoon bloating in the sun, its head reduced to a tire track.

With a sigh, he grabbed the flathead shovel.

If it wasn't for the union of skull and pavement, he would've preferred to just try and bag it. The stink of roadkill would cling to his tools, and in turn, his truck as well. The only thing his wife hated more than the erratic hours of his job was the smell that accompanied it. But it just paid *so good*; he couldn't believe people didn't last.

Chaz looked at the expired rodent and checked both ways before making his move.

The scuffs of his boots on the pavement. The buzzing flies on the corpse. The grind of the steel blade against pulpy asphalt. Another successful patrol.

It was easy money. Fifty an hour, twenty-four hours a day. You chose your own hours, with the understanding that all roadkill must be rounded up and incinerated within forty-eight hours of expiration.

They didn't elaborate, and he didn't ask. The pay alone was enough to keep his wife content, albeit reluctantly. It wasn't the proudest work, but he never missed a carcass. He would drive the length of Hitchcock every four hours, scraping and bagging every carcass on its two-mile stretch. Nothing but tall trees and swamps on either side. Drop the roadkill off at the local landfill to be burned from existence.

Chaz lobbed the carcass into the bed and tossed the shovel after it. Another successful run, more money in his pocket. He hummed his makeshift tune as he climbed in, only to find himself stopping. In the weeds beyond the shoulder, something caught his eye.

It was so insignificant, so easy to miss. He couldn't explain why, but the sight unsettled him greatly.

A slight part in the weeds before the swamp, so lush it almost disguised the divot in the earth. The disturbed vegetation already trying to right itself.

Poking out of the water was the rear-end of a motorcycle, the exposed tire perfectly still.

Beyond it, a humanoid shape skittered across the water on all fours, its body twisted and covered in moss. Dozens of seaweed tethers trailed after it, spilling out of the swamp's surface as it glided soundlessly over the surface.

Chaz turned to his truck, only to see it getting pulled away. Vines slithered around the tires and tugged at the axle, inching it off the road's shoulder. Bringing it to the swamp, taking his tools and phone with it.

Behind him, he heard trampling over the weeds.

POLYFEROUS

I thought the people putting on the award show for social media influencers would have picked a better location than this.

Polyphemus, of all places. The eater of moons.

I didn't expect an invite to such a prestigious event. I don't have much of a following, not compared to the other people here, anyway.

There's so many other faaaamous—

Cough—sorry. Getting used to the atmosphere. It's in retrograde, I guess.

There're so many famous people here. Most of my shit is follow-for-follow, that sort of thing. So yeah, my invitation was a bit of a surprise. I'm just happy they paid for the flight. The sandwiches though, there's just... cheese? Bread and cheese? What the f—

Anyway, yeah. Just happy to be here. Yeah, I'm pretty big on some socials. Mostly just write creepy stories, sometimes stage some photographs to go along with it. A Hawaiian shirt hanging from a dead tree, that sort of thing. People seem to dig it, I even have a few people pledged to my patre

other's eyes beneath the flesh you just have to peel it to see—

Cough—God in Heaven. This atmosphere is thick am I right? *Cough*—Yeah, a water would be great, thank you. No, no ice. Thanks.

Anyway. Yeah! Catch your boy on Polyphemus, from now until Sunday. Or whatever it is your time. I'll be **seeing** you there, I'll have plenty of

~~*EYES EVERYWHERE THEY LEAK FROM MY SOUL*~~

Make sure to like, subscribe, hit that motherfuckin' bell—you know the bell helps, and—*yes, Sherry, for the monetization, you have any idea how, HOW MANY TIMES DO I HAVE TO TELL YOU*—anyway.

Come and hang out with me.

So you can see every step of the way.

Walk in my ~~skin~~ shoes, follow the path to ~~the real almighty God, Polyferous~~ success.

I RAN OVER A BIRD

On my way home from work, I ran over a bird. It's not the impossible dumb luck of its flight path, the odd color of its feathers, or the look of its beady eyes burned into my brain that haunts me.

It's the sound. The sound of a hard-boiled egg crunching under my tire.

Briefly I could see the splotch on the road behind me, almost insignificant once it was no longer in the rear-view mirror. Things like this happen all the time, but I still feel terrible about it. I couldn't swerve, it had happened so fast. No amount of rationalization can quell the guilt that I feel.

I've felt physically ill since, or at least that's the only way I can describe it. I hear the sound echoing off the walls of my brain, the crunch that seems to follow me wherever I go.

It's not just the sickness it seems but my vision as well; it feels as if there's a film covering my eyeballs. Like a hint of color I couldn't see before. It only adds to the nausea. I'm going to surrender to my room for the night and hope some sleep will rid me of this affliction.

I couldn't sleep. I tossed and turned all night, and my only moments of respite were spent dreaming of flapping wings and that fucking crunch under the wheel. No matter how hard I try, I can't seem to shake it off.

I called in sick today. The nausea is gone, but in its place is a severe feeling of uneasiness. A hangover-anxiety feeling that cranks up every time I get close to the window. I'm afraid to go by the windows and look outside. I thought I heard the sound of something pecking on the window, but when I checked, I saw nothing. I'm just going to try and sleep today.

During the night, I heard pecking again. It's louder, but it sounds... far away. I can't explain it.

I took another day off. I feel like I'm being watched, no matter where I hide inside the house.

The pecking won't stop. I hear it in the shower. I hear it over the TV. I can't block the noise.

I decided tomorrow I will try to leave the house. Maybe I just need some fresh air.

I can't leave the driveway. I can see it clearly, like it's *outside* of the sky looking in. The neighbors can't see. I've called friends, and they can't see it. But it's there, standing on the horizon, towering above everything, so far away. Like it's in the background.

It's pecking at the sky. It's like it's stuck behind a sheet of glass, and it wants in. Every time its beak touches, I hear it inside my head. It's looking right at me.

Why don't they see it? Why can't they see it?

The glass... it's starting to crack.

WHATEVER YOU WANT, BABE

"What do you want for dinner tonight?"

"Whatever you want, babe."
"Are you sure? Nothing sounds good?"
"Whatever you want, babe."
"Nothing? Nothing at all?"
"Whatever you want, babe."

Sebastian listened to the same monotone response from the other room and looked up from his phone. As much as he enjoyed his wife's complacency, he couldn't remember the last time she had an opinion of her own. How long had it been? Days? Weeks?

He heard the running water in the kitchen and assumed he'd find her doing dishes. Getting up from the sofa, he followed the sound of the faucet and rounded the corner to find her. Just as he thought, she was standing there with her back to him, hands busy with a sponge and plate. She was looking out the window in front of her, into the woods in the backyard.

"Are you sure?" he asked, his words seeming unusually loud in the kitchen.

His wife froze, nothing but the sound of running water filling the void between them.

"Since when do you care what I want? It's always been about you. What you want," she said, holding her frozen pose.

Sebastian felt nauseous, and the throbbing warning of a migraine swelled behind his eyes.

"No, no, it's—it's not like that," he stammered, taking a step towards her. She flinched at the sound of his footstep.

"I'm afraid it is," she said, letting the plate and sponge fall into the water.

Despite her lack of movement, the faucet ceased to run.

"No, please. Whatever you want, really! Let's do it. Whatever you feel like, hon." He took another step toward her.

"Really? You mean that?" she said quieter, standing still as ever.

"Yeah. Yes. Of course. Whatever you want," he said, almost close enough to touch her.

She said nothing for a moment, and Sebastian waited. What she said next was barely a whisper.

"But you already know what I want."

Then she was gone.

Sebastian looked at the empty sink, his wife vanished out of thin air. He sweat profusely, his hands jittering as he reached for nothing. The sink was full, flies buzzing around dirty dishes. Through the window, he saw the woods.

He found the shovel hidden under the stairs where he'd left it.

He made his way to the woods, breathing harder the deeper he went.

The shovel plunged into the loose soil, digging until the smell hit him. When enough had been cleared, he sat exhausted, looking at the hole in the ground. Twisting limbs contorted, cracking as she pulled herself free. The mangled face looked at him, pale and caked with dirt. With a whimper, he laid on his back and closed his eyes.

Sebastian listened to her approach, each awkward step until she was over him, the putrid breath on his forehead. As the teeth slowly closed around his eye socket, he felt her clammy arm and whispered.

"I'm sorry. Take whatever you want, babe."

EVERYTHING WILL BE BETTER SOON

Patricia squinted as the Doctor adjusted the overhead lamp. Through the blinding light she could faintly see the nurse rummaging behind them, as the man in the white coat flipped over the clipboard for the third time.

"Is this really going to work?" she asked.

The Doctor paused and looked up from the clipboard, his eyes large and intense behind his glasses. His first look was of irritation, but it slowly melted into a warm and comforting grin.

"Ms. Hayworth," He began.

"It's Mrs."

The Doctor cleared his throat, "Right. *Mrs.* Hayworth. I've treated over a hundred patients with the same procedure, and the results have been nothing but extraordinary. There's been much research on the subject, and it's proved to be the most effective treatment *by far.* You must trust the *science*, Mrs. Hayworth. My goal is to make you better. Do you trust me?" he asked, putting a hand on her shoulder.

Behind them, the nurse wheeled up a tray covered in a fine cloth. She looked at the tray, then back to the Doctor. Despite her heart thumping in her chest, she felt herself soften a little at his touch. He was a man of medicine, after all.

"I'm just very worried, is all. Will it hurt?" she said, looking at the nurse as she approached. Without a word, the nurse started fastening restraints, looping the thick leather straps around her wrists. Patricia felt the instinctual need to place them on her stomach.

"It's normal to be nervous. It's a big step we're taking here. But I'll have you know, several people signed off on the procedure, including your parents *and* your husband. They trust me to take care of you. Before you know it, this will all be a bad dream."

Patricia nodded, and the Doctor turned back to his work. She heard the *snap* of latex gloves and looked at the ceiling in hopes of calming her nerves. The nurse brought the tray closer, and the Doctor removed the white cloth. Patricia decided not to look. It was better that way.

The nurse brought the lamp closer, brighter. Patricia squinted harder, and the outline of the Doctor drew near.

"Doctor?" Patricia asked, and he paused again.

"Yes, Mrs. Hayworth?" he said dryly.

"Will this stop the visions?"

"Immediately," he assured.

"I'm sorry, just one more thing," Patricia said, feeling the knot in her throat. She tried to see him, but the light was too bright.

"Of course. What is it?"

"Will my baby be alright? Will I be able to take care of it?" she asked, feeling a tear trickle down.

There was a moment of silence, then he cleared his throat again.

"Mrs. Hayworth, after this, I expect you'll make a full recovery. Everything will be better soon."

Patricia nodded and closed her eyes.

The Doctor watched her for a moment before proceeding. When she seemed content, he raised the pick and hammer, slowly aiming for the inner corner of her eye.

TROUBLE SLEEPING

I've been having trouble sleeping lately. I feel like I keep hearing something in the middle of the night, but every time I open my eyes, there's nothing there. My feet are always exposed and freezing, no matter how many times I make sure they are covered.

Nothing to be seen, nothing to be heard.

My mother says I'm paranoid. *Too many scary movies,* she says.

But I don't really watch them, not really.

Each night I am rousted from a dead sleep, only to find my dark, empty bedroom. It happens the same way every time, like a snap in the silence that I can't make out.

I've checked outside to make sure it's not just someone walking down the street. I checked the closet and found nothing but hanging clothes.

I sleep through my alarms. I yawn through my classes.

Still, the problem persists. My mother says it's just a phase. One I'll get over in time.

I cut out caffeine and minimized my screen time. Whatever was keeping me from sleeping through the night, I was determined to change it.

Even still, I find myself awake. I hear it, whatever it is, and I sit up instantly. Only to find nothing in my room but the cold, empty air.

I tried Benadryl, I tried melatonin. The drugs lull me to sleep, but I can still hear it through my heavy sedation. Something whispered, but I just can't make it out.

No one believes me. It's just a phase. It's just a phase. *It's just a phase.*

It's not a phase.

Last night, I set up a camera. I had to be sure. It's one of those old ones with the VHS camcorders, and I let it run on my dresser while I slept. At first, I didn't think I was going to find anything. But after fast-forwarding two hours' worth of footage, I saw it.

It slides out from underneath my bed, its many folds squirming as it worms around at the foot of my bed. I can barely make out its eyes because of the wrinkles, but it watches me for a time before uncovering my feet. From the folds protrudes horrible teeth, a mouth consisting of nothing but jutting molars. After moments of gnashing quietly it speaks, a hiss escaping its bulky maw.

You gonna eat that?

In the video I'm sound asleep, perfectly still as it looms before me. Even as it leans in and peels the covers from my feet. Even as it chews my toenails.

It doesn't pass up a single toe, its large molars chewing delicately on every digit.

The worst part is the end. Once it's done with my toes, it worms its way over to my bedside and leans over my face. It watches me again, almost thoughtfully. Then it opens its jaws once more, wide enough until it's hovering around my entire head. Then it mutters a word, right before retreating back under the bed.

Someday.

DAYLIGHT SAVINGS TIME

Tom couldn't shake the feeling of something being *wrong*.

It persisted throughout the day, a nagging that he couldn't quite place, no matter how long he pondered upon it.

A slow sinking. A downward pull. Something looming.

It didn't make sense.

Tom sat at his computer, hovering the mouse over an array of icons, wondering which one would make the feeling go away. He felt incapable of making the decision. Tom leaned back in his chair, wiping an anxious sweat from his brow. Then, silently, looked at the icons once more. There had to be an answer in there somewhere.

Outside for a cigarette. 4:58pm.

Why can I see the moon? Now of all times? Tom thought to himself, looking at the encroaching night sky. *Where did the sun go?*

Even when he was in the sun, it was too bright. Too *piercing.* It made him angry. If it was the answer, why didn't it make him happy?

Tom leaned against the rail of the balcony, looking up at the sky. He stared at the moon, the lurking feeling still burrowing inside him.

Why? *Why?*

5:00pm. Full moon. Bright moon.

"Why are you here?" he asked aloud, looking at the moon. He heard no answer, and silently dragged on the cigarette. The exhale was slow, almost exhausted.

Then it hit him.

Daylight savings time.

"Ah, that's the problem. Old seasonal trying to get me again," Tom said to himself. It made sense now—why everything felt off.

"The last one, it would seem."

The voice came from nowhere, like it was an echo on the wind.

"Ah, yeah. Heard they're doing away with that. Good riddance," he said, presumably to himself. He looked up at the moon, but something looked... off.

"They're not doing anything. It was just time, after all."

Tom's head started to hurt. He looked at the moon and realized that the voice was coming from *it*. His stomach suddenly felt upset.

"Time for what?" he asked, suddenly feeling uncomfortable. He looked at the moon, but it wasn't really a moon, was it? It was just a white dot. There was a noise, like wind without the breeze.

Tom gripped the old wooden railing, his fingernails cracking the faded paint.

"The end. The end of time," it spoke again. The clouds and light pollution started to fade, letting Tom see clearer than he ever had before. Letting him *truly* see.

Tom looked at the ~~moon~~ white dot, focusing harder than he thought capable. It wasn't a moon, it never was. It was just a glimmer, a reflection of the light from the planet. Like a twinkle in someone's eye.

An eye the size of the solar system.

Tom looked at the Eye, the massive pupil and iris so clear he didn't know how he couldn't see it the whole time. The air... was getting louder.

Tom felt himself crumble, but he couldn't look away.

"Will... will it hurt?" he asked.

Above, the eye blinked.

HOME SWEET HOME

*T*his *used to be a wonderful place to live.*

Jackie stepped out of the sedan and looked up at the house from the sidewalk and felt himself shrinking under the sight of it. It stood amongst the dozens of other cookie-cutter houses like a spire reaching toward the sky, something horrible radiating behind the cloak of beige paint and colorful curtains.

He made his way up the driveway, readying his badge, but not even needing to flash it. The usual crew he had seen many times before occupied the lawn, but he had never seen them like this.

Ten years as detective, and never a call for Birchwood. A place for khakis, cookouts, and Coors Lite. Everyone's home-sweet-home.

Neighbors wailed to the sky, rocking themselves in the grass in the fetal position.

The reporter for the local news crew was shaking, an unlit cigarette shaking in her fingers as she stared at seemingly nothing.

The officer that should've been guarding the door was vomiting in the bushes. Crime scene tape blew in the wind on the ground next to him, never quite making it to its destination. Jackie was called to the scene for a homicide. This looked like a terrorist attack.

Ten years and not as much as a domestic dispute. Why? After all this time.

Jackie stood in the open doorway, his gut twisting so hard he thought he'd join the officer in the bushes. He had long been used to the smell, but the sight alone was enough to peel the long-dried paint on his soul. He felt the urge to draw his gun and turn it on himself.

"Detective," his partner mumbled, sitting with his back against the wall. In his hand was a bottle of whiskey, frost congealing the glass from the victim's freezer. In his hand, his revolver.

"What—*what the fuck happened here, Boris?*" Jackie said, his eyes frantically taking in every horrible detail, every grisly stain.

Boris knocked back the bottle, tears trickling.

"It seems after sustaining the shotgun wound, she slit his throat and tried to climb inside it. We don't know who expired first."

Neither were recognizable. The struggle was impossible to comprehend. At their feet lay the stained Remington 870.

How... how the fuck.

Jackie's mental gears tried to scatter, but he forced them to turn. Boris drank and raised a hand.

"Detective,"

"We need *forensics*, Boris. We need... help."

"*Detective,*" He pleaded.

"What?!"

"We can't... we can't seem to locate their *child.*"

"Oh god."

Behind them both, a beastly groan echoed from the basement. Like a Kodiak being flayed alive.

Jackie reluctantly drew toward the blackened doorway, and looked down the wooden steps.

"Boris... call *S.W.A.T.,*" Jackie said, the sweat freezing on his brow.

Another groan rattled the steps, much deeper than the last.

"*He* said they can't stop him." Boris giggled behind him and set the whiskey down. Before he could stop him, he stuffed the revolver in his mouth and pulled the trigger.

THE GARBAGE TRUCK

It had been idling there for hours.

Angeline observed it from the safety of her window, wondering why it had been chugging away for so long. She hadn't seen it when it initially pulled up, and there had been no sign of someone coming back to claim it. Or shutting the damn thing off. It wasn't even garbage day.

Thick black smoke billowing from the tailpipe.

Yellow hazards blinking at an empty street.

Nobody behind the wheel, no one hanging off the side.

A whisper in the wind.

She looked up and down the street, bare lanes and empty windows lining the subdivision as far as the eye could see. It wasn't so much the truck itself that bothered her; it was the fact that *nobody seemed to be home.*

No school buses ferrying children, no parents returning from work, not even a mailman.

Angeline turned it over in her head, fighting the nagging urge that felt less taboo the longer she thought about it. After taking turns looking between the rumbling truck and the wall clock that ticked away... she found herself doing the only thing that made sense.

She took out the garbage.

The bag in the kitchen was hardly full, but she tied off the bag anyway. She slipped on crocs and opened the front door, letting in the sound of the worn-out exhaust. The street looked more deserted now that she was outside, and the impulse to close the door and retreat begged at the back of her mind.

Despite her mental logic, she closed the door and made her way to the street, the rhythmic slapping of crocs echoing her determination over the grass. The thing looked rougher up close, peeling paint and cancerous rust riddling holes throughout the structure.

It was only a garbage truck.

There isn't even anyone driving it.

It doesn't even smell.

Nothing to be scared of.

These thoughts drove Angeline on as she marched towards the truck, eager to prove to herself that she could handle this menial task. Hefting the bag to lob it in, Angeline approached the loader and stopped.

Dozens of swollen black bags filled the ass end of the truck, each bag stuffed to the point of bursting. She looked not at the mound but underneath it, puzzle pieces in the plastic forcing themselves together in her mind.

The vibrant pattern of a crocheted sweater.

A cold, outstretched hand.

An exposed half-face.

The details were so loud she didn't hear the boots thumping behind her.

Heavy hands grabbed her shoulders and shoved, pressing her into the mound of swollen plastic. Before she could resist, more bags toppled over her, heavy grunts followed by burying weight.

Behind her the loader compacted, forcing her into the mound of clammy bags. She kicked and screamed, but the bags silenced her, beckoning with clammy feet and hands behind the film as it consumed her.

Screaming against the cold dark, Angeline felt the truck pulling away.

INSIDE-OUT JEFF

I got a new job and then I saw a ghost. Nobody believed me at first, and I was still on probation, so I didn't want to make too much of a stink about it.

But after a few times of him appearing, almost in spite of me, I couldn't help but ask questions.

"Do you see that guy over there?" I said to Percy, who was puffing away at a cigarette.

"Who?" he asked, coughing a little before giving me his attention.

I pointed across the street, where another shop was located. The man waved in the opening of the bay door, his enthusiasm a little overkill for a Thursday night workday.

"Oh, that's inside-out Jeff," Percy said, putting the cigarette out on his heel before flicking it away.

"*What*?" I said, watching his unnatural smile continue.

"Yeah. Rumor is he died years ago. Someone wasn't paying attention or something. He got crushed. It was a whole thing then, but you shouldn't have to worry about it now. As long as you focus on the job," Percy said, heading inside.

Alone, I watched the man across the street, his smile fading as he tilted his head. He started to twitch, a convulsion that led to his insides spilling out from every orifice. No matter how hard he tried, he couldn't get them all back in. Then he twitched again, and everything was fine.

He waved and walked away, and my pocket rumbled as my phone went off.

I LEFT THE LIGHTS ON

Killian looked at the house from the sidewalk, swaying a little. It was late, and he was tired. A triple-pub-crawl landed him in front of his friend Ryan's house drunker than he cared to admit. The lights were out, something he expected showing up after midnight.

He made his way to the front porch and dialed his number, rocking slowly as the dial tone drummed in his ear. It went to voicemail.

Killian hung up and texted instead, squinting against the phone's brightness in the dark. After correcting several misspellings, he sent a simple text.

Hey mate, Sophie and I had a fight. Too drunk to go home. Using the spare to crash on your couch.

He locked his phone and lifted the smallest potted plant on the windowsill. Underneath was the spare key. As quietly as he could muster, Killian unlocked the door and shambled in. It wasn't the first time he had done such a thing.

The house was dark. It was a bilevel home, the lower level and upper level in view from the kitchen. Ryan slept upstairs, and Killian looked to see his bedroom door was shut. He would catch up with him in the morning.

Every step creaked loudly despite his attempts at silence. After quietly removing his boots, Killian sprawled on the couch in the front room, opposite the kitchen. He stretched out on the couch and closed his eyes.

After minutes of tossing and turning, Killian sat up. He could not sleep. Something about the lack of white noise, and the big quiet house. His eyes were adjusting and making sense of the shadowy furniture on the lower level. The longer he looked around, the creepier the lone furniture looked.

After a sigh, he got up and headed to the fridge. He opened the door and looked inside, disappointed to find no food, but relieved to see a mostly full bottle of red wine. His mouth watered, and he whipped out his phone to send another text to Ryan.

I owe you a bottle of wine.

Killian unscrewed the cap, then downed some of the chilled warmth, feeling immediately better about the creepy, empty house. After this, he'd sleep just fine. Bottle in hand, Killian turned, letting the fridge door close itself. In the fridge's light he got a glimpse of the stairs and froze.

Someone was standing at the top of the steps of the upper level.

"Jesus, mate, you fuckin' scared me!" Kilian called, wiping his mouth as the door shut behind him.

In the dark he could barely see them. Just their outline above.

"Mate? I just texted you," he said. Only more silence.

Without a word, they started heading down, skipping three steps at a time.

"Ryan?"

In his hand, his phone chirped and lit back up.

Oof. Sorry mate, out of town for work. I left the lights on so it looked like I was home. Feel free to crash. I'll call in the morning.

DO YOU HAVE ANY FOOD?

Just as Benny was pulling foil over the brats, he heard the knock at the door. After a day of grilling out on the back deck, he didn't expect any visitors, especially at nine o'clock at night. He looked at his wife, who had paused with the fridge open to offer a shrug.

"I'll get it," he said, setting the tray of food on the counter.

Benny opened the door to see a young woman standing there, awkwardly hugging herself. She looked lost, and the bags under her eyes made him think she hadn't slept in days. He looked past her and saw no car in the driveway. She had arrived on foot.

"Hi, how can I help you?" he asked nervously. His wife had joined him at his side, cautiously peering around his shoulder.

"Do you have any food?" she asked weakly, her eyes barely focusing.

"Is everything alright, dear?" his wife asked, subconsciously reaching for her phone.

"I smelt the grill... and it's just, we haven't eaten in a few days," the girl said, placing both hands on her stomach.

The couple exchanged looks of concern and let her in.

Benny watched in disbelief as she ate, no—*gorged* ravenously. Two burgers and three brats, buns and all, with a hefty side of potato salad had all been consumed in minutes. For the most part they just watched her eat, marveling at her appetite. They tried asking her questions in between helpings, but she mostly waved them off and stared at the food. Almost drooling. When she was finished, she pushed the plate away and leaned back, placing her hands back on her stomach.

They asked if she needed to use a phone or needed the police, but she refused additional help of any kind. After sitting a moment, she simply got up and headed for the door.

"I'll be going now," was all she said.

They insisted on a bit of money as well as the address and number of the local woman's shelter, which she was still holding in her hand when they walked her out. They closed the door behind her and watched her go, both of them concerned but equally confused. A confusion that grew when she stopped halfway down the driveway.

For a moment, she just stood there. Then, without warning, she started sprinting.

Back towards the house.

"What the fuck?" Benny said, instinctively locking the door.

Just as she hit the porch, she made a hard left and ran around the house.

"Call the police!" Benny said, grabbing a flashlight and heading out the back door.

Rushing out back, Benny flicked the light on and found nothing but darkness. The girl had vanished.

That's when he heard the squelching.

He followed the noise until it took him to the deck next to the pool. It was coming from underneath.

Benny shined the light underneath and gasped.

Underneath was the girl, hands shaking as her jaws opened painfully wide, a dark mass forcing its way out of them. Her eyes were bloodshot, rolling into the back of her head as her throat bulged. The beady eyed projection was extending out and reaching toward the ground, an open beak of sorts presenting a mound of soggy chewed food. Below it was identical offspring, several little malformed bird monstrosities bobbing up and "pecking" at the contents. The sounds they made were awful, like nails on a chalkboard.

Benny stared in disbelief, the single statement repeating in his head as he backed away.

I smelt the grill.

The girl's eyes darted to him, and her head started to shake. Like a warning.

The offspring's screeches stopped, and one by one their heads turned towards him.

As did the mother's.

LEG DAY

Noah pulled up to the gym, fired up and ready to go. He put his car in park and knocked back the rest of his pre-workout, already feeling the itch in his face. The late winter chill was freezing in his tank-top and gym shorts, and the door to the gym was over fifty feet away. Even though he shivered, he kept his chin up.

Today was leg day; the cold wouldn't bother him much longer. He put in his air-pods and started making his way. As he scrolled through his music, he noticed someone at the door ahead was entering the gym, and had stopped to hold the door open for him. Noah motioned for him to go ahead. He was still all the way across the parking lot. Seemed a little far away to be worrying about it.

Noah returned to his phone, decided on soft and sweet. He would warm up with a few miles on the treadmill. He selected Brian McKnight.

As the song started playing, he looked up to see the man still holding the door. He was still only halfway across the parking lot. Still too soon. Annoying, even.

"I'm good!" Noah's words were swallowed by the wind, and he waved him off again.

The guy just stood there, one hand holding the door with the other hanging limp. Noah noticed then that not only was he pretty tall, but he was also hardly dressed for a workout. And his hair was long as fuck.

Huh?

Old, black leather duster whipping in the wind. Faded, army-camo cargo pants with... white boots?

"Go for it man, c'mon! I'll catch up!" Noah shouted, unable to hear himself over the lullaby in his ears.

The man just held the door and stared, his mouth opening slowly, as if to say something. But his mouth formed no words, only kept opening wider. And wider.

What the fuck?

Noah stopped, now only twenty feet away. The man watched and waited, his mouth unhinging like a snake. The pre-workout pumped through his blood, heating his face despite the chill. If he didn't work out, he'd get nauseous. But the man at the door, and the... gym?

He didn't know how he didn't notice before, but the lights were off in the gym. There wasn't anybody inside, either.

Ahead, the man's jaw opened so wide it would fit his head if he tried. His limp arm reached for him, waving him in. Noah swallowed hard, and he started to sweat.

"Ah shit, I forgot something. Maybe next time!" Noah chuckled awkwardly, turning on his heel. He'd decided to just jog back to the car and bail—

The parking lot was empty, all the other cars gone. All except his. The only thing stranger than the empty lot was the door to the back seat opening just a crack. Long limbs and wispy hair slithered across the pavement, impossibly slinking into his car.

White boots tucked in, and the door closed.

THE LAST TAG

Rick was just about to call it when the doe walked into view. After a long morning of sitting in the blinds with his ass going numb, the beautiful white-tailed deer almost looked like a mirage at first glance. He rubbed his eyes and looked again, this time through the scope of his Remington 870 Super Mag.

Sure as shit, there it was. Two-hundred pounds of walking venison, right into his lap at the last second. Immaculate hazel fur with a white shine, fully grown and fattened for the season.

Feeling his heart pound in his chest, Rick stifled his excitement and focused on the kill. Slowly and carefully he shouldered the slug gun, each movement delicate and precise. He looked down the scope and lined up the shot, positioning the crosshair steadily like he had done dozens of times before. Just as the doe stopped to sniff the air, his finger hovered over the trigger.

A single shot, right behind the deer's front leg.

The three-inch slug dropped the deer immediately, and the gunshot echoed over miles of dead woods. A perfect shot, and an assumedly painless end. Rick looked up from the smoking gun to see the doe already motionless on the ground.

What a turn of events. Rick ejected the spent casing, his head already swimming with thoughts of venison steaks and hot sticks.

It would be enough to fill the freezer, for sure. Just as he was about to set the shotgun down he stopped, an uneasy feeling creeping over him as he looked ahead.

The deer was moving, strangely. Slow at first, followed by jerky, delayed thrashes.

Rick watched the deer cautiously from the blinds, waiting for it to pass. Death throes weren't uncommon in a kill, but these seemed... *different.* The shot was true, though. It wouldn't be long until it was over.

Without a sound, the deer got back up and looked around, seemingly unphased. It blinked lazily and twitched, even as the bloom of the gunshot wound oozed into the grass. Even as its right front leg fell away from its body.

What the fuck—Rick thought, shouldering the gun again to look through the scope. The deer awkwardly hobbled to look the other way, like it was looking for who shot it. Rick felt a twist of sickness when he saw the other side of it, a side that looked much less beautiful than the other.

The hide of the deer was covered in horrid bite marks, where many pieces had been ripped away crudely. The deer's other eye was cloudy—infected, a coagulated stream oozing as it looked in his direction.

Rick wanted to take the shot but couldn't. He wasn't looking at the deer now, but *everything else* in the trees behind it.

A limping mangy coyote, missing half of its face.

A human man, shambling from the bushes with a missing arm.

Several half-eaten squirrels.

All around him, the trees began to stir.

NOISE COMPLAINT

Officer Moore pulled the squad car next to the curb and took a moment to survey the property. Through the lens of his sunglasses and the beating sun outside the car, the only thing he could discern about what he saw was that it was *hot,* and the particular house he leered at needed a fresh paint job. He sat listening, hoping for some kind of hint as to what exactly he was walking into. Nothing but cicadas, and the faint drone of a lawnmower down the block.

Moore checked the laptop on the center console, glancing over the information before looking up at the house again. There was something odd about this one, something that didn't quite make sense. The houses in this neighborhood were old, sure. But it was a nice neighborhood, a place one would spend their years retired. On the other hand, it's not everyday you get a call for a noise complaint from not just one, but *four* consecutive callers simultaneously from the same street.

Each saying something like "it sounded like a scream, but horrible". Words that would haunt even the most seasoned of police.

The humidity washed over Moore as he got out. A thick, unmovable misery that started to collect on his skin immediately. He moved up the sidewalk and towards the front door, hands resting on his belt as he glanced around. It looked like there was nobody home. Moore knocked and waited, listened, even peeked through the windows. Not a soul in sight; nobody pacing around inside or hurrying to the door. Only silence.

Moore knocked again before proceeding around the house. The backyard was fenced in, but it was short enough to look over.

"Police department, anybody home?" he called as he made his way around, taking in everything as he went.

A beautiful garden—a collection of trellises, vines, and blooming flowers— made up most of the backyard. Nothing out of the ordinary. Moore considered leaving and calling it a wash when something caught his eye. He only saw a fraction of it between the clutter of petals and shrubbery, but it was enough to make his hand drift toward his gun.

The undeniable glimpse of a blouse fluttering in the wind, the bright fabric contrasted with dark specks of blood. Moore steadied his breathing and drew his sidearm, holding it tight as he advanced and mustered a calm but authoritative command.

"Police department," he started, but felt his words catch in his throat as he rounded the trellises, gun ready. He could hear a groaning, like a faint, disoriented plea.

A woman was lying in a writhing heap, blood matting her long auburn hair. Her eyes were unfocused and swollen, and the crimson seemed to be leaking from every orifice in her head. Her hands were contorted at her sides, each filled with matching clumps of dirt and grass she had seemingly ripped from the earth. She continuously mouthed the word "help".

When Moore announced his presence and reached for his radio to call for a paramedic, something rustled in the weeds beside her, next to a neat row of freshly pulled carrots. He approached it cautiously, training the gun on it as he nudged the weeds away.

Wiggling in the soil was something of the likes the officer had never seen. The petiole and stem were identical to the carrots next to it, but the bulbous orange skin was replaced with a horrible brown disfiguration. The vegetable moved on its own, little nub-like appendages squirming as it looked up hatefully with cloudy eyes, its wrinkled face twisted in anguish.

Before Moore could make sense of the thing, it opened up its mouth and started to scream.

THE CONSUMER

"Would you like to round up today?"

"Save and get better benefits with a subscription!"

"Would you like to donate to the 'Contribute Maybe Fund' today?"

"It's just gonna ask you a question real quick."

"If you don't want to, just hit *no*—"

"For better, more genuine content just for you, consider subscribing to our—"

Dennis closed the driver's side door and rubbed his eyes, feeling a tension building behind them. He couldn't stand going to town anymore, but it was his only day off, his only chance to do something other than punch the clock and rush home to *still* not get enough sleep. He used to find pleasure in his slow puttering around town and browsing shops in his free time, but now he couldn't help but feel like everyone and everything was trying to target him and wring him for all he was worth.

The man on the corner with the cardboard sign, staring him down as he did every time he turned onto the main street. The debit-card terminal asking him if he wanted to donate to a cause that was too hard to read. The advertisement on the little screen built into the gas pump that slowed the fill to a trickle and raised the volume as it asked him about a membership program.

Sitting through traffic and finding a far away spot at the local mega-mart, Dennis felt crushed by the invisible weight of currency. When he was younger—fifteen years ago, when the overtime actually felt like it meant something—one of Dennis's coworkers told him he "couldn't leave the house without spending two-hundred bucks". Although the man was twice his age at the time and it was most definitely a flex, he couldn't help but hear the voice echoing in his head as he shuffled across the parking lot.

Things were different then. Overtime wasn't used to waste on fun now, it was used to keep up.

He sulked as he grabbed a cart and pushed it through the second set of double doors. He thought of how things used to be, back when he made way less and things felt achievable, when the future felt wide open instead of like a lidded container with no holes drilled in it. His annual review boasted of the company's appreciation for his hard work and perfect attendance and netted him a whopping 2% raise, one that was eaten by the tenfold increase in cost of living. Watching his checks net him less and less over time with tax inflation made him wonder why he even tried at all, if there was even a point to the long hours and slow expiration of his tendons, with the looming threat of a medical bill if one of them ceased to operate.

Dennis filled his cart with things that would last him through the week, both products for his work lunches and easy meals at home. He scowled looking over the brands, the dollar increments rising and rattling his brain. Even the old reliables—the cheapest of cheap meals—had found a way to either downsize in portion or increase in price. By the time his cart was barely half-full, he knew he'd already be over his budget. He felt the migraine in his skull building as he made his way to the checkout, wishing he had remembered needing socks before the ingredients for tacos and lasagna. It was easier to go without than to walk back and put everything on the shelf where he got it. He'd get them next payday, for sure.

Before he knew it, he had waded through the self-checkout line and found himself scanning and bagging and watching the total rise. Each barcode chime raised the hair on the back of his neck, and he felt sweat congealing on his brow. He could feel the eyes of people behind him boring into the back of his head, making him self conscious as he fumbled with the cheap plastic film in the bagging area. By the time he was done, the numeric total stared him in the face with bold black font. Even though he tried to be mindful with the selection, it still felt like far too much.

Fuck it, fine. The voice in the back of his head grumbled as he reached for his wallet and inserted the card before entering the pin. As he withdrew it and returned it to his pocket, he watched the buffering sign and waited to see the magic message so he could leave and go home.

TRANSACTION APPROVED

Instead, he saw another prompt.

CONFIRM AMOUNT?

"Yes," Dennis sighed, tapping the touch screen. He loaded all the bags back into his cart and reached out expectantly for his receipt, only to see another prompt. One that asked if he wanted it printed, text to him, or emailed.

"Chrissake," He sighed again, selecting the print option. He waited for the familiar *whir* of the printer and only heard the start of it. After seconds of silence, Dennis was left still holding his hand at the empty mouth. When his eyes lifted to the touch screen, he found another prompt waiting for him.

WOULD YOU LIKE TO DONATE?

There was no message following the request, only big black letters. Usually they'd at least tell you what for. Dennis scratched his head and sighed, ready to be on his way already. He hit 'NO' and reached again for the receipt.

ARE YOU SURE?

Dennis started grinding his teeth, looking annoyingly behind him. The ones that weren't buried in their phones were trying hard not to look directly at those still bagging their things.

"*Yes,* I'm sure," Dennis said aloud, tapping harder than before.

He saw the screen change before he had the chance to reach for the receipt.

PLEASE?

Dennis scoffed at the question and looked behind him for a representative. There was only one, a younger kid carding someone fifty-plus for beer. He groaned as he turned back to the terminal, and found it had given him options for a donation under the large question:

$1 $5 $10 $20 OTHER

"You're fuckin' kidding," Dennis growled at the terminal, before jabbing his finger at **OTHER**. He had to tap three more prompts before finally getting the prompt he desired:

I REFUSE TO DONATE

As soon as he tapped it, he heard an audible thud in front of him. He looked over the scanner and shelves in confusion. He shot a glance behind him, thinking momentarily that someone must have been pranking him, like an employee or maybe even a Youtuber. None of the other customers seemed to notice, and the associate had moved on to a woman having trouble scanning a bag of avocados. He wearily turned back to the terminal.

The thud sounded again, louder this time. It wasn't until he looked down in anger, to the glass interface housing the scanner, that he saw the source of the noise. On the other side of the glass, through the old chicken juice and dried condensation, was a human hand. It was pressing against the glass, leaving just enough room for Dennis to see the glimpse of a face underneath it.

Inside the self checkout, was a man. His limbs were contorted, and his neck was cocked painfully, like he had literally no room to move. The longer Dennis looked, the more painfully impossible it seemed.

"Please, help me..." the man said. His only form of clothing was a loose-fitting blue vest, the name tag obscured by a contorted limb. One of his eyes was swollen up like a plum, like he had been beaten.

WOULD YOU DONATE TO SAVE A LIFE?

Dennis was sweating more now, looking once again behind him. No one seemed to notice. He turned back to the machine. The prompt was waiting for him. He could almost feel it laughing, taunting.

"What the fuck? What happened to you?" Dennis asked in disbelief.

"Please, *please*—" He begged, hitting the glass.

"This is bullshit," Dennis chuckled in disbelief. It had to be a hologram, an optical illusion, something. He hit the 'no' button again, and not a second later, he heard the crackle of a taser. The wail that followed carried throughout the store, but it might as well had been noiseless. The only eyes he saw on him were the irritated ones of impatient customers waiting for their turn.

"What do I need me to do—let's get you out of there," Dennis scrambled, looking around for an associate. Nobody seemed to notice the extra noise or even see his reaction.

"Please... I have a family..." the man moaned again, weakly. From underneath the glass, his eyes were locked onto him, assessing his next move.

"What do I need to do? I'm trying to—" Dennis was looking frantically around when he stopped, trailing off as he saw the man pointing with a shaking finger. Pointing at the terminal. He lifted his eyes to the screen and felt a cold sweat trickling down his brow.

"Please..." The man from within echoed again, echoing in Dennis's mind.

WOULD YOU LIKE TO DONATE TO SAVE LIVES? (YES) (NO)

He could feel the eyes of the self-checkout-man burning into him. Pleading. Begging.

Dennis lifted a finger and pressed **NO**.

HUMAN GRAVY

Rafael felt immediately sick as the car sputtered. He looked at the fuel light, wishing, *pleading* for it to hang on long enough to at least get out of the thick of the woods. He could feel the last gasps of life fleeting in the pedal, the final chugs of a tank running dry. Before he could even fathom the possibility of being stranded in the middle of nowhere, he found the car shouldering, and the headlights slowed to a still snapshot of tall, unmoving pine.

"No, no, nononono shit-*shit*!" He cried, squeezing the steering wheel in despair.

This can't be happening. This can't be happening.

For the past hour, Rafael had been trying to get gas, watching as the fuel needle drifted closer and closer to E. In the beginning, his cross-country trip had gone according to plan, cruising comfortably down the highway with no problem at all. Then, as if an unseen hand had intentionally steered him to misfortune, his luck took a turn for the worse. At first the subtleties were mildly inconvenient, but it wasn't long until it dove headfirst into disaster.

The highway construction that forced him into an unexpected detour. The closest gas station being closed for the night, with its pumps oddly shut down. In his desperate search for the closest fill-up stop, his phone's battery had depleted unnaturally without him noticing, powering down into a useless brick. When he tried to locate the charger, it seemed he had misplaced it. In a last ditch effort to find a solution to his sudden problems, he relied solely on the vehicle's GPS system, but the digital screen only seemed to plunge him further away from civilization, deep into the country. Now there wasn't a car in sight, and the darkness surrounding seemed to encroach around the headlight's glow. Like something was trying to snuff it out.

"Fuck. Fuck!" He beat his hands on the wheel once more, wishing he could teleport out of the nightmare and back into the safety of his home. If only he hadn't gone on this trip, *if only* he'd caught a flight instead. The *ifs* continued to taunt him as he mentally struggled with the realization of what would come next. He looked into the darkness past the light's reach, a backwoods void that seemed to stretch forever.

He would have to walk.

Uttering a long, angry string of curses, Rafael searched the car for something—anything to help him in his time of need. No phone, no flashlight, no flares. He found a little lighter in the center console, but the flint refused to spark. He searched the glovebox but found nothing but his registration and maintenance receipts. After minutes of searching and delaying the inevitable, he found himself reaching hesitantly for the ignition.

If he killed the lights entirely, he wouldn't be able to see. If he left the lights on, the battery might be dead by the time he made it back. He thought of the hazards and wondered if the light would be enough to chance. If someone passed by his car, maybe they'd find him further up the road and would be able to help him. With a deliberate sigh, he pushed the triangular button and shut the door behind him.

Bullshit, this is bullshit.

After taking a long look both ways, he started walking, in fear that if he didn't push himself to do it he'd return to the car and hide forever until the sun came up. He walked quickly, wiping the sweat from his palms on his jeans. He checked back often, watching the blinking lights grow smaller and smaller until they were specks in the dark road. He looked above to see the trees towering above him, the scuffs of his sneakers echoing in the night.

Crickets chirped; an owl hooted. Off in the unseen distance, something rustled in the brush and made him jump. He wondered if it was a squirrel. A coyote. A skinwalker. He let out a nervous chuckle and focused on the walk, rubbing his palms together in a vigorous attempt to feel cool and collected. By the time he looked at the car again, he couldn't even tell if it was there or not. It was like the weeds had drug it off the road, or the night had gobbled it up—

When he looked back ahead, he froze. Not in fear, but disbelief. Through the trees ahead, he could see the glimmer of a porch light. He rubbed his eyes and looked again—and sure as shit—there was a house coming up, one he hadn't even noticed. He couldn't have walked that far in such a short time, and surely he would've seen it from further away.

No matter. Filled with a newfound sense of hope, Rafael quickened his pace to a jog, feeling the trees pass with a rush of relief. Just when he thought the universe was conspiring against him, it had thrown him a bone. He just hoped the residents of the lit-up house didn't collect them as a hobby.

Arriving at the mailbox, Rafael looked up the drive. The bright porchlight painted an uneven path of mud and gravel, the kind that would bottom-out the vehicle of a delivery driver. He walked up slowly, minding his steps so he didn't add a rolled ankle to his list of inconveniences. He focused on the door to the house, each stride bringing him hopefully closer to a way out of this ordeal. They had to have a landline, even out here. Maybe they'd surprise him by having a smartphone. *Everyone* had one these days. He focused on the thoughts of hope and ascended the rickety porch steps, paying no mind to the tattered shingles on the house's exterior. Or the collection of junked vehicles that crowded their yard. A light was on in the garage addition of the house, with a little bit of light poking under the door. Maybe they were a mechanic?

The front door was open, but a see-through screen door hung weakly. From the inside, Rafael could hear the faintest drone of a television set. He took a deep breath, cleared his throat, and knocked on the frame of the screen before announcing himself.

"Hello? Anybody home?"

There was a moment of silence before he heard a groan, followed by the familiar *ba-dong* of someone declining the footrest of a recliner.

"Just a minute," the voice rang out. It sounded like anyone's old aunt or grandmother, with a hint of a southern drawl. It was dark inside, and there were only a few slivers of light streaking into the breezeway. He couldn't see her, but he could hear her approach, the methodical whine of floorboards heading his direction. He hoped she was nice. She sounded nice.

From behind the screen, an elderly woman stepped into view. She was shorter, rounder than she sounded, and peered up at him from a thick set of bifocal glasses. She looked him up and down before looking past him, breathing heavily as she took her time observing her visitor.

"Can I help you?" she asked.

"Hi—so sorry to bother you. I ran out of gas, up the road. I was wondering if you had a cellphone, or maybe a landline I could use to call a tow-truck? I just need to get to the nearest gas station," he pleaded, his hands gathered in front of him. He hated this, every part of it. But if it got him out of here...

She looked at him long enough for him to wonder if she actually heard him. By the time he wondered if he should ask again, she adjusted her glasses and spoke.

"Fraid I don't have one of them fancy phones. But I do have my house phone. My cousin Skeeter's got a tow truck, I'll give him a ring. You poor thing, he'll get you straightened up."

"Oh, you don't have to bother him. I can just call TA if you don't mind, they'll be able to—" Rafael started, but she cut him off.

"Nonsense. Skeeter loves helpin' out people 'n need. He'll be happy to do it. Come on in, I'll give him a ring," she said, holding open the screen.

Rafael tried to control his sigh. Everything in his being urged him to make a run for it, but he didn't know how far it would be until the next house, if there even was one.

"I appreciate it, if it's not too much of a bother," Rafael said, and stepped in. The woman led the way, walking him past a cracked door on his right, to a dimly lit kitchen on his left, talking as they went.

"You just have a seat here for a minute, I'll go give him a ring. Are you hungry? I've had a stew going. A good one, been simmerin' all day," she said as she waddled.

"No, thank you," he said, looking around the kitchen. It was cluttered and dusty, the counters completely covered in miscellaneous junk. Newspapers littered the kitchen table. Stuff that looked like it hadn't been moved in years.

"Suit yourself. One of my best ones yet. You hang tight and have a seat. I'll give Skeeter a call."

She said, disappearing into the dark domain that was the rest of the house. Rafael thanked her and stood awkwardly in the kitchen.

His skin startled to crawl. It wasn't like the house was filthy, he just couldn't shake the sense of not feeling welcome. The whole situation screamed every cliche he'd seen in the movies, and he knew if he was watching himself on the screen, he'd be ranting about how he was still standing there. Despite the nagging feeling he had, there was nowhere else to go. Rafael looked for a seat, but when he noticed not only the table was covered in newspaper stacks. The chairs were too. He resolved to just stand there, tucking his hands in his pockets.

Impatiently, he looked around the room. There was nothing immediately alarming about the place, aside from what was probably a hoarding problem. The kitchen was interesting, though, furnished with appliances and dishes that must have been around since the 1950s. A bulbous refrigerator that looked like it broke down ages ago. A dusty Coca-Cola machine covered in heavy dust. A stove that looked like it ran off chopped lumber.

As Rafael waited for the woman to return, he found his eyes lingering on the stove. It wasn't the age of it that intrigued him, or the obvious neglect. It was something she said to him before going to use the phone.

Been simmerin' all day.

There were no pots sitting on the grates, no bubbling concoction. Not even an open flame. But he could *smell* it, the lingering odor of something stewing. But he was in the kitchen, and there wasn't even a crock pot plugged in—

A voice pulled him away from his thoughts, so quiet he thought he imagined it.

"Free us."

It raised the hair on his arms and riddled him with goosebumps. Rafael looked around, expecting someone to be hiding around the corner. But there was no one. He was alone.

"Hello?" He called out, hoping to hear the old woman. He walked back into the breezeway and leered in the direction she had disappeared to. Looking into the dark of the next room, he could see nothing but the glimmer of a television against old China cabinets.

"Granny? You there? Helloooo—"

"Free us."

He heard it again and whipped around, facing the screen door. He expected to see someone standing outside the screen, brandishing an ax or a gun. He found nothing but an empty porch, and the chirp of the crickets outside. The smell was stronger now, so strong he couldn't believe he didn't notice it as soon as he walked in earlier. It smelled of boiled chicken and burnt hair, or copper and broth. The smell changed with every inhale, sometimes enticing, sometimes repulsive. A savory gravy one second, then aged vomit the next. As his senses reeled to put a finger on what could produce such a thing, he found himself looking at the cracked door in the breezeway, where the stench was wafting in.

It was coming from the garage.

"Hello?" Rafael called aloud, nervously. He heard the call again, a whisper that seemed to carry on the whiff of the unplaceable scent. *Free us.* What if someone needed help, and he was their only chance?

He pushed the door open, the light from the garage filling the breezeway. After taking a precautionary glance towards the living room, he stepped into the garage, squinting against the bright light that enveloped him. The sight before him made little sense, as he had never seen such a thing in that particular scale.

In the center of the garage was a cauldron.

The pot was massive, like a mythical brazier crammed where a car would normally be parked. It hung from a heavy tripod of what looked like welded scrap, simmering over a dugout bed of red-hot coals and freshly split wood. As flames licked the sides of the cauldron, Rafael could hear the contents within boiling, a wet thrashing that seemed to be barely contained by a heavy rattling lid. Steam hissed with every rattle that sounded of the screams of deflated lungs.

It sounded like someone was in there.

Rafael approached it slowly, feeling sick to his stomach. Something was wrong here, *very* wrong. His thoughts of a phone or a tow truck went out the window as the urge to help possessed him, and he looked around in a panic to see if there was anything of use. There didn't seem to be a way to lift the lid directly. He'd have to think of something. After a frantic moment, he removed his jacket and wrapped his hands with it, deciding maybe the best he could do would be to just push the lid off entirely. He swallowed hard and approached the rumbling cauldron, his hands shaking as he drew near. Cursing to himself, Rafael took a deep breath and readied himself—and gasped as the cauldron burst open.

The mass that exploded from within reached for him with several hands, each slimy and steamy and *fast.* Before he could run, he was met face to face with a dripping horror, hollow sockets and exposed teeth that echoed a silent scream. The amalgamation was on him instantly; a wave of tar-covered bones and greedy fingers that snatched his clothes, his skin, his hair. Limbs of all sizes wrapped around him before he could cry out, the secretion of the slithering monstrosity melting his skin with theirs as it drug him painfully to the boiling vat, their gurgling home of human gravy.

Just as quickly as he arrived, Rafael was gone, and his final thought as the heavy lid closed above him was the realization he had misheard the whispering. He could hear it clearer now, not as a voice in his head, but from the chattering mouths that shrieked silently in his ears as they melted away.

Feed us.

THE SPIDER

The Wanderer looked up at the cathedral, the torrential downpour soaking his clothes. It didn't take long for the storm to magnify, the indignant gloom of the forever blackened sky churning scornfully until powerful winds ripped through across the infinite plain, carrying with it the reek of ash and mud and death. But the powerful gale meant nothing to the Wanderer, for it felt like silence against the malevolence that slumbered within the parish.

An aura so putrid, he felt a delighted shiver in his veins.

Like the storm, the cathedral itself reeked of unbridled rage. The structure—once assumedly pious and hospitable—had turned *fowl,* the stonework plagued by a wicked expansion in the form of cracked lumber and bent nails. Crudely constructed and grotesquely overlapped, the addition reached for the sky like a perverted monolith looming above the steps in a portrayal of venomous spite. It mattered not to the Wanderer what testament was held or what God it belonged to, but if they were worthy of the saw.

Rain pelted his melted mask and trickled off the rusted blade, past sins and atrocities fading away like a distant memory. He found a final affirmation of the challenge ahead in the steps themselves; while his weapon wept a gentle crimson, the stone stairs had been bathed in it. Whatever had happened here, happened in such a volume it had seeped out from under the church's doors, and run down the flight until it reached the end of the domain's reach. The endless expanse of tall grass that never grew or withered, but simply seemed to endure.

Even diluted, the blood seemed to scare the grass, as if it wished not to bathe in it.

In silent determination, the Wanderer tightened his grip on the saw's hilt and began climbing. With every step he felt the creeping rigor loosen in his limbs. It had been a while since his last encounter, perhaps the longest stretch of his seemingly endless journey. As the hours stretched and the days melted without any notable cycle of time, his steps grew slower, heavier—but never ceased. Even as his fingers froze depressions in the foam. Even as the blade drug limply against the earth. There was always a reward at the end of his persistence, this just being the latest in a long string of pain and contested strength. However brief, the taste of admirable blood was always worth the journey, as it was all he could think about. The chainsaw's unquenchable thirst. The wielder's undying lust for battle. A perfect harmony of codependent addiction.

The Wanderer took the steps two at a time, his rubber boots squelching against the sticky granite. The wind whipped at his tangled hair and butcher's apron, and the rain fell in sheets, as if the storm itself were trying to thwart his arrival. Lightning forked and thunder boomed from the clouds above, so loud it shook the stairs as he climbed. Despite the severe weather, his gaze remained on the door, his iron visage watching through closed eyes. By the time he reached the top, his chest heaved with every breath, the thrill of the coming fight rejuvenating his muscles.

The doors to the cathedral were massive, nearly twice his height, and several inches thick. He took note of the heavy metal brackets bolted into the door frame, a sign that it had once been barred. He placed a gloved hand on the weathered wood, feeling the energy emanate from the grain. As he felt the power radiate, he felt eyes upon him, and he turned to see something lurking around the corner to his left. Behind the stone something peered curiously, and the Wanderer watched with disinterest. Although insignificant, the creature was familiar.

The pest that looked upon him frowned with an upside-down face and hairless brows that raised underneath scarred eye sockets. A merman in the cruelest form, the monstrosity carried itself on its hands, its torso ending in a spill of ruined intestine. Even cowering against the storm, it couldn't resist its own curiosity. The Wanderer regarded it as he would an annoying fly, the question of whether it was plotting or merely bored didn't make it past his judged insignificance. Without as much as a word, the Wanderer placed both hands on the doors and pushed.

The doors groaned as they opened, immediately giving way to the heavy stench of iron, candle wax, and murder. The flickering light inside was tossed from the wind, painting a dance of shadows across the long stretch of stone columns, each decorated with dozens of horribly defiled bodies. Wrists, eyes, and mouths bound in metal twine, so tight it buried into the skin. Their knees had been dissected and the kneecaps removed, and their torsos looked to be viciously hollowed out. The Wanderer didn't understand the damage, nor did he care to, only taking note that whoever was responsible had done it with such force it had stained the tapestries lining the walls. He didn't linger on the viscera for long, for his attention was quickly pulled to the far end of the room.

Kneeling before a grand altar was a man, his back turned, his head bowed in worship. He was wearing what was left of a priest's robe; the back ripped open to expose a mess of scars and fresh wounds. One hand was held in front of his face, the other holding a flogging strap that dripped from recent use. He muttered a chant softly, one that only ceased once the Wanderer walked in, his heavy boots thudding against the creaking floorboards. Even as the priest stood, the Wanderer continued to close the gap between them, the patter of runoff from his clothes and hair mixing into the stained wood.

The priest turned to face him, dearly clutching a long rosary of harvested patella. It was wrapped around his fingers like a knuckleduster, his thin digits engulfed by the blood-stained bone. He was bald and grinning, looking down on the Wanderer with horribly malformed eyes. They were bulging and misshapen, like something had laid eggs in them. Despite the bulbous stare, he regarded The Wanderer's company as a threat and made a show of the flogging strap in his hand. The Wanderer dismissed it silently, unimpressed.

Outside, the wind whipped against the cathedral, with lightning and thunder so loud it shook the building. As the candles flickered, the priest rushed toward the Wanderer, raising the flogger with an angry growl—only for it to be cut short. The priest's infected eyes widened in surprise as a hand gripped around his throat, the gloved fingers squeezing until they nearly burst from their sockets. The Wanderer raised him off the ground, and in three bounding steps, slammed him into the base of the altar so hard it rattled the candles on the walls. Usually he would experience a surge of gratitude with the snapping of a spine, but as he looked down upon the crumpled man, he felt nothing but utter disappointment.

He had come here to feel power, to fight a *real* opponent, but this one was already nearly defeated. The priest gasped at his feet, the flogging strap clattered uselessly to the floor, the rosary held weakly. As he looked down on him, he met his gaze with his bulbous eyes and started to laugh. Mocking him.

A burning anger welled within the Wanderer, but the priest only laughed harder, an echoing choke of a gasp that bounced off the walls of the sanctuary. He kept laughing, even as the Wanderer shoved him against the stone, drew the rusted blade against his mouth, and started to manually saw back and forth. Even as the jagged teeth tore and ripped through the taut cheeks of his face, and his jaw rattled against the blade. Even as the top of his cranium lolled against the last remaining sinewy straps.

The Wanderer seethed against the mockery. Only when he rolled the priest to the floor and brought his boot down on his skull did the laughter finally cease. The stomp nearly flattened the head entirely, mashing both halves against the wood until it was reduced to nothing. He felt no pleasure in the destruction, even as he raised the boot to inspect the sole. Whatever had been festering inside of his eyes had been reduced to jelly, blending in with the rest of the pulp that was now soaking into the boards.

Before he could lower his boot, a loud slam sent the flames flickering once more, some of them extinguishing entirely. The Wanderer looked to see the doors to the church had closed, showing him nothing but his shadow dancing in the candle's light. Another shadow danced into view, and with it, the sense of power he had longed for.

It was coming from the ceiling, in the shape of the cross.

The Wanderer felt the heat next, a well-restrained glimmer of someone much stronger, *worthier*. Disregarding the destroyed priest, he turned back to the altar, eager to see the true master of this domain.

It came in the form of a woman. Arms wide, palms facing out as she glided to the floor, the flowing skirt of her habit obscuring her feet as she floated. She looked down upon him with a set of bleeding eyes, black orbs of absolution that held a piercing stare like nothing he had ever seen before. Behind the wicked guise was a sense of curiosity, like someone long-awaiting company. While the white of the Nun's garments was horribly stained, her skin was as smooth and pure as porcelain, like she had recently cleansed herself. As the skirt fluttered to the floor and she towered above him, the Wanderer looked up at her in silent marvel.

Behind the bleeding eyes, he could sense the same desires of insatiable violence. As she looked upon his cold metal mask, he could feel her assessment. Her judgment. Perhaps she, too, had longed for a worthy opponent.

Perhaps the two were the strongest they had come across yet.

The wind whistled. Rain pattered the windows. And the Wanderer felt for the ripcord.

The chainsaw roared to life, the familiar sputtering scream vibrating in his hands. The Nun licked her lips slowly, even as he rushed towards her and thrust the blade toward her stomach. The Wanderer worked the blade in, but it didn't move, and he found himself struggling against the weapon. He looked to see the amused smile of the Nun, her hands brought together in the rusted steel of the bar, not even an inch away from the churning teeth. As if in prayer. With the trigger squeezed, the Wanderer applied pressure with the front handle to overpower her, but it refused to budge. She looked down on him the way a mother would as her child struggled.

And she started to get taller.

The flowing skirt of her habit started to billow, and one by one legs reached out, each like a black beckoning finger. He felt the increase of power next; a nuclear heat that blasted against him, way stronger than the Butcher's, and the Laborer before him. Despite his struggle, the Wanderer beamed at her astonishing strength. Three legs per side, with a single one arching over each shoulder like a stinger. By the time her robe fluttered once more above the floor, the abdomen appeared: large, bulbous, and bigger than his body. It ended with a set of acidic spinnerets, and the floor bubbled against the dripping secretion. With the bar held firm between her hands, the Nun reached across her chest with one of her overarching legs and sent it rocketing towards the Wanderer's face.

Hitting with the force of a steel bat, the leg sent him reeling, tumbling head over heels until he collided with the darkness of the front door. He was on his feet immediately, lurching from the shadows, the saw revving over his head. He brought it down and it met the cross of the two shoulder legs. A flurry of sparks danced over her veil. With her hands free, she snatched fistfuls of his long, tattered hair and slammed him face first in the column closest to her. Before he could react, she yanked him back and catapulted him over her shoulder, using the strength of all of her legs to whip him around by his hair. He crashed into another column instantaneously, the roof shaking against the explosion of mortar and dust as he toppled to a heap on the floor. The skittering of her legs echoed over the floor as she gave chase, looking to ram him while he was down.

The Wanderer pushed off the floor and met her running, shoulder checking her before she could get the satisfaction. The Nun gasped as the air fled her, and one of her razor-sharp legs shot out like a stinger as it stabbed directly through his thigh. She erupted in a scream as the Wanderer worked over one of her legs, the teeth cutting clean through. Just as the leg thudded uselessly to the floor, her scream turned to an almost orgasmic laugh, and he looked just in time to see the windup of her backhand. The blow hit him hard enough to chip his teeth, the flesh behind the metal mask bruising instantly. He swung wildly with the saw, and the blur of the blade whisked just inches away, only for her to close in and seize him up by his hair again, this time grinding his face into the floor as she drug him across it. Blood leaked behind the mask and erupted out of the sides in a spurt as she shoved him through another column, keeping the same smile even as they worked through the rubble.

Pinned against the many bloated corpses, the Wanderer punched and kicked, only to be rewarded with a retaliated stab from one of the many legs. The Nun continued to punish him, slapping and dancing around him in an endless onslaught from above. They raked and pulled and stepped on him, the heat of her aura suffocating as she beat him relentlessly into the ground, just as she had the many victims before. His grip on the saw weakened, and he struggled to get a word in, and he reached blindly for one of the legs that punished him, eager to push back. Only when one of the legs pierced through his hand and pinned it to the floor did he find any sort of opportunity.

With all his might, the Wanderer rammed his shoulder into the tibia that had gored him. With a sickening *snap* the leg bent backwards, and the Nun shrieked in pain as the digit went limp. The Wanderer climbed to his feet and embraced her in a strong bear hug, lifting her off the ground until her legs squirmed in a panic.

The slam to the floor cracked the boards beneath them, and before she could overpower him again he brought the chainsaw down on her shoulder. The reddening teeth released a spray of dark blood that painted the stone around them. The Nun twisted and swatted and palmed at his face until the legs found their footing and she was able to shove him off. The transition was all she needed for the upper hand, and as the Wanderer fought to bring the saw down. Again, he felt the four remaining legs constrict around him in a tight embrace. The Nun rolled on top of him, both of her hands trying to wrestle the saw free while the top two stingers jutted into his ribs. As the Wanderer felt them root around and dig through his insides, he felt the gravitational shift of his body dangling in the air. He looked to see a spindle of strands attached to the stone above, the same kind of wire that was wrapped amongst the several victims littering the floor.

She was bringing him to the ceiling.

Suspended in the air like a pendulum, the Wanderer fought to get free. He kneed her stomach and elbowed her face, but nothing seemed to stop the working spinnerets. If anything, her grip only seemed to get stronger, and soon he felt the rush of wind as the chainsaw sparked across his own metal face as she worked the tool in her favor. The sensation rattled his skull, and he jerked his head away, the greedy blade shaving strands of his hair and shearing the leather of his apron. When he tried to muscle it back to her she broke several of his fingers, her gentle hands snapping them like twigs. With a giggle of pleasure, the legs dug further into him, prodding through his organs and weakening his grip until he felt the saw slipping away entirely. When an additional leg stabbed into his back, the Nun ripped the saw from his grasp, letting it tumble to the floor below.

The chainsaw clattered uselessly, sputtering until it inevitably died.

As they reached the top of the grand church, the Wanderer clasped both hands over her throat and squeezed with all the strength he had left. The Nun playfully took his face in her hands and caressed the clammy steel with black painted nails, almost lovingly, before shoving her thumbs into the eyes of the mask. The eyes remained closed, but the force dented the steel against his brow, painfully splitting the skin beneath it. The Nun shed a single bloody tear as he struggled, right before she kicked off the ceiling with determination.

Together they launched toward the base of the altar, the many legs releasing and maneuvering him until he awkwardly crashed into the stone, bones breaking against it as she slammed down on top of him.

The floor shook and mortar crumbled between the bricks, sending a shower of brittle cement cascading over them. The improvised shingles of the roof outside shook loose and stuck into the mud, while the stained glass cracked against the sheer might.

The altar wobbled and stabilized. And before it, standing tall, was the Nun.

The Wanderer reached for the saw, unable to drag himself closer to it. Stark white bones protruded from his skin in multiple places, a collection of fractures the Nun looked upon with gratification. Her long fingers ran up her stomach and over her breasts, smearing the blood on her face before holding her arms out as she had when she had first descended. Blood wept from the mask as the Wanderer reached for his weapon, only to be restrained by the weakness of his body.

Slowly, the Nun hefted him up and thrust him against one of the remaining columns, letting his body crumble against the stone as she turned her back on him. With the abdomen aimed, a flurry of wire engulfed him with a hiss, the tight wrap digging into his skin and constricting against the pillar like a fly caught in a web.

The Nun bent one of her arachnid legs and bowed to him, hands brought together as if to show respect. The candle's wicks burned furiously and bright, and the tattered tapestries flapped in her presence. She offered another single bloody tear before plucking the chainsaw from the ground. She regarded it in magnificence, taking in its wear, its rust. She ran the jagged teeth over her tongue before resting her cheek against it, her hand drifting toward the rip cord.

Stunned and broken, the Wanderer watched in heresy as she started it on the first try. An inkling of admiration vibrated in the mask before it shed a bloody tear of its own. The Nun held the chainsaw tight as it chugged and coughed its smog, the upper legs flexing like wings as she moved toward him. Confined to the column, the Wanderer stared as she squeezed the trigger and plunged the wailing blade into his stomach.

The blade ate hungrily, chewing through the apron and blending his insides with trembling joy. The miasma that burst from the masked man's stomach was black and potent, and the Nun stared intently into the mask as the eruption washed over her. She drew closer as she felt the blade rend his muscles and grind against his vertebrae, relishing in the undeniable victory over her helpless victim. The Wanderer tensed and jerked against the decimation, staring back defiantly as the tool shook in her hands. She took in every seize, every throe, even as the mask itself seemed to drool as well. The metallic lips parted slightly, the bubbling of blood seeping through in gurgling spurts that even she didn't understand. She leaned closer, curiously inspecting the anomaly of the iron visage.

With a final erupting cough, the chainsaw's blade burst through the lips of the mask, and the hungry teeth struck right between the eyes. The bite was quick but *deep,* shaving through the bridge of her nose and liquifying her stare immediately. She let go of the saw with a shriek, flailing and clawing at her eyes that were reduced to nothing but hollow cavities in an instant.

The rusted blade revved before retracting, a devil's serpent slinking back to the depths behind the mask like a tongue. As the Nun flailed against the fatal wound, the Wanderer flexed against the constricting wires, his skin parting and weeping before they ultimately snapped against his strength. Shambling to his feet, his body jerked and thrashed as he righted himself, taking only a moment to watch the Nun scramble across the vast expanse of the church. When she worked her way back towards him, the mouth on the mask bubbled once more, this time in the form of a violent, full-body purge. The pungent blood covered her like a hose, seeping into her wounds and soaking her clothes with the scent of muddied fuel.

In her chaotic fit, the Nun tore down the tapestries and stumbled into the altar, all the while raking at her eyes in an attempt to quell the pain of her newly found blindness. In her desperate thrashing, she raked the candles from their shelves, sending them tumbling to the floor.

With an igniting burst, the Nun went up in flames. Impatient tongues lapped at her robes and the tapestries alike, feasting on everything the fire could find as she continued her rampage. The Wanderer watched as her robes were reduced to ash, the fabric burning away until they exposed a slender body wrapped in wire, a shibari tie that reached across both the human and arachnid frame. The wire itself continued to burn with the oil, melting until it ran scoring lines across the charred skin.

In slow, deliberate steps, the Wanderer jerked his limbs, resetting the bones until the tendons acclimated and secured them in place. It was an agonizing but welcomed pain, and as the Nun drug herself across the cracked floor, he found himself looking towards the altar that shone above him.

He brought it down with an angry pull, his limbs barely stable enough to bend the steel and break the wood that held it upright. As the Nun pleaded for life, the monument came crashing down, a final act of pulverization that crushed both her and the floor with it. The boards crumbled and broke away, opening a void beneath the ground that swallowed it all.

Fire snaked over the walls and columns, engulfing the remains of the church in a wicked fire that couldn't help but spread. The Wanderer watched the gaping hole with heaving breaths, stopping only to admire the destruction before the stoic mask turned its attention to the saw sitting quietly on the ledge. He walked over to it slowly, the feeling of the teeth in his stomach still fresh in his mind. Like himself, the saw was forever hungry. He couldn't bring himself to hold that against it.

With a weak hand he picked it up, his fingers reluctantly settling into the depressions left behind from his endless march. Lost in the symphony of cinders and crumbling stone and victory, the Wanderer couldn't hear the enraged skittering emanating from the pit. He couldn't defer the remnants of heat from the raging fire that had become the church itself. Looking at the ruined altar, the charred tapestries, the smoldering boards on the roof, he only felt the satisfaction of the domain crumbling in on itself, just as the others had before it.

When the Wanderer turned to the door, he found nothing but the embrace of barbaric, angry legs.

The Wanderer smelled the stink of the earth behind his mask. He still felt the grip of the saw, the other clutching a fist's worth of dirt as he struggled to push off the stagnant soil. It carried a scent of rot with it, a history of unchallenged suffering that hadn't as much seen the gloom of the sky above. Long had this ground been covered, cherished... *hidden.*

Above was a single ray of light, a dying cast of the smoldering church above. Even though it burned brightly, he knew it was a matter of time until the plains reclaimed it, and the world righted itself once more. He worked his way to his knees and found he wasn't alone in the poorly lit crevice.

Laying in the light was the Nun, her body limp and charred beyond repair. Her face was twisted in a final look, but whether it was of pain or pleasure, the Wanderer could not tell. When his eyes followed the trail of her body, his grip tightened around the guard once more.

Behind the lifeless Nun, stirred a set of furious, glaring eyes. Purple slits blinking above a row of bared teeth, each dripping with a saliva that fizzled into the dirt below it. A face once hidden by a gorgeous, flowing robe. A horror obscured beneath the mirage of a beautiful savior.

A frenzied, hateful spider. It moved closer, dragging its charred companion along. Much like the dead weight, it moved without regard to its broken leg, its skittering appendages trampling both as it calculated its own survival. By the time the Wanderer got to his feet, its teeth were already bared, and a set of mandibles clacked excitedly as it circled its prey.

As the Wanderer's hand rested on the ripcord, the Spider reared back with a hiss.

It was on him immediately, the many legs and teeth gnashing wherever they could. It screamed a primal chorus of rage and resentment, dominance and delight. It stabbed and prodded and thrashed, taking advantage of the Wanderer's fatigue in an all-out assault to eliminate the threat that had wandered into its home. He felt his hair drag into the dirt and the flesh rend against the many claws and teeth of the monster, but he only focused on one sole objective amidst the onslaught.

The rip cord.

His thick fingers clutched it like a lifeline, curling around the puller like it was the last thing he would ever feel. Under the shadow of the Spider, he yanked with determination, each time more desperate than the last.

Once. Twice. Three times.

The engine coughed, sputtered, then roared to life at the squeeze of the trigger. The Wanderer propped it against him and pushed out, feeling the immediate spray of hot entrails against his apron. The Spider howled and retreated, gushing uncontrollably onto the dirt beneath it. The Wanderer felt the acid sizzle on his skin, and when he touched the exposed skin behind his long gloves, he watched as the flesh pulled away with ease.

As the Spider limped away, the Wanderer descended upon it like a madman. The saw screamed as it slashed horizontally, hacking through one leg, two, a third. The Spider teetered to one side, flailing helplessly against the smoking beast that chugged ever closer. The Wanderer looked upon it; the acid cleansing the filth and corroding the metal of the mask as it remained the same expressionless stare.

The purple eyes watched as he hefted it up like a dagger and buried it into its abdomen. The chainsaw ate without remorse, splattering the Wanderer in a bursting uproar as he broke through the armor to the delicate bits beneath. He reached in with his other hand and pulled the carapace apart, tearing through the strands of wire that held it together on the inside. With an ear-piercing shriek, the husk gave way to a tide of underdeveloped offspring, human and arachnid monstrosities that wailed at the first taste of the damp oxygen. The Wander sawed and crushed them as he went, relishing in the desperate groans of the beast that had pinned him down several times before.

He ripped and tore and sawed until there was nothing left, and the Spider cast its last look of hatred upon his cold metal mask. As his finger left the trigger, he stood there heaving, and he caught his breath as the chainsaw sputtered into stillness.

Collapsing to his knees, the Wanderer gazed upon the Spider, now reduced to a ruined, useless carcass. The fire burned above, and he looked toward the inferno in victory—a thirst finally quenched. But as the flames reflected off the mask, he felt the undeniable nag of the momentary abatement.

In the pit around him, he heard a skittering. It was slow at first, but eventually the blinking light was enough to pull his attention away from the celebration. He looked upon the sets of purple eyes until there were dozens, hundreds, each blinking to life and crawling closer in the darkness. His head hung low, not in defeat, but in calling. His hands shook and his knuckles cracked, but in the end, they found their way to the weathered handle of the pull-cord.

The Merman watched from the steps as the cathedral collapsed on itself. Fireflies twisted and turned amongst the wreckage, extinguished by the droplets of the dying storm.

Like it, the battle was over, and soon the land would forget it had ever happened in the first place. Another quarrel, another clash of swords forgotten by the Etch-A-Sketch of time that was the creed of this miserable land. Another cesspit of misery snuffed out by a more determined, more tenacious evil.

The Merman watched for a time, observing the ruins as it burned and withered away. He had followed this one for a time, witnessed many atrocities in his boundless search of a worthy opponent. Maybe this time, he had found what he was looking for. He watched the ruins with his upside-down face, with a look usually mistaken as sadness.

There would be another. One worth watching as they struggled. The Merman sighed and shuffled down the stone steps, ones that would soon be claimed by the shifting sands—ashes—of the world before. Carrying his entrails behind him, he hopped gingerly down the steps, careful not to fall and tumble. As his calloused hands reached the last step, he heard something stirring amongst the wreckage. After a deliberate pause, he turned towards the collapsed church and stared with hollow eyes.

Beneath the crumbled stone and embers was a set of hands, each garbed in melted rubber gloves. One felt blindly for the earth, the other clutching a chainsaw.

FINAL FLESH

I find my spot in the sand and set down the cooler. I take a moment to bask in the scenario, feeling the golden rays on my skin, enjoying the view of the grayish-blue reaching toward the horizon. The sky is clear, spotless. The sand is warm, and feeling the grains between my toes is soothing, grounding. I close my eyes, breathe the fresh air. Listen to the gulls chirp on the wind, the soft crashing of the waves.

I've been doing so good. Great, even. Best I've ever been.

The beach is... packed.

Families and couples of all shapes and sizes bustle around, play in the water, lay in the sun. The pier and the lighthouse are on my left, filled with people casting lines, walking the concrete structure, and taking pictures. On my right, there's an ice cream stand, where children giggle as they try to contain melting soft-serve. Next to it is a set of bathrooms, little brick structures just off the sand. A little further down the shore, a family's radio plays softly, not too loud. Whitney Houston, from the sound of it.

This is a good day. A good spot. I'm glad I made it out of the house. I'm glad I made it here.

Not long after I lay out my towel and plant myself next to the little cooler, my stomach rumbles. I'm hungry, like I haven't eaten in days. I flip open the cooler and get my sandwich, freeing it from the Ziploc bag. I get out the bag of chips and root around in the ice for a soda, shaking the cold runoff from it before closing it and setting everything on the lid.

The tear of the foil packaging is satisfying. The crunching press of corn chips against dense bread and lunch meat is satisfying. The crack of the cold aluminum can is satisfying.

For the first time in a long time, I'm satisfied.

Some gulls linger nearby, eyeing me in a group. I toss them some chips, and they flock and fight over them, inhaling the food in a way that seems dangerous and unhealthy. One of the gulls among them doesn't have any feet, and is peg legging around in an attempt to get a piece of its own. I try to throw some directly to it, feeling a strange sense of connection to it. Both of us, trying our best to stay afloat.

A teenager stumbles into the group in an attempt to catch a foam football, and the gulls disperse in a flurry of frantic cries and flapping wings. The walls are meat. As the teen brushes the sand from the football, I take another bite of my sandwich and divert my attention elsewhere. I decide to look back at the pier, but something down the shore catches my eye. It looks like there's something floating in the wind.

Tumbling over the sand is a Hawaiian shirt, like a kite struggling to catch the current.

I choke on my food. An unchewed piece of chip fights against a series of coughs, and my eyes water. When it passes, I tilt the can to my lips to wash it down, and I suddenly feel like I've lost my appetite. As I pack up the food and return it to the cooler, I see the ice cream stand. I can't remember the last time I had a cone.

The cooler and towel should be fine, not going anywhere. People should leave it alone. I brush myself off and head towards it, patting my shorts to make sure I have my wallet. I do. I wonder what kind of flavors they'll have. Something special? Just a classic swirl would be enough. That would pick me right up.

I weave around the little base camps families have made. Heavily sunburned dads nurse on beers in fold-out chairs. Girls take selfies angled at the horizon. Tired moms apply another layer of sunscreen. I feel a pain in my foot and my ankle rolls awkwardly to avoid it. I look down, expecting to see a rock or a stick and see blue fur and wide eyes instead. Half buried in the sand is an old children's toy, one that looks like a rabbit, or used to be. Its little limbs operate on a dying battery as it wiggles, and its broken voice box mutters something about children and knives.

How strange.

When I get to the ice cream stand, I'm second in line. There's a man ahead of me wearing a floral shirt, sun hat, and designer glasses. He's hunched over a little plastic boat of food, I can't tell what kind. I wait patiently. I look towards the lake, trying to focus on the waves, the music. A young couple splash playfully on a sandbar. The man stands there for a moment, seemingly enjoying his food, before walking away abruptly. I guess he wasn't in line after all.

I walk up to the counter, where a younger man smiles and waits. I try to see the menu, but I can't seem to focus enough to read it. I'm starting to sweat.

Get it together.

"A cone, please," I stammer, wiping my forehead.

The young man nods and makes his way to the soft serve machine slowly. Almost robotically. The dispenser groans as he works the cone. I dig out my wallet, fidgeting with it as I return my gaze to the sandbar. The couple is gone. The young man returns, holding the cone out with a smile.

My wallet is empty.

I stare into the fold, wondering where my money went. I start to feel sick. I realize it's not just the money that's missing. There's nothing in it at all. No license, no credit cards, nothing.

"What seems to be the problem?" the young man asks, in a voice that sounds pretend.

I feel dizzy. Like the ground is moving. The earth is spinning too fast. I want to say something, but the words choke as I look at the man. He's staring politely, but something's off. The more I look, I realize there's no menu at all. Or that the man looks like his limbs are made of plastic pieces. *Or that he's held up by strings.* The cone held out in his plastic looking hand is not chocolate or vanilla. It's maggots.

No.

My skull vibrates. The bile rushes up my throat and I barely suppress it with my lips. I rush to the bathroom close by, dodging kids and parents alike on uneasy legs. I struggle past the sinks and rows of stalls, taking the only one that's open—the last one. I hunch over the toilet in time to feel the dry vomit roll into the toilet, a compacted mess of lunch meat and chips. I heave until there's nothing left and my head swims.

I've been doing so good, I'm good, I—

I take a deep breath and wipe my mouth. It's fine. Everything's fine. It's *been* fine. We're good. I unlatch the door, open it, and freeze.

The sinks, mirrors, shower heads, they're gone. In their place is a sprawl of washing machines, stacked three high, all the way to the ceiling. Each of them are off, and they look like they haven't been used in a while. They're painfully still, horribly rusted.

You don't belong here.

"You don't belong here," I say to them. My reflections in their sideload doors don't mouth the words. It's not right. Can't be right. It's just dark.

I decide to go, and they watch me do so. Need to get back into the sun. Back to the cooler. It's fine, really. Back in the sand, it's not fine.

The people on the beach—all of them—watch me. They're standing still, like someone paused them. Why aren't they moving? I'm fine, you can move. I don't need your help.

I don't need your help, stop looking at me, I'm ok—

"Excuse me, coming through," I mutter as I walk in between them, keeping my eyes on the cooler. It's not far. I can make it.

The pier is empty, and the fishermen are replaced by a single man running in reverse. I don't focus on him; I look for the cooler.

"Excuse me, sorry."

"Let me squeeze right past you."

"Please, just let me through."

"I'm *fine,* alright?"

"Stop *fucking looking at me!*"

At the cooler, I can hardly breathe. It's alright. We made it. Everything will be okay. The music is gone, just a distant scream now. I know I have them around here somewhere, they never go far.

I flip open the cooler and stare into the bobbing interior. The food and drinks are gone, the ice is melted, the water luke-warm. I rifle through the pill bottles floating on top. They're empty, all of them.

"Why? *Why?!*" I scream, backing away from the cooler. I want to be angry, but my lip quivers weakly, the tears well. The people say nothing, do nothing. They're not even looking at me anymore. Their eyes are dead, their faces blank. They're looking at the water and I don't want to. I know, eventually, I will.

Standing in the water, at the end of the sandbar, is a woman. Albeit blindfolded, she looks directly at me. I can't make out the details of her clothes, what little she's wearing. But it's wrong. The whole thing, it's wrong. One hand is clutching the shaft of a scepter—no—a staff, held firm in the water. It looks like it's made of bone. It looks like it's *moving.*

"I don't want to do this. I *can't.* Not anymore," I say, the words choking. And I'm not going to. I'm going to pack up my towel and cooler and go home.

I reach down to grab them, but my fingers grasp nothing but vibrating, trickling sand. It's not fair.

"Help me! Why doesn't anyone ever help me?!" I shout to the people, and I'm not surprised when they're gone too.

I look back at the woman. Her arm is extending, one delicate finger pointing behind her, to the water.

My skull rattles and my brain screams. I feel it flay into strips, a slow, maddening pull that never ends. The wind chills the sweat on my back, and I feel it pushing me closer to the shore, my wobbling legs trying to keep up. When I open my eyes, it feels like they're bleeding.

Behind the woman, the water is shifting. Like the impossible parting of the sea, the water reaches towards the sky, leaving behind an uneven trench of muck and bones behind her. Above the sunlight shifts, the golden rays dimming and fading, and I feel like I can never breathe again. I feel the wet sand under my feet, the pokes and prods of shells and fish bones. I can see her clearer as I approach, unable to do anything but follow an unexplainable soundless song.

Standing next to the woman, she looks like an oracle, or a priestess. Her hair is long and wispy, her blindfold heavily stained an old, faded red. An intestinal robe hangs on her thin frame, one breast covered, the other seemingly ripped off. A skirt of human skin billows in the wind, revealing a leg tattooed entirely black. The staff's head is alive, a shining gem hiding amongst a network or pulsing, reaching nerves. In her other pointing hand, I see something clutched in her fingers.

A single set of eyeballs.

Without a word, she beckons me to follow. I don't want to go, but I know I must. I need to see what she wants to show me. She leads me into the trench, and I follow. Above the sky is black and the sun secretes an awful red, darkening everything behind us.

Walking into the lake, the walls are meat. An absolute finality of flesh.

We walk for hours, descending deeper into the desolate path. Things churn within the walls, screaming and shifting. Winged eyes and gargantuan worms dance in the mess, watching as we delve into a long forgotten place.

I want to say I've been doing well, that I'm getting better. But I don't even know anymore.

The further we go, the more I feel a clarity in the derangement. I don't understand, but I don't think I need to. Maybe I was supposed to be here all along.

When the woman stops, I realize we've arrived at our destination. A bit of water lies ahead, a dispersing whirlpool that makes me think of laundromats, straps, and needles. When the water dissipates, I can see it clearer. I can hear it. An ultimate form, and old god, a supreme being. I try to make sense of it, but I know it doesn't matter.

It changes before me, like it's trying to decide. A beating heart, a staring eye, a pulsing brain. The form shifts before me until it grows a row of serrated teeth, that parts the membrane like a zipper. A maw opens, and I find myself inching my way towards the edge of its jaws. I can't see what's inside, but I can hear it calling. The groan from within is unlike anything I've ever heard, cavernous and otherworldly.

I look at the gore priestess, but she doesn't speak, doesn't point. She takes a step back, leaving me to look into it alone. The red light starts to fade, and I take a deep, shuddering breath.

I seem to have misplaced my pills. I don't think I'll be needing them anymore.

AFTERWORD

Hello there. It seems you've made it to the end. If this is your first time reading my work, thanks for taking a chance on this book. If this isn't the first time you've survived the meat, welcome back! It's good to see you again. Either way, I appreciate you taking the time to read this note.

Undulating Flesh was originally a little flash fiction book I wanted to do for fun. Somewhere to dump all the shorts I was writing on the internet, Reddit in particular. I used to write as many as one a day, two on some occasions. Looking back over all of these stories, I'm reminded of where I was in my life when I wrote the individual pieces. *Miami Night,* in a South Beach hotel on my first real vacation, to *The Wandering Saw,* in a basement after a major surgery. Some were more of an exercise, while others I felt compelled to make sure they made it to paper. Each have their own memories tied to them, whether they are good or bad, and when I read the titles I can't help but smile. As the years went on, especially after *Aggravated Flesh,* it became harder and harder to write something so quick, something crammed in under 500 words. The stories would still trickle in, once a week, once a month, every few months. Until it came time to write *Human Gravy,* and

I was literally incapable of squeezing the story down to less than what I had.

So, in a weird way, this book represents my growth. And for that, it is very special to me.

What was originally going to be a funny one-off, then a series, eventually ended up coming into its own and making its own blueprint. Its own flesh. And as I've grown through the years, so has this book, slowly standing on its own with its strange backbone stories, its wild chainsaw fights, and fleshed out with all the scenarios I could possibly pervert. While writing the little shorts was fun and helped me develop as a writer, I don't feel like I have to do it anymore.

So, in a weird way, this feels like goodbye.

Three years of flash-fiction, tossed into a washing machine, and neatly folded by **Velox Books.**

I wanted to say a special thank you to my family and friends, who have supported me through the ups and downs of this journey and have encouraged me to push forward. Particularly my wife and son, who make this whole thing possible. I love you guys.

Secondly, I would like to thank Velox for repackaging this nightmare into the beast it is today. A mega collection of so many terrible things, all dolled up with a nice face. They make a pretty damn good looking book, I must say.

Third, I would like to thank everyone I've met on my writing journey who have helped me through the years. You know who you are, and I appreciate you more than you'll ever know.

Last, I would like to thank you, the reader, for taking a chance on this little book. I hope you enjoyed it as much as I did creating it. It really does mean a lot. Maybe we'll meet again, and I'll entertain you in the future. There's a few more books to dig out of the pit, and many more horrors I'd like to see hit the page. See you next time.

The walls are still **meat.**

—Jesse Pullins